Praise for *The Book Against God* by James Wood

"Wood, a distinguished British critic interested in the expansive nineteenth-century novel about big things like literature and faith, has written his own big-thing novel, his first, which has to do with literature and faith, but is also, happily, laden with wit, forceful images, and English eccentrics."

—*The New York Times Book Review*

"Intelligent, skeptical, occasionally tender in spite of itself, Wood's novelistic persona reminds one of Nick Hornby or A. N. Wilson— fellow Brits who straddle easily the sorrow and hilarity of the human condition."

—*The Boston Globe*

"A small quiet novel, a piece of music for solo voice. That voice is often unpleasant, all too human, and rarely likable, and Wood's success is in the degree to which he redeems those very qualities . . . a considerable artistic victory."

—*Harper's Magazine*

"Wood proves himself to be a delectably witty writer . . . his dialogue is crisp and his characters irresistible while in his lush descriptions . . . every judiciously selected word carries emotional, moral, or spiritual weight."

—*Booklist* (starred review)

"[Wood] has a genuine comic gift."

—*New York Observer*

"Wood is the rare novelist able to dramatize the life of ideas and give it human dimension."

—*Publishers Weekly*

"[*The Book Against God*] seems designed to fascinate, irritate, and disturb just about everyone from Karl Marx to Billy Graham. And whose beliefs couldn't stand a little reexamining now and then?"

—*The Times*

"Deftly and beautifully written."

—*Books & Culture*

"The novel delight[s]."

—*Philadelphia Inquirer*

"Wonderfully done . . . [Wood] is a tremendous talent."

—*The Buffalo News*

"*The Book Against God* isn't stilted, safe, or derivative; it's real flesh and blood, rather old-fashioned, considering Wood's tastes as a critic, with humor, passion, and some serious flaws that strangely serve to make the novel more endearing."

—*San Francisco Chronicle*

"*The Book Against God* impressed me enormously, with its intellectual liveliness, its metaphysical awareness, and its subtle use of the unreliable narrator."

—Paul Binding, *The Times Literary Supplement*

"[*The Book Against God*] had me smiling and sometimes made me laugh aloud . . . a book that I shall certainly reread, for its comic realism, its warm intelligence, its lack of pretension."

—A. N. Wilson, *The Daily Telegraph* (U.K.)

Also by James Wood

The Broken Estate: Essays on Literature and Belief
The Irresponsible Self

James Wood

The Book Against God

PICADOR

FARRAR, STRAUS AND GIROUX

NEW YORK

www.picadorusa.com

Picador® is a U.S. registered trademark and is used by Farrar, Straus and Giroux under license from Pan Books Limited.

For information on Picador Reading Group Guides, as well as ordering, please contact the Trade Marketing department at St. Martin's Press.
Phone: 1-800-221-7945 extension 763
Fax: 212-677-7456
E-mail: trademarketing@stmartins.com

A chapter of this book previously appeared in *The London Review of Books*.

Desgined by Barbara Grzeslo

Library of Congress Cataloging-in-Publication Data

Wood, James, 1965–
        The book against God / James Wood.
            p.   cm.
        ISBN 0-312-42251-2
        EAN 978-0312-42251-6
        1. Truthfulness and falsehood—Fiction. 2. Children of clergy—Fiction.
3. Graduate students—Fiction. 4. Fathers and sons—Fiction. 5. Authorship—
Fiction. 6. Young men—Fiction. 7. Atheists—Fiction.   I. Title.

PR6123.O527 B66 2003
823'.92—dc21

                                                        2002042600

First published in the United States by Farrar, Straus and Giroux

First Picador Edition: June 2004

10 9 8 7 6 5 4 3 2 1

For my parents, and for C.D.M.

For whom the Lord loveth he chasteneth, and scourgeth every son whom he receiveth.

—HEBREWS 12:6

THE BOOK AGAINST GOD

1

I DENIED MY FATHER THREE TIMES, twice before he died,
once afterwards.

The obituaries editor of *The Times* was responsible for my
first denial. That was almost two years ago. I was still living
with my wife, Jane Sheridan, but we were constantly arguing.
At University College, where I was teaching philosophy, I
had become one of those figures whom students romanticize
and sometimes even pity. I didn't have the proper qualifica-
tions, and the classes I gave were printed on the curriculum
brochure—grudgingly, I felt—in a different coloured ink
from the main lectures. Insultingly, the university paid me
by the hour! The faculty was beginning to look at me as if I
were dead, the students as if I were somewhat grotesquely
alive, but it amounted to the same thing.

We were in debt, and my childhood friend Max Thurlow
offered to help. He is now a successful, what you might call
intellectually deluxe columnist at *The Times*—the type who
mentions Tacitus or Mill every other week—and knew that
the newspaper prepared its major obituaries in advance of
the subjects' deaths, and that most of them were written by
freelance contributors. So Max proposed my name to the
appropriate editor, Ralph Hegley, and said that I could write
obituaries of philosophers and intellectuals. And Hegley
asked to have lunch with me. We met at a restaurant in Covent
Garden—expensive Italian, snowy tablecloths, steam room
hush, Pompeian ruins of cheese on a silent trolley—and sat

at a window table. On the street, where the cars were parked in convoy, a traffic warden was going from car to car, pen in hand, like the waiters inside the restaurant soliciting orders. Hegley had a huge head, was middle-aged, sickly lugubrious, pale. He was dressed in a double-breasted suit as thick as a straitjacket, and a rich silk tie plaited in a fat junction. But he wore oddly childish shoes—they seemed as soft and rubbery as slippers. "I have bad feet," he explained, when he caught me looking down.

"I'll order for you if you don't mind," he said. "There are certain do's and don't's at this restaurant. It takes years to acquaint yourself with this little civilization." As he said this, he looked around with a strange contempt on his face.

Hegley explained that freelancers wrote advance obituaries of selected "candidates." He was especially interested in philosophers who were known to be unwell, or rapidly declining with age. He became impatient, and irritably coaxed the keys in his trouser pocket as he put names to me.

"How's Althusser? He's the killer, right? Maybe *his* number's up now. And that other chap in Paris, the Romanian, Cioran. I hear he's not too well, it's the Romanian genes. Any Americans? We tend to miss 'em, then we have to do a rush job once they've gone. I don't like rush jobs. That is for other papers, all right? Oh, and we need someone to update our Popper piece, pep it up a bit. I've heard he's a wee bit poorly."

Catching on, and knowing nothing about the apparently welcome illnesses of various world philosophers, I invented several ailments.

"I'm told," I said, "by various colleagues at UCL, that Gadamer is not very well."

"Jolly good. Add him to the list." As usual when lying, I felt warm, light-headed.

"And Derrida has never had tremendously good health. That's well known."

"*Is it?* Right, let's snatch him before he . . . self-deconstructs—isn't that his word?"

I left lunch with four commissions—Cioran, Popper, Derrida, and Gadamer—each paying £200.

But I never wrote one of those obituaries. Other things got in the way. Look, I have been trying to finish my Ph.D. thesis for seven years, and I seem to have a distaste for finishing things. Recently, I have been neglecting the Ph.D. for a private project which I call the "Book Against God" (I think of it now as the BAG). In it I copy out apposite religious and antireligious quotations, and develop arguments of my own about theological and philosophical matters. It has swelled to four large notebooks. It has really become my life's work, as far as I am concerned. And whenever I was about to begin one of those damned obituaries, I found myself drawn to some crucial novelty in my BAG, and the day would disappear into theology and antitheology.

Eventually Hegley got tired of waiting, sent me an irritable letter. It had been three months, he complained, and he had received nothing. Should he still consider me the writer of the proposed obituaries? I don't cope well with pressure. I was keen to stay on Hegley's order form, and suddenly I realized that the most decisive way both to explain my tardiness and to appeal for sympathy would be to tell him that I had been lately dealing with my own rather more proximate obituary: I told Hegley that my father had died a month ago, and that I had not had an ungrieving minute to

deal with the work in hand. Hegley wrote back with his con-
dolences. Of course I should take as much time as I wanted.

This worked so well that I told a similar lie a month
later, after I received a letter from the Inland Revenue about
outstanding taxes payable on various part-time jobs I had
had over the years. Usually I ignore these kinds of communi-
cations, but this one had an imperious glower and for some
reason my name was printed in bold capitals: THOMAS
BUNTING. I opened it to find myself summoned to attend
a "hearing" in Wembley. There I would be "assessed" by
government auditors. If there were any extenuating circumstances, any good reason for the tardiness of my payments, I
should explain myself in writing, and at the hearing this letter would be read out in my defence.

That was how I found myself three weeks later sitting at
an unnatural table—that caramel-municipal sheen found in
so many offices—opposite four men in suits, one of whom
was reading out my letter. It explained that due to the recent
death of my father, and the heavy business related to the
tidying up of his estate, I had fallen behind in the paying of
my taxes. I was truly sorry to have found myself in this position but the last three months had been a period of grief and
shock as well as distraction, and might I presume on the le-
niency and compassion (this word underlined) of the asses-
sors to grant me another six months to get my taxes in
order? This was read out in a flat, bored voice so that, if one
closed one's eyes, one would swear that the reader—a terribly thin man—was simultaneously doing something else. I
kept my eyes down and strove to appear slumped in grief.

The stay of execution was granted. Of course, my father
was alive then. I had calculated that an extreme measure
would work. I would not have written those letters had I

known that my father would be dead within a year of my writing them.

But we can't schedule the consequences of our lies.

The third of these "denials" took place after my father's death, and was not a lie, but by then it felt like one. When I recently told Jimmy Madeiros, the manager of the underground porter-packer division at Harrods, where I worked this summer, that my father had just died, and that therefore I couldn't continue with the job, I was telling the truth. But it seemed like a lie, because I saw at once that he didn't really believe me. So I felt cheated. When I'm not lying I think I should almost get credit for it; it is like that wise saying in the Talmud—"The thief who lacks an opportunity to steal feels like an honest man."

2

IT IS SEPTEMBER NOW, September 12th, 1991, to be exact, four months since my father died; and it is longer since things began to sour between Jane and me. And now—what a mess I'm in, really. I'm reminded of my old history teacher in Durham, Mr. Duffy. One day he came into the classroom and upturned the wastepaper basket on the table. Then he took off his gown, pleated in the corners like a napkin, and threw it onto the pile of papers and dust. He walked over to the timid little boy whose parents were divorcing and took the contents of his desk and added them to the pile of rubbish. Then standing behind the table, and putting one leg before the other, he declaimed: "In 1381, England was in a mess!" All these years later, I know what he meant.

At the moment I'm living in an unpleasant little room, a bedsit I suppose, in Swiss Cottage, in a 1930s building on the Finchley Road pounded by traffic. I moved here in May, just after my father's funeral, and after my estranged wife put me "on probation." At the service, with Father's body barely cold, Jane told me that she would have me back only if I could prove to her that I was no longer a liar, an operation which, I see now, has more than a touch about it of the famous Cretan paradox. In four months nothing has happened yet on that front, so here I am on the Finchley Road, alone. The landlord asks for the rent in cash every

Saturday morning. My bed is next to the bathroom door, which can't close all the way, and I hear the lavatory dribbling day and night. It makes me think of a little boy with an eternally running nose. I am on the first floor, above a karate studio, of all things. During the day, yelps of triumph and pain can be heard. I miss the flat Jane and I lived in when we were together. It was in the hilly area of Islington, on the top floor of a gabled Victorian house. From the high window you could see a piece of the policeman's helmet of St. Paul's dome, and further on a glimpse of Parliament, and its loyal river, obeying the crowded banks, selflessly flowing. At dusk, holding a drink by the window and feeling luxurious and waiting for Jane to return from work, I loved to see the city streetlights going on all over town in amber hesitations.

Jane was always frustrated by my extravagance and by my inability to earn any money. I don't blame her for getting angry. What did her husband amount to? I was barely tolerated at UCL; I moped and bunted (yes, I invented the word) about the house all day in a dirty paisley dressing gown (but made of very good silk); and instead of finishing my Ph.D., I fiddled in ecstasies—and they are ecstasies—with my BAG. Jane teaches the piano at Trinity College of Music, and she used to get occasional lump sums when she played recitals. I had my shillings from UCL; in those days, they still felt like employing me. But London, and my expensive ways, swallowed everything we earned. I can't help blaming my late father, Peter Bunting, for my extravagant tastes. In 1959, Father, who had been teaching theology at Durham University, resigned his job and became a priest. He was bored of teaching and keen to have a parish. He took command of a little church in the village of Sundershall, about ten miles west of the town. No doubt he reckoned that the difference between a university lecturer's salary and a vicar's stipend was small enough that no sudden impoverishment would consume his family. But my parents' finances were sickly; in my memory, Father seems to be continually driving in to Durham to meet "the bank manager," to arrange for "another lease of life." Though my parents weren't ascetic, indeed quite worldly by instinct, our life was materially thin. All our textures were strained through the sieve of their finances.

That necessary rationing has produced extravagant tastes in me, and an avoidance of the ordinary wherever possible. For instance, I never blow my nose into a handkerchief because the nasal trumpeting has always sounded plebeian to me. (I clean my nose quietly and secretly.) I like beautiful objects, rich foods, rare atmospheres. It sometimes seems to me that I'm on a quest to naturalize and enhance all the materials and substances with which I grew up: where my parents had a reproduction of a Russian icon, I yearn for the real thing; where they wore nylon, I will wear cotton; their wool must become my cashmere, and their *méthode champenoise* only ever my Veuve Clicquot. The upright piano must become a grand. The secularist, as I certainly consider myself, has a duty to be worldly, to take the pagan waters at spas of his own choosing. Don't I have Nietzsche, one of my favourite philosophers, to support me? And Camus, the Algerian bather-seducer. Now, it's true that in my present circumstances—all day that blasted traffic races past my window, up the awful Finchley Road—I do not have much opportunity for extravagance; I have very little income, and whatever I earn (or am given) I have to send off to Philip

Zealy, a crook and usurer in Durham. Zealy has taken nearly
all the money I earned this summer at Harrods. But my day
will come.

Anyway, to return to our marriage. My lavish habits, not
to mention the requests of the Inland Revenue, had indebted us pretty badly, and this was one of the reasons for
the frequent arguments that Jane and I had. We had decided
to try to have a child (or rather, Jane had made the decision), and this momentous choice had made her even less
tolerant of my lies. "Our child cannot have an untruthful
father, Tom. What example would that be?" Well, I dislike
my lies, too. Morality aside, lies add to the general confusion of my life, a confusion I sincerely want to reduce.
Quite often, I might be happily minding my own business,
and then suddenly a mental irritation reaches me, and I
remember some little deceit I have committed, and I realize that I still have to extricate myself from the confusion it
has left in its wake. This happens less now, because I see so
few people in my present life; but when Jane and I were still
living together my lies were always getting in the way of har-
monious relations. I might, for instance, have declined a
supper invitation with the Impeys by quickly inventing a
prior engagement with the Davidsons; but then the Impeys
happened to know the Davidsons and might discover my
untruth; so, as an alibi—and this happened on one occasion—
I had then to phone the Davidsons and fix up supper for
the same night on which I had originally declined to see the
Impeys.

Not long after the incident with the Inland Revenue,
Jane and I quarreled about a foolish situation. Catrine
Hillier, apparently one of Jane's "enemies"—in our four
years together I never properly ascertained who was an en-

emy and who an ally, since there were weekly demotions and promotions—phoned to ask us to a small drinks party two weeks hence. Jane was out at Trinity; I was in the middle of writing a long entry in my BAG about Kierkegaard. I was fathoms deep in his repulsive brand of Christian masochism, wrestling with assertions such as this: "Did Job win his case? Yes, eternally, for the fact that he *lost his case before God.*" No one else in the world *resists* these vile paradoxes! The task has fallen to me alone to fight the Danish knight of faith, and I was knee deep in the necessary struggle when Catrine rang. Caught off guard, and not forthright enough to refuse, I said that we would go, making a mental note to phone her nearer the time with an invented excuse. Then I went back to the BAG, and didn't look up from it until mid-afternoon. When I came up for air, I noticed with dismay that the flat was untidy, that chores Jane had asked me to do—to vacuum the carpets and wash the breakfast dishes—were mysteriously untouched. I couldn't really face domestic work, so I went into town to get a book and also bought, on impulse, a rather pretty necklace for my beloved, who loves jewels of all kinds.

Jane returned late that evening, with her usual emphatic bang of the front door, and the sound I knew well, of her music case—with a loose metal buckle that rings—being stored away in the front hall cupboard. Vivid with the city world she had come from, and carrying a little urban ghost of cold air behind her, she entered our warm sitting room. She was wearing a short brown leather skirt (my suggestion) and a white silk blouse. Looking at her, I thought that her male piano students were very lucky, and had probably never had it so good.

I was excited about the necklace, but before presenting it I told her that Catrine and Danny Hillier had invited us to drinks and that I had mistakenly agreed to the invitation.

"All right, Tommy. I know we've agreed that there won't be any more lying." She reached forward, gently subtracted my cigarette from my hand, took a drag herself, smiled, and shone her very dark eyes at me. She kissed me, and then nipped the cigarette out. "Sorry," she said, as I watched the pinched foam filter in the ashtray, "I can't stand it in the house in the evening. Now, although we've agreed, you're now going to have to pull out one of your lies again to get us out of Catrine and Danny's party. I can't possibly go!"

"Tell me again why Catrine is now in the enemy camp?" I asked, amused. "And do you want a drink?" I asked, noticing Jane's eye on my large scotch and soda. "Alcohol is permitted, I assume?"

"Well, it's *perfectly* clear," she replied, rather haughtily, and with great emphasis, as if I were testing her.

"Yes, my love, but not to me," I said.

"Catrine has been horribly mean to Roger about his choir. She said hurtful things about their last concert."

"I see."

"You're teasing me."

"Well, because you move your friends—"

"They're your friends, too—"

"You move your friends from one camp to the other for only two reasons: it's either something murkily musical, or something elusively ethical. In Catrine you've managed to fuse the reasons into one." I could hear my voice sounding like my father's—clever, too buoyant.

"Tom, not everything can be put into words, something that probably comes as a shock to the Bunting family. I don't like her at the moment and that is that. We can't *possibly* go to Catrine's. So pull one of your stunts for me, will you, darling?" She wandered into the kitchen and I suddenly remembered that I had neglected the domestic chores.

"Oh, darling, it is a bit *grim* to come home and find the place a complete *tip*. Didn't I ask you to do the dishes?"

"Yes, you did, and I forgot, and I'm sorry, but I had to be out this afternoon, in town, where I bought . . . this!" I handed her the plush little box. She tilted open the flimsy sprung lid.

"You bribe me, you bribe me . . . Oh, it's beautiful! Tommy you're so extravagant, and I have *far* too many lovely things, most of them from you."

I murmured to Jane, in the interest of truthfulness, that it was largely her money.

"You're not supposed to say that, you silly thing."

A good liar needs strength: strong nerves, strong ethics (precisely so as to be able to keep the lie separate in his soul from the truth), and above all a very strong memory. I have the nerves, the ethics, but unfortunately I am forgetful and disorganized. I promised to do something about the Hilliers' invitation, and then forgot about it, and suddenly it was the day of the party, and Jane saw the time and name written on our kitchen calendar (written by her, of course).

"What did you do about that in the end?" she asked me.

"Ah. Nothing . . . as yet. But—*but*"—I held my hand up to calm her down—"we can still cancel."

"Of course we can't. It would be awfully rude. You did nothing at all?"

"Yes, I suppose it *would* seem rude," I muttered to myself.

"Tom, I asked you to do this. Two weeks ago. I asked you. I have to do *everything* in this house."

"I have a plan," I said.

"Oh dear," said Jane—not, I think, without some fondness.

"Look, tonight we won't even try to attend the party, and if the phone goes we won't answer. But tomorrow night let's go to Clapham and appear at Catrine and Danny's at exactly the time that they want us there tonight."

"That's utterly silly."

"No it isn't. It merely looks as if we got the date wrong by a single day. An easy error. Now, in the best possible world, Danny and Catrine will be out and we can leave a note; but if they are in they will forgive us for our honest mistake, offer us a drink that politeness dictates we refuse, and then we are on our way into the night. I know, we can have dinner round the corner in Wandsworth, in that new restaurant that was just in the *Standard*."

"We can't do that. I asked you to lie on *behalf* of me, not to lie with me at your side. I couldn't do it. And I asked you to lie before the event—not after it! No no no, I refuse to go along with this, this silliness. Oh dear, this teaches me a lesson."

"What lesson?"

"You know what I mean," she said ominously. Then she lightened, and I thought we might be through the worst of it. "And who's paying for supper, Croesus?"

I struggled to get Jane to accept this plan. She would

not. We went to the party, and she got gloomy again, and was cross with me all evening for not having the courage to have declined the invitation when I first received it. Of course, we had a perfectly pleasant time at the Hilliers', a fact which Jane refused to accept.

TEN YEARS AGO AT UNIVERSITY COLLEGE, when I was a student there, Professor Syme called me "the Great Pretender." What did he mean by that? I think I was a pretty good philosophy student at London—rather idle, very plausible for sure, picking at odd tufts of learning. Asked to read Plato, I would spend instead a few days with Plotinus. That's my way of doing things. It was not deception so much as a disdain for the bridle. I liked to be free. I *like* to be free! Syme predicted that I would win top marks or fail badly in my finals exams. I won top marks, and then had the pleasure of frustrating expectations by not staying on to do a doctorate.

But once out of university I was afflicted by a real eagerness to study. I sat at home, reading and reading. Well, not at home, actually, but at Uncle Karl's house in Chelsea. And Karl is not my real uncle, either, but was my father's best friend, a refugee from Germany who came as a mere boy to England in 1939, and met Father in the early 1950s, when Karl became a student at Durham University. Father took the young Karl under his wing. Later, Karl made money, a lot of it, in the 1960s and '70s, as an art dealer. He has a house in a street behind Sloane Square. After university, I lived with Karl for three happy and decidedly childlike years, in an enormous bedroom whose walls were covered with outrageous contemporary paintings. It was an easy existence, during which I sat and read a great deal, spoiled only by the odd necessary job when money ran out and by the unannounced entrance of uniformed deliverymen, who came to take one ugly painting off the wall and replace it with another. But there was a quality of desperation in the way I consumed books at Uncle Karl's, beginning each in the hope that this was the one which would tell me how to live, how to think; as soon as I realized that it would not, my reading of it began to slow, precisely as if my heartbeat were slowing from its initial race. More often than not, I put it aside.

Eventually, partly at the urging of my parents, I decided to go back to university and begin a Ph.D. dissertation. I worked quite hard at first; but then I lost interest and hope, and in the last two years the BAG has become more important to me. The problem is that I started reading books that were utterly beyond the scope of my academic work—the early Church Fathers, the Psalms (again and again), certain Buddhist and Islamic texts. And then I couldn't stop reading these "irrelevant" books.

It was while I was most blocked on the Ph.D. that I met Jane, five years ago now, and began to develop some of my bad habits—the irresponsibility, the lying when it was not necessary, not replying to bills, and so on. I was twenty-six, she was six years older. I won't deny that I'm irresponsible— though not actually as irresponsible as I probably seem. For instance, while we were married Jane and I always argued a great deal about my failure to pay bills on time, and yet they *were* always paid in the end. In my teens I read somewhere that Erik Satie never opened any bills. Now, I am cowardly, so I was unable to go as far as Satie. But I thought that a little of the Satie style would be a good thing. Again, I can't entirely divorce this quality of my temperament from my secularism. If one believes that one has only seventy years or so on this earth and no afterlife, one cannot spend one's time observing all the proprieties and rules. My God, if I were scrupulous about paying bills, balancing my cheque book, cleaning the lavatory, answering letters and telephone messages, changing my clothes, bathing, and the rest, I would spend my entire life rolling the rock of diligence up a hill of someone else's making.

No, life is always a struggle for freedom. Whenever I sign a cheque for some idiot company or other, I feel a little like a man in an electric chair or in a hospital bed, streaming with wires and connections and linkages. All these smothering tentacles: the gas company, the electric people, the landlord, the tax man, the credit-card officials, all of these needy babies pressing down on me and demanding that I turn my life into one long liegedom. So I leave bills unopened, and it gives me a small thrill to come upon them on the kitchen table, and to know that although inside the envelopes lie all these hysterical flashing demands, from the outside they are as calm as chess players. Then, having done nothing, I watch the second wave, the repeat requests, arrive a couple of weeks later, and enjoy placing the second wave on top of the first wave of bills on the table. Once I have resisted this, I am primed for the third wave, exactly ten days later. These requests are not from the original companies but from collection agencies—the bailiffs—and come in special envelopes. This is the moment at which I sign my cheque like a good little bourgeois, and enclose it with a pugilistic note, a bit of a challenge: "P.S.: Since I have finally paid up, you can call off your thugs."

Obviously, this is less of a problem than it was, because I have fewer bills to pay in the Finchley Road bedsit. But it was always coming between me and Jane when we were to-

gether. The Ph.D. is clearly to blame. It forced me into an
unnatural and weak position with my wife. Her husband had
no income, no power, and no status. All he did was sit at
home trying to finish the unfinishable. The more I look at
it, the more I see the Ph.D. as the reason for everything bad
in my life.

Often, I think, Jane enjoyed my spirit of rebellion—
though she has never been a secularist like me—and used to
laugh with me at some of the scrapes we got into. That's what
has made understanding her so difficult: for the first two
years of our marriage she seemed to cherish my irresponsibility. She herself is exceedingly law-abiding. So I think she
enjoyed living with me, with this younger man who was obviously a creative and blithely lawless presence. I think she
almost encouraged me not to pay bills and so on. I have a
memory of her standing at the doorway and laughing wildly
while I answered one of those telemarketing calls on the
phone. "Am I speaking to Mr. Bunting?" She knew what I
would always say in response to that question: "I'm afraid
you're not. I am house-sitting for Mr. Bunting, and he's in
Hong Kong for a month. Perhaps you'll call back when he
returns?"

It's true that Jane began to get angrier with me about my
financial irresponsibility. Last year, about six months before my father had his first heart attack, we argued about my
credit-card payments. Someone from Visa had started phoning me. Day after day the phone went, and it was always the
same man. So on the fourth or fifth day I performed a trick
I had used before, and which Jane had previously enjoyed.
As soon as I heard him speak, I said, "Hello?" He replied:
"Yes, hello, is that Mr. Bunting?" And again, with more
puzzlement, I said, "Hello?" as if I couldn't hear anyone on

the line. And again, he said, "Hel-*lo*, Mr. Bunting." Then, for verisimilitude, I kept the receiver near my mouth and shouted to Jane, "Jane, what is wrong with this bloody phone, I can't hear a thing. Someone has phoned and I can't make out a word he is saying! This is the *third* time today. We *have* to get it fixed." And then I put the phone down. Jane, of course, came to me and asked what was wrong with the phone. I told her that I had simply been using my old trick to get someone who was "after me" off my back. But Jane reminded me that we were married, and that if someone was after me then that person was also after *her*, and that if we ever had a child that person would also be after our *child*. That was what being a *family* was. Her sarcasm was rising like floodwater. To calm her, I explained that it was nothing more serious than the Visa people chasing a late payment.

"But you told me that you had paid the bill," said Jane.

"Did I? I find that extremely unlikely."

"You looked into my eyes last week and told me that you had paid the bill and posted it in . . . I think you said in Gower Street."

"Ah, no no, it wasn't the Visa bill I was referring to. No."

"What was it?"

"Another bill."

"The lie you are telling me to cover up the first lie is more repellent to me than the original one. Just so you know." Jane seemed almost to be shivering with disgust.

Now, there are liars who will tell you that they were pleased to be forced to confession, that as soon as they began to tell the truth it bubbled up wantonly from their mouths. I am not one of those liars. Caught, I tell another lie to hide the first. I surrender a lie with great unwillingness and feel instantly nostalgic, once it has gone, for the old comfort it offered me. But I also know the value of a tactical surrender.

"Okay, I hadn't paid the Visa bill."

"And you lied to me when you said that you had."

"No, I don't think I did lie. I'm sure I imagined when I spoke to you that I *had* indeed paid and posted the bill."

"Oh, Tommy." Jane looked at me with amazement. "Tell the truth! Don't you understand that I care much more about your lying to me than about your lying to the credit-card company?"

What surprised me was not Jane's anger but her distress. And, frankly, although practically I understand the distinction between lying to one's wife and lying to a corporation, philosophically the difference seems slight. Surely both lies were so tiny, so opportunistic, that they hardly merited examination, let alone rebuke? The problem is that Jane has no sense of proportion. It's a curious aspect of lying—looking at the phenomenon philosophically—that for most people the size of a lie has no relation to its perceived potency. People like Jane cannot distinguish between small lies and large lies; for them, the act of lying is always *itself* an enormity, and comes in only one size. God did the same in Eden. After all, Adam's sin was actually very small, but God inflated its consequences ridiculously. Jane treats every lie as if it were asparagus, which, whether I eat one spear or ten, makes my urine smell with exactly the same pungency.

IT WAS MY FRIEND ROGER TRELAWNAY who introduced me
to Jane. Roger runs an early music choir. He is eager and
gentle, a happy schoolboy. He speaks very fast; his upper
front teeth are slightly twisted. They look as if they are trying to escape from his mouth under the pressure of such fast
speech and have got caught up in themselves in the process.
I can't always understand Roger, because he treats the music
world as if it were school, handing out nicknames and judg-
ments to players and conductors. "This one is conducted by
Hitler!" he says eagerly, as he puts on a record for me to listen to. He has a set of wholly musical assumptions, most of
which are nonsensical to me: "It's all in D major, which is
really boring." Or: "B minor is the key of suicide." So I
tend to listen to about half of what Roger says. But I heard
him talk about Jane Sheridan, one of his "music friends,"
and finally he dragged me to hear her give a little concert in
Bloomsbury. I was unwilling to go because I almost always
dislike Roger's music friends. "You won't be disappointed,
Tom," he said. "She's a marvellous pianist, and also quite
dishy, way beyond my league."

I thought that Jane was not very attractive as she came
onto the stage; she was heavily involved in one of those
large, parachute-like concert dresses made of puffy blue raw
silk, the kind that only female musicians wear. As she passed
the piano, she patted its black hood, which was raised as if to
catch the sun, bowed, sat on the red, buttoned-leather seat,

scratched her cheek, and began a quiet piece, which I didn't know. Her neck and back were thin, her hair was gripped in a severe ponytail. The short sleeves of her bunched and hilly dress throttled her thin upper arms, whose white skin caught the light as she lifted her hands—lifted them gently, in paddling movements, as if trying to calm the piano. Her face was lovely; I could see that, and I was beginning to find rather an erotic contrast between the angular arms and wrists, probably as thin as they had been when she was a teenager, and the more rounded, certainly adult deposit on which she sat. As she concentrated, the tip of her tongue emerged like a middle lip. She sat as if at a loom, calmly weaving and shuttling. By the end of the concert, I wanted to meet her. I was tremendously attracted by the sight of this woman so completely at work, so much the mistress of her instrument.

Roger and I approached her as she stood by the piano after the concert, talking to a plump man in a light-brown leather coat, with white creases in it like the striations of fat in a piece of meat, whom Jane later identified as the organist of St. James's, Picadilly, "where Stokowski was once the organist." (I made myself look as if I knew who the hell Stokowski was.)

"Well, what did you think?" she asked Roger, in a flash of that difficult pride I would come to know so well.

"Super," said Roger. "Beethoven a *bit fast.*"

"Yep, I need fingers like a millipede's legs to do bits of 109 anyway," she said with great briskness. "God, those trills!" I was surprised by this firm easiness, because I would've been irritated had Roger criticized me in that way.

There was a silence. Roger, who can be socially incompetent, had not introduced me.

"I thought the concert was brilliant, beautiful," I offered. The last adjective made me awkward. I think of myself as moderately attractive, neither handsome nor ugly. Epicurus speaks of *katastema*, the stable condition of the flesh, and argues that the achievement of this constitutes the highest joy. My looks, neither striking nor quite dismissable, had enabled such stability, since they protected me from extremes of emotion: I had tended neither to be rejected by women nor to be jumped on by them. And in parallel, my emotions towards women had tended away from extremity. But about Jane I felt extreme, quite quickly. Jane's eyes had a quality which immediately made me anxious. She turned amazing, dark eyes on me. Such thick long lashes! I had seen her only in profile, and was shocked.

"I'm Thomas Bunting, by the way."

"Oh yes, I've heard all about you," she said.

I think I was immediately attracted to Jane. To begin with, she has those remarkable eyes, densely dark. So intense are they that if I look only at them, she seems to be always angry with me. The rest of her face is almost tyrannized into blandness by them: for a long time I found that I could not recall any aspect of her face other than those black concentrations. She has a habit of pushing her chin out, as if catching something with her teeth. Her hair is very dark, fiercely commanded into a ponytail which hangs quiveringly, like the needle of a delicate instrument designed to monitor her moods. I got to know this shaking sleek ponytail very well indeed, because Jane has many moods, and there is no way to predict when or why she will laugh (at which point her ponytail, laughter's tassel, swings and rocks) or become angry (the ponytail, now pride's brush, stiff and unmoving, as she tilts her head to the left and closes her eyes in fury). Her noise is quite long—something suggestive of erotic prolongation in a long nose, I think—and her neck is long, too. At its base is a teaspoon declivity. There are freckles on her collarbones: eager touchmarks, sexual dapple. Her accent is very proper.

Roger proposed a drink somewhere.

"Not in this—party dress," Jane said firmly. "I feel ten years old in this thing, and as if the clown were about to turn up and keep us happy. Give me a moment."

She disappeared to change. The only sounds were the distant London traffic, and the wet collapse of a cleaner's mop on the floor of the now empty hall. Five minutes later, Jane appeared from a heavy side door twice her height, and came towards us. I was astounded by the transformation. The ugly concert dress had compiled a superfluous commentary of silk around her, and obscured the truth. But in tight-fitting black jeans and a white blouse with oversize buttons she was closely revealed—slim, tall, elegant. She had exchanged her ponytail for a brilliant crimson hairband that glowed as if painted there. I noticed a tiny hesitation of the left foot. Not quite a limp. At the piano she had been utterly graceful. Away from it, she was a little physically awkward, with this tiny hesitation in her step. In my infatuation, I thought this was beautiful, as if the piano were calling her back to her proper place.

We went round the corner to a pub on the Tottenham Court Road. It was almost empty. In a wooden corner, a young man was duelling with a bleating machine; he stood with his legs apart like a belligerent midshipman and said "Fffuck!" every so often. The barman vaguely wiped the table before we sat down with our drinks. My hands shook as I held my glass.

Roger and Jane talked about musicians, some of whom were famous enough for me to have heard of them, though Roger would insist on his nicknames: a famous conductor was introduced as "Doris Godunov" (deliberately pronounced "goodenough"), and then repeatedly called "Doris." Others were friends and colleagues, teachers at Trinity or the Guildhall, organists, young conductors, pianists making their first recordings. I was struck by the viciousness with which Jane discussed some of these pianists. I would discover that her reputation in the music world, indeed the whole question of her musical talent, was a painful matter. I've grown familiar, over the years, with her appeals for reassurance and her bitter complaints about other players. She used to sit on the floor next to a loudspeaker—her habitual position for listening to music—and say, "I'm just as good as she is," or "What's so great about this chap? Very ordinary digital technique." Her usual dismissal of a competitor was: "Nothing much to write home about!" With her fists clenched and her eyes closed, she sat furiously, and her tassel of hair moved from left to right in an angry shiver. "Why don't these people"—usually a critic or music administrator—"give me more respect?"

Music brought Jane and me together, but perhaps it, along with the Ph.D., drove us apart in the end. Jane once told me that talking to someone else who "really understands music" made her feel as if she had met someone of the same religious faith. She didn't mean me; I was a pagan, unable to pray with her. But it was lovely to touch the hem of that faith, to approach her single passion. In those early weeks, after meeting her with Roger, it was very exciting to watch this passion, and to wonder about its force if it were ever shared between me and music.

And that is what happened. When Jane realized my intentions, she responded to me as she treated her music, with ferocious seriousness and daily devotion. My own love suddenly seemed feeble in return, secondary. It was she who phoned me many times a day, her voice made small, made junior, by the plastic receiver; she who left notes under the door at my dirty room in Bloomsbury. She was, in those days, superbly tolerant of precisely those characteristics which would later frustrate her. She seemed to be amused by the squalor of my Bloomsbury room, in a flat I shared with a very neat Indian scientist who pencilled his initials on his eggs so that I wouldn't steal them. She used to tease me for my musical incompetence. And I happily failed four of her five tests of musical ability. These were, in ascending order of difficulty: Could I recognize a piece of music a week after I had first heard it? Could I recognize what century a piece belonged to? Could I sing, without losing the note, a simple tune, such as a hymn? Could I sing, without losing the note, a more complex tune, such as the viola's opening theme in Bartok's Concerto, or the violin's in Glazunov's, or a difficult Beatles song like "The Fool on the Hill"? (She loves the Beatles.) Finally, could I sing the bass part to a simple tune, such as the National Anthem? I passed only the first test. I recognized a passage from *Rosenkavalier* when she played it to me a week after taking me to hear it at the Coliseum, because a fat man next to me had shaken with tears during the passage, and had made the whole row of seats move slightly, in sympathy.

I have always been afraid of her tremendous moods, of the abysses into which she can fall, especially when she used to blame herself for not being a good enough pianist and threat-

ened to close the piano lid on her fingers. Perplexed by her
uncertainties, and lacking the necessary expertise, I tended
to assert that she was as good as any of the great pianists.

"As good as Schnabel? Pollini? Richter?" (Richter is
one of her favourites.)

"Well, I don't really know what they are like."

"Then don't say foolish things!"

"But tell me, then, my sweet, what is it about these pianists that you lack?"

"It's impossible. You wouldn't understand. First of all,
they are inhuman. Kempf could do the Forty-Eight Preludes
and Fugues in different keys. Transposing fugues at will!
'Oh, today I'll do it in F-sharp minor, just for kicks' . . .
And he could do that at the age of twelve, did it when he was
examined for his place at the conservatory, a little boy,
dressed probably in shorts, I should think."

"You mean they don't make mistakes?"

"Oh, no, they make mistakes. Well most of them, except
Michelangeli and Brendel. They make mistakes, even Schnabel
made mistakes. That's the terrible thing: they are human,
too. If you ask me what makes a certain pianist great, I can't
say. Sometimes it's as simple as applying all ten fingers
with equal pressure and command on the keyboard. Pollini
has that. There are generally one or two fingers that are lag-
gards—"

"Runts of the litter." I often provide metaphors for
Jane. It is a bad Bunting habit, learned from both my father
and mother.

"Exactly. Well, in his case—"

"All his fingers are firstborns."

"You could put it like that. Listen to this." And she
would jump up and open her cabinet, where her hundreds

of records were tightly packed in big metal racks. And she would play me Schnabel and Richter and Rubinstein and Rachmaninoff, and so on. All the greats, I suppose. It was quite an education.

I generally become solemn when listening to music, partly because that is what I think is demanded of me. But Jane was more often brisk than solemn, swiftly appraising the quality of the performance. She would cry out "Mistake!" and then try to get me to hear it, but I was a poor witness. "There! There! Can't you hear how he's late with that E-flat?" And she tried to get me to hear faults in intonation. "Most singers are slightly flat, just slightly, but *you're* not going to be able to tell, I'm afraid. Lennon, McCartney, Harrison, and of course Ringo, *all* sing flat."

Jane so often became downcast that I quickly took it upon myself to make her laugh, to lift her out of the realm of adult responsibility, to be the lover—and then, with less controllable results, the husband—who provided her with what she lacked. This made us happy for quite a long time. From that first, ecstatic year, I see vividly the moment I decided that Jane had to have a new concert dress. We were sitting in the Islington flat, London beneath and beyond us. She mentioned a forthcoming concert and I told her that she looked fabulous in everything except what she wore on stage. Why not get something black and slinky, instead of blue and puffy? Jane responded with laughter. Then she became serious.

"It's very important, darling," she said, "if you are a woman in classical music, not to get a reputation for frivolity and lack of seriousness. Look how all the record companies are marketing these new attractive female violinists. And sometimes pianists, too. These baby dolls have two years in the sunlight, and then they *completely* disappear."

"So you're saying to me that it is advantageous in the world of classical music to look dowdy."

"Oh, Tommy, that's a mite brutal of you."

"Well, you said it."

"Yes, it *may* be advantageous . . . particularly . . . no, I won't say it." She had a tiny smile.

"Go on."

"No, I won't say it."

"I know what it is. *Particularly* if you are an attractive woman, this being completely unusual in the classical music world."

"*Quite* attractive," said Jane shyly.

"Extremely attractive, I think."

But I wasn't going to listen to Jane's objections, and I forced her to look for another dress. I said that it should be beautiful and very expensive, and that buying such things was a proper exercise of what Saint Augustine calls "the imperial will," which made her laugh. We went to Chelsea, which I know well because of my time with Uncle Karl, and I marched a reluctant but giddily amused Jane from boutique to boutique, until we found a long Valentino dress in grey silk barely embossed with tiny lozenges of white. Jane, of course, was horrified by the price, and refused even to consider buying it. I played along with her. But the next day I borrowed some money from Uncle Karl (who lives just around the corner) and went to the shop on my own and bought the lovely, airy, silky distraction. Jane has worn it ever since, and her career, at least, has not suffered.

5

THAT FEELS A LONG TIME AGO, NOW. Jane and I have been separated since our terrible argument last Christmas. Then, in May, at Father's funeral, she led me to believe that there was some hope. I remember very clearly her words: "I want you to prove to me over the next few months that you can be honest with me, honest about absolutely everything, from the highest matter to the lowest." But she has not kept her side of the bargain, because she never phones me or sees me. So I have good days and bad days. This week I have been in despair. I can't work on the Ph.D.; I can't seem even to work on the BAG. Empty days. Generally, I go to bed with the best intentions, and I am optimistic that something will work itself out. At night, I sit in bed surrounded by many books as if by a flotsammed sea: I believe in stocking the unconscious for its nightly winter. But nothing is right after that. First, because it is September and still quite hot, I must have the bedroom window open, and insects come in. And I have to kill them. I cannot sleep with an insect nearby; I have a phobia that it will land on my face as I sleep. As soon as it announces itself I leap from my bed. I have spent a good deal of the nights this summer squashing insects against the wall: mosquitoes fluffing along the walls with dizzy legs, flies with their cloudy wings and that disgusting way in which they stick to the wall and cudgel their front legs at me, beetles as greasy and shiny as coffee beans, and wasps, many many wasps, so menacing and yet so oddly slow and easy to kill. All of them must be exterminated.

And then I find that I can't sleep, and the "neutralizing" technique which has helped my insomnia in the past proves useless at the moment. The traffic is only really silent in the early morning. Didn't Heine say that Germany kept him awake? Well, London keeps me awake all right. So I abandon sleep and get up early. "Man's first duty on rising—to blush for himself," says a favourite philosopher of mine. I don't blush; I look at my dark morning beard in the mirror of the mouldy bathroom and smile because of something silly Max said to me when we were both seventeen and first beginning to shave. Max told me then, in a voice as masculine as possible, that sometimes he shaved "three times in one session," even if it made the skin sore, because this chased the stubble away for three times as long.

I look out of the window at the Finchley Road. At dawn it is finally quiet, for about an hour. A kind of grey caul hangs over the buildings. Far away, I can hear the distant glamour of London's constant noise, the soft, dashing, marine thunder. Soon Mr. Rowan will come, with his shuttlecock of many keys, to open up downstairs; and then Theo will arrive at the Olympus, the Greek café opposite. The day is starting—but to what end? For what? I light a cigarette, get my coffee from the catarrhal machine, and look at the shelves in the hope that somewhere is the book that might redeem my life. Perhaps it will be Spinoza the heretic, or Leibniz the justifier, or Hume the sceptic, or Schopenhauer the true Freudian, or simply Plato the first? And then I get out the papers of my Ph.D. . . .

Today was typical. I spent an hour reading some of my favourite Psalms, went back to bed to sleep, got up again, spent another hour looking vaguely at my books while wondering if Jane might phone. Then I had to collect my dole cheque; the office is a good way up the Finchley Road. After that it was lunchtime, and I dropped into the Olympus to eat, and to say hello to Theo, the waiter there. I love to ask him, with the seasoned privilege of the regular, "What's good today?" even though the menu never changes. Theo's thick, unruly eyebrows are like bunches of tobacco. He and I agree about religion. He hates Greece, hates the Orthodox Church.

"All those icons make me feel I'm being watched," he complained to me today.

"Well, that's the point, you *are* being watched."

"Yeah, that is just what I say."

Theo deliberately encourages new patrons into arguments about the Elgin Marbles, so that he can surprise them by arguing for their retention in the British Museum. "Leave them where the air is good and they have a hundred-percent experts who know what to do! Athens air is like this café, for crazy's sake."

After lunch I went for a long walk down Adelaide Road, through the curling backstreets to Primrose Hill, where there are little squares that suddenly appear, holidays from the city. Right now, because it is the end of summer, the pavements are clingy with mashed blossom. The trees made me think of Sundershall, which is so much in my mind at present. Sundershall is surrounded by a theatre of hills, and one of these hills is covered with trees, the most beautiful trees. In winter, they are rather terrifying: when their branches are bare and gnarled, they look inverted, as if their own roots are waving in the air. In summer, they exuberate into green, each leaf a delegate sent out by life, and the English oaks swell so that their broad stems seem only pedestals to the caught heaviness above them . . .

6

IT WAS SEPTEMBER 18TH, a year ago exactly, that my mother phoned me to say that Father appeared to have had a small heart attack. He was being monitored in the county hospital in Durham, a place, believe me, no one would want to die in. Peter Bunting inherited his father's bad heart; my grandfather, whom I never met, a headmaster in Kent, collapsed in his mid-fifties while saying grace in the panelled school dining room. Peter, like his father a grand smoker, was doing much better: he was seventy, still at work, and had announced that he wanted to die "in harness." There had been a daily rattle of blood-pressure pills which fascinated me when I was small—Father shaking out four capsules onto his hand and grimacing with a kind of odd gloat of the neck as the pills went down. Yet to me he was always the very example of energy and vivacity. One of the religious thinkers I like to read—when I am supposed to be working on my Ph.D.—says that baldness is merely the body's early preparation for death. But Father, who was very bald, seemed not involuntarily so; rather, it seemed that an excess of vigorous energy had willfully banished his hair to the margins of his head, as if throwing off a lazy cap. His big brow (on a small head) seemed to enjoy its clear freedom. Whenever I now picture my late father, I see first not his eyes but that bald, clear, strong head, with its little semicircle of demoted hair at the back, a grey nest of remnants. He fought with distinction in the Second World War, though only a young man in

his early twenties. Surely he enlisted because he had too much
energy; he could have avoided fighting if he had wanted to.
And surely he decided to become a priest in 1959 because he
had too much energy to be trapped in university life.

Of course, once my mother gave me the news I went
home as soon as I could, with the usual mixture of desire
and despair. I was keen to see my parents again, and eager to
walk in the remembered countryside. But I had taken so
long to accomplish anything that I seemed now only to dis-
appoint them. All our conversation was shadowed by their
anxiety about my future. I grew to dread the inevitable
query: "How is the Ph.D. coming on?" Even my evasive,
difficult, vain father could not hide his worries. Jane seemed
delighted that I was leaving; I felt she was struggling to appear concerned. And so I went. How vividly I *see* that journey northwards in my mind. Four hours by train from
King's Cross. Families of fields to pass through at great
speed. The station at Durham. Always quiet. Baskets of red
and yellow municipal flowers on metal chains, offerings
from the ceiling itself. When I arrived I saw the owner of the
ugly little sweet stall, which has been there as long as I can
remember, eating one of his own chocolate bars and reading a tabloid newspaper in a pompous way; he had half-
moon glasses on and looked up every so often, probably to
display his studiousness. The train pulled away, and in the
new silence I could hear somewhere a transistor radio's
plastic sizzle.

Yes, I can see it all, all again. The many roofs, and the
brown life of the river, and the grey cathedral which stands
over the town watching it, and its two enormous towers,
each of them showing a dark, louvred belfry—when I was a
boy I used to think of those belfries as God's lungs. Two of

the saints of the early English Church are buried in that cathedral. Over the centuries the authorities dug the poor fellows up, to prove that they had miraculously never decomposed, or to heal supplicants. Given the use they demanded of them above ground, why did that crowd ever bother to bury saints in the first place? My father used to joke that if all the limbs of Saint Francis of Assisi claimed by believers as relics were really limbs, he would have been a millipede. And below the cathedral, there is the grey main street, the cloudy café owned by the Italian family called Bimbi, the old cinema whose carpets were always moist, the bookshop run by the humourless man who left his wife for a man, and the Student Union building, looking like a restaurant kitchen, the many fliers and hurried posters pinned to its punished green door like patrons' orders.

People were walking along that main street: northerners, pale, generally reticent. The regular daily exchange between acquaintances is a wary glance, and a swift, simultaneous "Okay?"—the word being both question and its own answer. It always rains a great deal, and then the grey streets and grey bridges stream with greyness, and the ladies of the town emerge wearing curious transparent plastic head-scarves, as if they are cultivating their hair in little hothouses.

Outside the station was the usual line of shudderingly patient taxis. The driver looked oddly at me when I told him where I wanted to go. "That's a long drive, mind," he said. And that closed the conversation until, half an hour later, we entered Sundershall—barely more than a single corridor of low cottages opening out onto the green release of a lawn shaded by three or four unremarkable trees. It's said that a cricket team once played every summer on this green, but I have never seen one, and I'm pretty sure that no one plays

cricket in Sundershall. There are two pubs for every church
in this valley, something of which I approve; one of them,
The Stag's Head, looks onto the green. In summer, the
open door shows rows of wineglasses suspended by their
bases from the ceiling. When I was fifteen or so, Max and I
would nose around outside, keen to be let into this sour
cave, while the publican, Paul Deddum, standing behind his
row of tall, ornate ale-levers like a little boy behind toy soldiers, would yell at us to "get your nebs out of here"—and,
once, looking at me, "or I'll tell your da and he'll tell God."

The cab went up a gravel drive, and on the right a simple Victorian church came into view, built from big, grace-
less blocks of grey local stone. The crowded graveyard in
front of it looks with its grey slabs like the abandoned quarry
that furnished the church.

The vicarage is the same age as the church, but built of
sandstone, with leaded, ecclesiastical windows in a gothic
style, whose old glass is beginning to buckle with age. At the
door is the brass bell-pull that so delighted me when I was
young. It has always been marvellous to see the long cord,
which stretches from the door right along the hall, moving
so calmly while the sprung bell at its end convulsed. It
seemed so easy to request something: a simple pulling of
this wire, and people were summoned, came running. I
opened the door: the familiar gloom and heaviness of wood
as usual, the sparse pictures on the wall—engravings of the
cathedral, an architectural drawing of Guy's Hospital, the
copy of a Russian icon with all the battered allure of its false
gold—and the grandfather clock, still hypnotizing with a
calm pendulum.

My mother emerged from the dining room and charac-
teristically wiped her mouth and pulled her blouse down in

preparation for kissing me. I knew for certain that, on hearing the bell, she had lingered for a second to swallow, in one gulp, the remainder of a previously neglected lukewarm cup of tea.

"Thomas dear!" she said. "Tommy. Are you all right?" She held me. Unfortunately this has been her question since I went away to university.

"Yes, all in all, I am." Her grip relaxed a little. "How's Dad? Where's Dad? It's good that he's out of the hospital, right?"

"Look at you, you're a terrible mess. And you're dyeing your hair," she accused.

"I am not dyeing my hair. What colour?"

"It's darker than usual."

"It's been getting darker for the last ten years. My *hair* is dying."

"Oh, I see, your hair is *dying*." This was our usual happy routine.

"Mum, how's Dad?"

"Tommy, are you . . . bathing?"

"Bathing?"

"Yes, bathing, washing."

"Oh, now and then." I smiled, and disengaged myself from her small, strong grasp.

"Tom, it's not really something to make light of."

"Please tell me that I don't smell."

"No, no, but you don't *look* very clean, somehow."

"Well, I don't *feel* very clean," I said, smiling.

I put my bags at the foot of the stairs. I could feel, as I bent down, my mother appraising me, and sensed the cling of her anxiety.

"Daddy is feeling much better," she said. "He's in the study, I think he's preparing a sermon. But come and give me all your news in the kitchen and we can bother him later."

But I wanted to see Father right away. I rarely found my father at work, and sure enough when I entered, Peter Bunting was sitting in his armchair reading a newspaper, held up in front of his face so that he looked as if he were a hearth and the newspaper being used to make the fire catch. The air was cool and still in the study, an invisible reprimand to the room's material chaos. Papers were piled so extravagantly on the floor and desk that they no longer resembled paper; they now seemed like games, childish invitations to play and further mess the room. An old dog-basket had four or five large books piled in it, all of them wide open at a chosen page, and placed upwards on top of each other in a swift spasm of research, presumably abandoned long ago. Three drawers of the desk were sticking out, panting to spit their contents onto the floor. The only surfaces unmolested by anarchy were the books on the many bookshelves, whose clean rounded spines were as ordered as organ pipes. There was nothing hanging on the wall except a cheap, dove-coloured cross.

Of course, Father knew that I had been in the house for several minutes. He put his paper down, raised his round, bald head with its small ears and said: "Everything all right?" Years ago my parents had decided that I should call them by their first names, Peter and Sarah, but I always found myself unable to call my dad Peter to his face. So I said nothing. He looked thinner to me, but otherwise utterly unchanged. All the old vigour.

"How are you feeling, Dad?"

"Look at this!" he said, and directed me to a photograph in the newspaper. There were three bespectacled bishops, pompous in their skirts. The long cassocks seemed to be designed to hide things. "One of these men is a fraud. Which one, do you think?"

"How are you defining fraud?" I asked, feeling the familiar rise of irritation at my father's genial confidence.

"Intellectually vacant, crudely evangelical approach—'my saviour in Christ'—has personally healed eighteen cripples and cast devils out of teenage girls—always setting up youth clubs everywhere—"

"Okay, yes." I looked again and selected the man on the left, for no better reason than that his spectacles were larger than the others'.

"Wrong. It's the one in the middle. Can't you see him vibrating with zeal?"

Peter stood up, rustled the newspaper to the floor, and again asked, "Everything all right?" He looked away as he asked. It was generally the first thing he said when meeting people. It gave him the air of one who had just woken up in a hurry. "By the way," he said, "nothing wrong with me at all. Thus spake the good doctor. It's medical writ. I am free from their captivity, and not even on parole!" My father was a great Christian optimist. He liked to joke that "unlike many people, I am searching for the secret of un-happiness." He was very erudite, and rather prided himself on his worldly sense of humour, aware that this was rare in priests. For instance, he wrote book reviews for a journal of theology in London, which sent him advance copies of the books. He had removed a sticker from one of these and glued it to the favourite of his six different bibles. It read: "This is an advance copy sent in lieu of a proof."

This was pretty characteristic of his humour and of his faith. He was hospitable to all enemies. It was a family story that once a German plane was coming in to attack Peter and a group of soldiers who had become detached from their battalion. There was no time to hide. Young Peter had the idea of waving at the plane, in friendly fashion. It worked, or so he claimed, and who could dispute him? The German pilot, too high to see the uniforms, mistook the waving soldiers for Germans and flew by.

As pleasant as ever, my father took my hand and shook it. "I'm so pleased to see you looking so well," I said feebly, but meaning it. He waved my words aside, and I looked down at his shirt, which had two buttons open over his breast. His heart had obviously returned to its usual business; he liked to put his hand inside his shirt and palpate his chest, especially when involved in his favourite occupation, which was to sit in his armchair, legs immodestly splayed, and listen to Romantic music on his elderly record player. The reticent passion of Edward Elgar was the sound of my childhood, the sound of the Malvern hills in summer (though I've never seen them, in fact), the valleys as gentle as stomachs, fatherly oaks with their green brains. Peter had an old record from the 1930s, I remember, with a very young Yehudi Menuhin playing Elgar, the fifteen-year-old violinist ridiculously photographed in plus-four trousers, so that he seemed to have very long ankles, and Sir Edward Elgar, a stern, stiff old man, his white moustache a frozen waterfall over his lip. Menuhin, in a note written when he was much older, described this first encounter with the great English composer, how Elgar, at the piano, played a few bars of his Violin Concerto with the boy, and told him that he was quite happy with his playing, was sure the recording would be fine, and *he* was now going to the races. Peter Bunting loved that.

Not only was Father rarely seen writing a sermon, he was rarely seen reading a book. Yet I had never discovered any ignorance on his part. Growing up, I feared him, for there was nothing he didn't know. The stock of his knowledge was continually bubbling, and any novelty or spice could be added to it, without a fundamental change to the flavour. An extraordinarily sure mind, calmly enriching itself, very flexible and alert. He sat in his study, I now know for sure, and played puzzles and word games, and worked out in advance the puns and allusions and little jokes he loved to reveal in company. I remembered that he had made a teasing variant of the old English poem:

> Western wind, when will thou blow?
> The small rain down can rain.
> Christ, if my love were in my arms,
> And I in my bed again!

Father's version, the first line of which he murmured every so often when the television news showed long-haired Jews nodding their heads at the Western Wall, threw cold Anglican water on their absurd messianic hopes: "Western Wall, when *will* thou show?" And I would hear a contented little laugh from his high-backed chair.

Yes, I was almost always surprised, in conversation or argument, by my father's knowledge. When did he acquire it? And Peter, I suspect, knew that the mere display of that knowledge sufficed to subdue me. Once, in my early twenties, we were arguing in our usual way, by indirection, about some aspect of morality. I must have said something rash, for Peter calmly reprimanded: "That's rather a postmodern idea, I think, this collapsing of all hierarchies." The argument ended there, for suddenly he was describing *my* thought to me! Peter Bunting knew it instinctively, in a moment. He didn't need to read any books of postmodernism; he just absorbed this information swiftly and mercilessly. It was rather the way he watched whodunnits on television. Invariably, he fell asleep after fifteen minutes, because, he said, he had already worked out who had done it and was "jolly bored by the rest."

Mother was at the door. Her small frame was fronted by an apron, whose strings she had not tied but stuffed into each pocket of her loose, dark-brown trousers. Peter and Sarah were both trim, almost dainty, physically quite elegant (Peter's dishevelment existed only in his study). I was always struck by how closely they stood together. They had everything they needed. They had made a kind of joint-stock of each other's mannerisms so that the originator was no longer identifiable. For instance, I don't know which parent first began to purse his lips, but now they both did it. They communicated wordlessly. Sometimes, in the evenings, Sarah came into Peter's study, and with one hand vertical and another placed horizontally across it, made a letter T, while looking quizzically at her husband: it was the sign for a cup of tea. And though they drank tea every night, from the same art deco cups and saucers, the event seemed to give them the same pleasure every night; there was no death by repetition in their marriage, quite the opposite, it was as if only by repetition they knew the exact weight of everything.

Oh, if I could only have learned from this . . . I seem so incapable of repetition, so bad at sticking at anything, and I marvel now at this aspect of their lives, at their emotional resourcefulness. On one of the many dark days, as the general optimism was needlingly challenged by a northern rain (which quietly leaked through the window of the unheated bathroom, making a cold domestic silt in the corner of the window ledge), both parents sensed danger like animals, and said, seemingly simultaneously, "What about a fire? In the sitting room?" And that stopped the rain!

Mother, with flour on her cheek, was beckoning us to the dinner table. As I walked by her, I smudged the flour off with my finger. "What was it?" she asked. I felt my parents look at each other, felt them walking behind me, close to each other. An irritation, a burst of jealousy went through me, and then Sarah said:

"Dearest, how long will you be here?"

"I don't know, maybe a week. You know, I'm not teaching that UCL seminar this term, so I have lots of time. And Dad's health—"

"But next term you're back at UCL, yes?" asked Father quickly, with shrewd eyes.

"Yes, yes," I lied.

"Jane doesn't mind losing her husband for a week?" asked Mother, looking very directly at me, but smiling. My parents probably never spent a night apart.

"Well she'd rather I stayed, of course. But she's worried about you, Dad, so she's happy to let me come. She said she'd come up here next weekend. By the way, she played a very good recital last week for some of the students and also the general public. A lunchtime concert."

"Schumann?" asked Father, all-knowingly.

"Umm, yes, in fact, she did play some Schumann, I think."

"Probably the *Kinderszenen*."

"Exactly right, Dad, yes. And some Beethoven and Mussorgs—"

"*Pictures*?" asked Father.

"Yes, *Pictures*. Yes. Yes." I stopped for a moment, controlled my annoyance, and then went on.

"About fifty people there, and only one of them seemed to be eating his lunch, so for once it wasn't a picnic with Muzak. But there was a problem with an old man at the back—who started humming the tune quite loudly at the end of the Mussorgsky, and this same man came up at the end and bowed low and gave Jane a bunch of flowers he must have been hiding in his coat, because I had turned round several times to frown him down and hadn't seen them."

"Jane is so very pretty, I do awfully understand the impulse," said Peter, with an enthusiastic vagueness. "Who was he?"

"No idea at all," I said. Actually, it turned out, Dr. Wilkerson was an old piano teacher of Jane's, but I felt I had been obliging enough and it gave me an immature pleasure to withhold from my parents, especially my father, sitting there so receptively, information that would only make them happier and more genial than they already were.

"But tell me about the hospital, and everything else," I said.

"Oh no, let's not talk about that," said Sarah. Instead, she told one of her village stories.

She is wonderful at imitating the voices of neighbours and friends, with a high-pitched, soft snort of pleasure that makes her nostrils dilate. She creeps into people's accents like an aristocratic burglar going through someone's bedroom. Often it takes several seconds for me to realize that Mother has "disappeared" and is inhabiting another voice.

My father laughed at her story, and in far-flung amusement knocked over his wineglass. "Oh dash," he said, as the wine bloodied the blue tablecloth. He left the room, was gone several minutes, but returned only with a packet of cigarettes.

Father smoked every kind of tobacco; he passed that love on to me. At one notorious Harvest Festival dinner in the village hall Peter managed to smoke a pipe before sitting down, a cigarette between courses, and a small cigar with his coffee. Afterwards, Mother said that Peter was less like a smoker than a door-to-door salesman for tobacco, demonstrating its varied uses. I used to love watching him smoke when I was a little boy. When he exhaled, the cleaned, rare smoke took so long to emerge that his lungs seemed to be manufacturing it.

Sarah appeared not to care that he didn't choose to clean the stain on the tablecloth. She quietly left the room and returned with a cloth. But she reprimanded him for smoking in his current state of health. Peter ignored her and struck his match, holding the booming flame to the quickly red end of the cigarette for too long, as if he were lighting a pipe, so that it burned fiercely. Charred streaks journeyed along the paper.

"You know, Petie," Sarah said, "it's the cigarette that's having a cigarette, not you. It's half-gone already."

"Oh my dear, that's perfect, then, since you don't think I should have it anyway," he smiled. "And why shouldn't the poor old cigarette have a bit of a smoke? When I smoke my cigarette, am I smoking it or is it smoking me? Thomas knows who I am paraphrasing, don't you?"

"Yes," I said, irritated in spite of myself, and resisting the old family game by refusing to supply Montaigne's name or the sentence that Peter was adapting.

"One of the great Renaissance essayists," Father continued. "Possibly Christian, but more likely an agnostic and sceptic, and sensibly hiding his heresy from the authorities. But, then '*Que sais-je?*'" he finished, self-mockingly.

"I've always disliked that idea, of covert blasphemy," I said, perhaps a bit hotly, "like concealing a gun. It seems untruthful, dishonest." I said this, despite my own multiple dissimulations and deceits. I wasn't at all sure why I was saying it, except to resist my father. I didn't even believe what I was saying. My own "heresy," after all, was covert for most of my adolescence. It was still essentially covert when I was with my parents.

"Oh, I don't know," said Peter, in a sweet, singing tone. "After all, belief and unbelief are not absolutes, and not absolute opposites. What if they are rather close to each other, I mean belief shadowed by unbelief and vice versa"—he pronounced it "vicey-versa"—"so that one is not exactly sure where one begins and another ends? Then, 'lying' about belief is not like concealing a gun, is not really like lying at all, but more like telling your wife that you slept well when in fact you spent the night racked by insomnia."

"But it's still untruthful," I said, a little bewildered by my father's rapid thinking, and somewhat amazed that I was speaking these words about truthfulness so brazenly.

"Well, well," said Father soothingly.

One reason that he and I always found it so difficult to express our differences is that my father brought his immense capacity for evasion into our arguments. Peter, the supposed believer, the great parish priest, the former lecturer in theology, aerated his faith with so many little holes, so much flexibility and doubt and easygoing tolerance, that he simply disappeared down one of these holes.

After their tea ritual, my parents prepared for bed. There was a scene, repeated throughout my childhood, in which they liked to debate who should first use the bathroom (the house's other bathroom was unheated).

"Would you object, my dear, if I went first?" said Peter.

"Of course not, my love, but please do remember not to keep the hot tap running while you do whatever you do in there, or there'll be none left for the rest of us." Once, when asked more exactly "What is it that you do in there?" Father had replied that he read either the Gospel of St. Luke or seed catalogues, the kind sent by companies to gardeners for mail order. When Sarah laughed, he seemed not to understand, pursed his lips, and then burst out, mysteriously, "Yes yes, I see that the New Testament and a seed catalogue are essentially the same thing. But I'm telling the truth!"

In fact, my mother went first, and Peter, backing more amply into his armchair, crossed his legs at the knees. Glancing at the raised shoe, I saw the pavement-coloured sole, unusually clean. "It's," Peter hesitated, "marvellous that you are with us, Tom. How is the . . . er, the . . . the thesis, the Ph.D.?"

"It's going very well, Dad. It's nearly finished, actually."

"Oh, that is marvellous news, marvellous! You realize, don't you, that everything will be easier once you have finished it? Obviously." The last word was said matter-of-factly. Father used it a great deal, and it usually made me sad. But thinking of his recent frailty, his poor heart, the three days in hospital which he was refusing to talk about, I was grateful, and said, "Thank you, Dad."

Peter stirred, mended his legs, rose. "Well it's Sunday tomorrow, and I have the seven-thirty communion before the big service, so I shall push off now." Passing, he kissed me on the crown, keeping his hands in his pockets.

Left alone, I thought of nothing for a moment. My father's favourite word hung in the aftermath. Obviously. The obvious and the hidden. *Thou knowest, Lord, the secrets of our hearts.* Am I hidden, and my parents obvious?, I thought. Well, here I was, back at home again, the garden where I played as a little boy . . . There was rain outside, I could hear the first falter of it on the grass and on the old path leading to the church.

It was growing stronger now, tramping on the roof; a drop came down the chimney onto a log, and was hissed away. I climbed the stairs to my old bedroom, calling out "Goodnight" to my parents. Mother had turned on a light in the bedroom. I saw the familiar outlines of my childhood, confused by some of the furniture my parents had added in my absence. The single bed was innocently narrow, the white sheet turned down over the blanket like a Puritan collar.

There were two shelves of children's books, eagerly coloured. There was much heavy ugly furniture in the room. Really, my childhood was full of heavy, strange things. Father had always insisted on giving me "the best" available object for my birthday, despite my parents' poor finances. Armed with an order from me, Father planned his mission around "the best." As I opened it, the wrapping-paper crackled on the ground, and he used to say, "This is generally considered the best of its kind available," in a rather stiff, unnatural way, an important look on his round face. But Father's idea of luxury was never very luxurious.

When I was little, adulthood seemed a regime of such solidity. Lonely, I used to wander through the house, turning over the ungainly possessions my parents had acquired. In their bedroom was a heavy oak wardrobe filled to the limit with clothes that hung like dead curtains; this morbid plenitude was shocking, since my own little wardrobe was rather empty; there was a heavy bed, a dressing table with wing-mirrors like those of a giant antique car; a "gentleman's" clotheshorse, with a wooden arm that extended like a public sign, on which to hang trousers. For some reason this contraption reminded me of a scarecrow; it seemed to belong outside. In the bottom drawer of a large chest were rows of silver metal cylinders, each with an old, unsmokeable cigar in it. On the end of each cylinder was painted a rosy escutcheon, on which a knight on his horse gave a strange, shrunken smile. These had belonged to my father's father; now the objects that had killed him were kept as relics of his existence.

7

I HAD A HAPPY CHILDHOOD, I'm sure of it. I loved the vicarage; even the church. It was painful to witness my widowed mother having to abandon the vicarage this summer for a bungalow in Durham. Now that little church is vacant, vicarless, while the idiot bishop decides who should fill the post. I suppose I should take the bishop's tardiness as a compliment to my father's irreplaceability. To those few who bothered to come, Peter was surely irreplaceable. He dispensed a Christianity that was inseparable from life. The rhythms of the village, and of the seasons, were also the rhythms of my father's ministry: rising Easter, and sun-favoured summer, and census-gathering Christmas, when, as if in mimicry of the story of Caesar Augustus, all the villagers came to be counted and for once the church was truly full. When I was a boy, I enjoyed all the festivals except the most important, Easter. The brutality scared me, and when I was older, the unconvincing insistence of the hymns sounded like one of my own lies: "He has risen! He has risen!" Well, who says so? Don't those words resemble a school report about a delinquent who has finally moved up the class, something neither parents nor teacher quite believe? Accordingly, the little church's congregants intoned the words flatly, in mournful accents, without much joy.

Father conducted a gentle service. Mother and I usually sat in the front row, and Peter, newly plump in his henlike clerical frocks, stood not at the altar but with the congregation, in the middle of the nave. His clean, soft, bald head was filmed in light from several stained-glass windows. On Sundays he wore shoes with rubber soles (no one was quite sure why), so that he had a soundless and pious tread. Yet there was nothing else pious about him. He acted as if his church had no roof, as if it were an open theatre on which life simply shone its sun: his church, like his head, was uncovered. Into his prayers he folded every human occurrence, triumph, disaster, and banality. It was a Bunting family joke that Peter's prayers were like life, and, as Mother put it, "take almost as long." He stood, hands clasped and eyes closed, pursing his lips, and enjoined his congregation to pray to God for—everything. For the wonderful weather, for the lunch we will soon go and eat, for Muriel's swift recovery, and so on.

Bowing my head to the pew so that I could smell the gist of the wood, my right hand caressing the old heating pipe that ran along one wall, I would listen to these prayers. "And we pray," Peter intoned, "for the souls of the three priests murdered this week in El Salvador. Lord, hear our prayer. We pray also for the thousands made homeless by the recent flooding in Bangladesh, and ask you, Lord, to give them succour and shelter. Lord, hear our prayer. At this time, we also pray for Dr. Shields, whose cousin was involved in a car accident in Birmingham last Monday; and for Lance and Angela Menzies, whose son Austin died of leukemia on Friday. Lord, hear our prayer."

I always felt I was hearing a page of atrocious international news and a page of tragic local news, each ripped from the newspaper. When I was a teenager, I used to hear my father with a kind of vindictive horror, my mouth and eyes open with amazement, convinced that such a list of misfortune vandalized the very face of God. I'm more mature about these things now, I hope. Now I realize that, as far as Father was concerned, this catastrophe was God's world, vandalized by man. It was because there was so much evil-doing and pain that God's correction was needed. Pain was not an argument against but *for* God. To tell you the truth, this argument still irritates me. Why should we need correction from Him who made us? And why has He made us so very flawed, and then just disappeared? The most charitable image of this particular God I can produce is that of a father who breaks his son's leg just so that he can watch his son learn how to appeal to his dad for help in mending it.

At the end of the service, I used to greet the regulars: Terry Upsher (and, until two years ago, his deaf father), Susan Perez-Temple, Muriel Spedding. Terry did some gardening for my parents. He still lives on the main street in his father's old house. When Terry's dad was alive, they used to walk around together, Terry shouting at his unpleasant old dad, who walked always slightly ahead of him as if they were a Muslim husband and wife. Terry has never left the county, and has never been on a train. I am very fond of one of his verbal peculiarities. He says "the part of it is" when he means "the point is," or "the thing is." Sometimes, when I was little, we used to sit on the wall of the vicarage garden, and Terry might say, haltingly, "The part of it is . . . I don't feel very champion at the moment," or "The part of it is . . . that there bush is *finished*." Then he would stand up and wander off.

Muriel Spedding was always at church. She is a kindly widow who used to take hot meals to Terry and his father when old Mr. Upsher was still alive. Otherwise, people said, the Upshers would have lived off bread and butter and jam.

Muriel is very trim, with tiny black lace-up shoes that seem, as is often the case with old ladies, to have become her feet. It is impossible to think of her ever taking them off. It is as if her feet are entombed in two little graves. Yet she is very alive and spry, and keeps her shape by dancing, and by playing an enormous electronic organ whose sound trembles. Muriel is worldly in an unworldly way, has travelled, and enjoys proving to me that she knows exactly where I live in London. "And how *is* Islington?" she would ask me conspiratorially, pulling girlishly at the buttons of her blouse.

And pompous Mr. Norrington was a regular, and also the old lady, Miss Ogilvie, who, curiously, used three sticks, one for the left leg and two for the right.

At the end of the service the fifteen or so worshippers clustered by the door and walked down the graveyard path very fast, with fugitive pleasure, as people always hurry the last room in an art gallery, eager to be done with all that observant piety. My mother used to say that this urgency had to do with their need to prepare Sunday lunch, but I've always disliked Sundays themselves—the awful calm of those afternoons— and I am sure that the sensible villagers felt exactly the same. Nietzsche, my old companion, wrote that only the industrious English could have invented the deep boredom of Sundays, the better to make us welcome a busy Victorian Monday.

No, the only people who clearly enjoyed every aspect of Sunday were my parents. After the service, in the vicarage kitchen, as the Sunday roast—beef, lamb, pork, in strict rotation—was dying a second time in the oven, my parents used to talk through the service. On the Sunday of my return last September, Mother lightly rebuked Peter.

"My dear, your sermon was a wee bit long and obscure today. I lost count of the number of literary allusions."

"There were seven, precisely," said Peter, mock-woundedly. "A biblical number." He lit a cigarette, and dropped it.

"Twenty-five minutes is too *long*, my dear," insisted Mother. "And I hope that cigarette stays on the floor."

"Is it, now?" asked Peter gently, fiddling on the floor for the white cylinder. He stood up and smiled. "When I was a young man I once went to a church up in the Scottish Highlands, terribly strict and austere, where the antique minister, who must have been at least eighty, spoke for fifty-five minutes—fifty-five minutes!—on the text 'And Moses and Aaron fell flat on their faces.' Now *that* was a sermon! Not a dry eye in the house by the end."

"Nor an open one, I daresay," laughed Sarah. "I thought that the church in the Highlands was the place where the minister was retiring and was giving his last sermon."

"No, my dear, that was in Cornwall. Dick Hooper's old church in Truro. Yes, it *was* his last sermon before his retirement, and the vain blighter was feeling very loved by all and very sorry for himself, and certain he would be missed, so he chose for his text 'And they fell upon Paul's neck, and kissed him.' The vanity of it!"

Sunday always brought out my parents' most ecclesiastical wit.

WHEN I WAS A LITTLE BOY, Sunday was a visiting day, and Saturday a marrying day. On Monday mornings, I often took a piece of wedding cake in my lunchbox to the village school: this was the spoil of my father's work on Saturdays. It seemed to me then that my father was constantly marrying and burying people, joining and separating them. In my childish mind the dead and the affianced were equally half-alive; they all entered the vicarage as reputations. Each category was treated in the same easy, genial way. "I have to marry Clendennon's son," Peter might announce at the dining table, while I, wide-eyed, legs dangling from the slatted kitchen chair, trying to do my homework, looked on. "He's gone and got Joanna—you know, Joanna in the pub—pregnant." Or, once, as he came into the kitchen, with his overcoat on:

"Bill Clemons has died. What on earth am I going to say about him? He only came to church at Christmas."

"Adele Clemons we know far too well," said Sarah.

"Oh yes, she *is* most peculiar. When I went round there just now to offer the usual 'and God shall wipe away all tears from their eyes,' she gave me a cup of tea, and as I was sitting there I sensed a presence behind me just out of eyesight. I turned and there was Bill Clemons sitting upright in the armchair, the poor fig, utterly dead of course, but staring at me in a rather lively fashion, with a small photograph in his

hand. I suppose Adele called me before calling the undertakers."

"A photograph? How odd. Adele probably called you
both and you just beat them to it. That wouldn't be very
hard. The Pickerings are practically dead themselves."

"They are their own undertakers!" said Peter.

"With Bill you can always do the Japanese angle," said
Sarah.

"I'd thought of that. Three years as a prisoner of war did
him in, that's pretty obvious."

Death had no sting in the Bunting household, partly
because Sarah and Peter sincerely believed in the resurrection of souls (or "lift-off," as Peter called it), and partly because death was a technical matter which called for an
immediate flurry of organization, and a swift obituary. Most
of the villagers discussed were not members of the church,
since hardly anyone came to church; the village was Peter's
real church, and had to be. For instance, the couples who
came to the vicarage to arrange to be married were often
strangers to Peter. I used to love opening the door to them.
A young man and woman stood awkwardly. As if in preparation for their life of traditionally divided labour, it was always the young man's task to say the first words: "Is . . . is
the vicar in, then?"

As shy as them, I asked them inside, and they stood in
the hall, their heads bent as if it were raining, and looking
around naively at the walls. Peter emerged, bustled them
into his study. Then I heard that sound so familiar to me,
of quiet conversation behind a door. The house vibrated
solemnly as if a doctor were visiting. Behind that door, in
father's extraordinarily untidy study, these people discussed

their weddings. I used to press my ear to the wood, once in delightful consort with Mother, who held my hand as we listened. "This one will be our little secret," she said. A sentence or two could be heard occasionally: "No, we like the *old* service, with all them words," or "A week in Edinburgh is good enough for the two of us."

The visitors, the visitors! They came up the gravel path, past the graveyard with its look of tidy ruin, to ask for healing of one kind or another. Religion barely entered into it. In that traditional place, the priest was socially elevated. Going to Peter was a modern version of visiting the landowner to collect wages. Peter gave the parishioners the salary of his words, and rich words they often were. With gentle, undogmatic faith, he fit himself around the lives of his flock. Peter believed that most of his petitioners were in search of friendship rather than God. Mr. Tattersall, now long dead, used to come every week on Sunday afternoon when I was a boy. He had a red birthmark like a wax letter-seal across one cheek, and always carried a small umbrella, even when it was sunny. Father told me that Mr. Tattersall was "terribly alone." Mother told me that Mr. Tattersall had driven a bus for many years, the cream-coloured 54 that went every day between the villages. He had had an accident in which he knocked down a pedestrian. There had been nobody on the bus at the time—there rarely was—and Mr. Tattersall had accelerated away. The pedestrian recovered, and Mr. Tattersall, whom no one liked, was not charged; perhaps it was felt that he was already punished by the now shameful symbolism of his birthmark.

Terry Upsher was another regular Sunday visitor, always in the same clothes, as if, like a child, he had been dressed by a monotonous mother. There was the flat cap, with its dirty softness inside, a collarless shirt pulled tightly over a strongly mapped chest, and trousers that were too short, so that he seemed permanently excited. His face was grey; his high voice quavered loudly, and Mother and I could hear everything he said inside Peter's study. When Terry's father was alive, he was adamant that he never came for himself, only for his father.

"The part of it is, Vicar, me da's not been champion these last few days. He says nowt, never speaks to us except he says 'good morning' when he gets up. Rest of the day he's dowie, he just watches TV like it was all the one fil'm."

"And how are you, Terry? How are *you* bearing up?"

"Me? I'm okay, Vicar, it's just me da. I'm past meself with worry."

I used to follow Terry once he came out of the study. I was disturbed by his large, dirty hands; I had never seen anything like them. Terry swung one of those hands onto my head, and then often I accompanied him into the vicarage garden, and sometimes into other gardens, and watched him mend a broken rose, or build a bonfire, or clean a moss-sown wall. Terry was silent in a way my parents never were, except when they were eating. Yes, that was it, Terry worked as if eating through his jobs, with resigned hunger. Silently he did his occasional work in all seasons: in autumn (which he called the "back-end"), when the laburnum shed its poisonous tadpoles; in winter, when the frost candied the grass; in pricking spring and in powdery summer, when each full tree, busy with sanguine birds, became its own forest. And all the while, I looked at Terry's hands, broad with earthy seams.

I used to think that Terry spoke "funnily," and one day asked him why.

"I was born here," he said. "Me da's the one what talks funny, he has that many clever words from when he was down the pit." Terry told me that the coal miners had certain words peculiar to themselves, a whole language, and these were called "pitmatic." I loved this word as soon as I heard it; later, Max and I would name our philosophical group the Pitmatic Philosophical Society, in homage.

"With this strike on, it's just down at heels for me da now, he's angry at them in the pits, the miners, for striking, and he doesn't say much. 'I'm resigning my membership'—he said that yesterday, and I said to him, 'What you talking about, you're not a member of owt!' But when he talked pitmatic, like, I couldna get half-nowt from him anyway, so whor's the difference?" I loved following Terry around, brought him a sandwich and an apple from the vicarage. He hunched over his food as if he were crying.

Sometimes I felt I wasn't welcome. There was an awkward moment once when Terry asked me if my father helped me with my homework.

"Does he write it for you?" He looked strangely at me, closely.

"No," I said, lying. I could see a tiny straw of sleep in his left eye.

"I reckon he does. I can tell from your face. Well, that's not allowed, is it? He's doing it. That's clodding! You sitting on your honkers, with your da doing it! What's the capital of America, then, if your da's not clodding for you?"

"I don't know," I said.

I've won some of them pub quizzes," he said, rather

than supply the information. When I was older, I discovered that Mr. Deddum occasionally fiddled the answers so that Terry could win the odd pub quiz. Practically the whole village was in on the deception.

I will always remember that afternoon—I was ten or eleven, still small—when, alone as usual, I walked out of the vicarage, down past the churchyard, and turned left towards a little bridge that mounted the river. As I turned the corner, I saw Terry leaning against a wall, breathing heavily, while another man, a stranger, was trying to shake his hand. Both men looked as if their clothes had been shifted slightly to one side of their bodies. One of Terry's shoes was lying upside down on the pavement. Terry ignored the man, worried his shoe onto his foot—holding out his shaking hands like a diver as he did so—and walked away, followed by me. He was muttering, "I'll *lace* him, I'll lace him." I followed him to his house; I had never been there. Old Mr. Upsher was watching the television, a daytime sitcom. "I'm in a fight, Da," Terry shouted, in his high, nervous, unstable voice. "Good," replied his father, barely stirring. Before I left, Terry showed me what he called "the special room." It was sparse—a small table, a chest of drawers, and very thin curtains. They fluttered hopefully as the door opened. He turned on the single light, a bare torturer's bulb. On all the surfaces, and on the floor, were piles of many objects: boxes of chocolates, small decorative plates, a bar of fancy soap, a silver cannon, a framed antique map. I recognized the map. "We gave that to you," I said.

"This is where I keep everything what's given us by people for me jobs," he said. "I don't touch owt of this . . . paraphenayli." He turned out the light and shut the door.

"Me da's not allowed in there," he said, quite happily. "And divvent tell anyone about this."

It was a Sunday rule that someone from the village join my parents for lunch. Often these lunches were full of mishaps and misunderstandings. Peter and Sarah were exquisitely courteous, but in such a way that they imprisoned their guests. Father compensated for his shyness by making his questions refined and ornate. He adopted this manner only at the dining room table, almost as if he had been taught it by his parents.

"And your fair niece, whom I once met . . . Ah, is she still sans husband? She should hurry. You know that line from the poem, 'Too long a sacrifice can make a stone of the heart.' I always thought her eminently marryable, however." Muriel Spedding, to whom this question was once addressed, lost all her customary jauntiness and muttered into her soup. Mother's task was to translate her husband for others, so speedily and instinctively that many never noticed it. Peter might ask of a guest: "Are you talking about that oddly uncherished little path that bifurcates the top field?" and my mother, sensing that the visitor was lost, would insert: "You mean Pilgrim's Path, by Harrison's farm?"

In my memory, these Sunday guests were always single, middle-aged women, hungry for company but made clumsy by Peter and Sarah's obvious fulfilment in marriage. Demurely they stood in the hall, fiddling with coats whose buttons seemed too large for their fingers, their screenlike spectacles magnifying their anxious eyes into bullets of panic, their long, obscuring skirts a kind of lay equivalent of Peter's chaste cassock. Only their thick grey strong metallic hair, simply cut by the one salon in the valley, seemed to be in its prime, greedily nourishing itself at the expense of the soul.

On the Sunday of my visit a year ago, Susan Perez-Temple, who was not at all shy, was the guest. Everyone knows about Susan because of the exoticism of her background. Her father was a valet in the royal court in Madrid, and she grew up practically in the palace. She arrived in her usual lemon coat and a string of huge, flamboyant amber beads which had been given to her mother by a Spanish nobleman.

"How's my favourite philosopher?" she said, offering her dry cheek to me. And then to Peter, "How's my favourite vicar? Don't overdo it, Peter. There was absolutely no need for you to take the service today."

Susan is highly conservative. She carries with her a constant suggestion that she might at any moment complain about something or other, because her favourite conversational gesture is "Don't get me started on . . ." "Don't get me started on South Africa and Mr. Desmond Tutu"—she would snap his name as if she were teaching numerals to stupid children. "Don't get me started on the United States of America," spelling out the words as if the union were a recent chimera. But in fact she never does "get started" on any of these controversial subjects, and I've decided that this is perhaps the unconscious strategy of a shy woman with strong private opinions, in the way that a small country might boast about the power and professionalism of its army without often deploying it.

As we sat down to lunch, she said:

"Imagine, Sarah, I was sitting in the village hall last Thursday. Actually, I was thinking about you, Peter, stuck in that awful hospital in Durham. Don't get me started on the hospital! You remember that a string quartet were playing? Before the concert, the schoolchildren had had a tea party, and it was a dreadful rush to get them out in time. During the concert, I became aware of a very strange smell, an odour really, and I began to look around, and couldn't see anything. Well, then I saw the radiators: on every one of them there was a large, wet, dirty tea towel drying out! Can you think of anything more primitive? Really, this village! The hall isn't some kind of nomad's tent, it is not a yurt— do you know the yurt? I sat in one last year on my Mongolian trip."

Susan had just come back from Uganda, where she had seen twelve corpses, all from the same family, laid out on the grass. No one would tell her what had killed them. The authorities had arranged them as a series, according to height, from the tallest to the shortest.

"They were a bit like those cheap nests of Russian dolls I once saw on my trip to Moscow. I imagine it was some kind of virus, because they were immediately buried, and then all of their belongings were set on fire."

The image powerfully struck me.

"Christ," I said, perhaps too enthusiastically—and saw out of the corner of my eye Father's disapproval of that blasphemous invocation—"what an amazing and awful notion. The absolute destruction of everything, and the completely irrelevant fate of losing everything *after* one's death, when one is already totally extinguished."

"But in fact not totally extinguished," said Susan. "The Ugandans, so I was told, have a word for the grave which translates roughly as 'hiding place.' So they may consider themselves to be hanging around after death. Anyway, they are usually buried with some of their favourite objects."

Peter started at this, and as he moved, so a long arm of ash broke off his cigar, suddenly, and fell on to the large blue tablecloth. It made me think of a sailor who has walked the plank and suddenly fallen into a blue sea. I laughed to myself.

"You know, don't you," Peter asked, and looking be-musedly at me as if I were a little strange to be laughing at this moment, "that the locals have a word not dissimilar for the grave? They call it a lair. A northern and Scottish word. It is not applied to the grave per se"—he pursed his lips—"but to one's slot in the graveyard, the place you book with me before you die."

"Why are you sounding *quite* so jolly?" asked Sarah, with a smile in her voice.

"Well, it's interesting, isn't it? Obviously a lair suggests that the dead are waiting down there to rise up again and attack the living, like bandits. Awfully pagan really, I ought to discourage it, but they all use it. It's important that they book now, because we are running out of space."

"I'm already booked," said Susan.

"So you are, in the northwest corner, I believe, with me!" said Peter. "Just as New York can only expand upwards, our churchyard can only expand downwards. We don't have the room to put man and wife next to each other. No, now we have to rebury old corpses further down, and then put a new corpse on top of the old one."

"So, 'lair' is actually more precise than 'six feet under,'" said Sarah.

"It's more like twelve feet under. For instance, Dr.

Braun. Now, his wife, remember, died, what, ten years ago? Anyway, Braun has booked a lair—of course *he* doesn't use the word—in the same grave as his wife. But there is no space alongside. So when old Braun pops off, we will have to re-bury Mrs. Braun farther down, and then put her husband on top of her. It'll be tighter still for Terry when he dies, because both his father and mother are down there already. Braun is much better off in that respect."

"No democracy, even in death," said Susan with satis-faction.

I shuddered at all this blithe talk of burial and reburial, because at that point in my life I had attended only one funeral, my grandmother's, at which I behaved very poorly. I was six when my granny, Peter's mother, died. Father took the service, said "Ashes to ashes, dust to dust," and threw soil down into the pit. I could make no sense of anything. Why was he doing that? My friend Richard threw gravel at my bedroom window in the same way, to get me to wake up early so that we could go and play behind the big tree on Pilgrim's Path before breakfast. Was Daddy throwing soil to get Granny to wake up? Down the path from the church-yard I saw a man in a grey cap polishing with an invisi-ble cloth the doors of the hearse. It looked like he was writing playful letters on the car. I envied him; he had escaped our miserable responsibilities. Daddy sternly in-toned the words of the funeral service, and everyone looked very intelligent, staring and frowning at the coffin, as if it were Granny's *fault* she was dead. Suddenly I broke away from the mourners and ran fast towards the hearse—why, exactly, I don't know. I fell on a tree root or stump of stone, twisted my ankle painfully, and cried out. Behind me, my father, dressed from head to toe in a black cassock, a column of night, strode towards me with a furious look on his face. Furious. Simultaneously, the driver approached, and the two men, converging, picked me up, each holding one of my arms. The driver started to ask me if I was all right, but Father spoke over him. "Come back to the grave," he said, still frowning like everyone else gathered there. I stood next to him at the graveside throughout the rest of the service, and his black cassock thinly brushed me.

I could never forget my father's stern face as he strode towards me. After that disgrace, I had a recurrent nightmare, in which my father, dressed again in his black robes, walked angrily towards me, and my grandmother then woke up from the dead, pushed open the coffin, pursed her lips as my parents did, and began to whistle a horrible tune—it was the hymn "Crimond," which we sang in church. I wanted to tell my parents about it, but they seemed so happy, and I didn't want to spoil their happiness. I was silly, because if I had told them I am sure my parents would not have been cross, as Peter once was when he caught me telling a lie. "Now, my little man," he said very solemnly, gripping my arm firmly with the pincers of muscular Christianity, "we won't have lies in this house. We absolutely *will not have lies in this house.*"

I was so shocked that I cried, and Mother came to comfort me.

"Oh really," said Peter, "if you indulge his tears, he will become as bad as Saint Ignatius—weep, weep, weep."

"Was Ignatius especially tearful?" asked Mother, interestedly, turning away from me.

"My hat, yes. Saturated in tears. Endless tearful self-punishments. Ignatius couldn't get up in the morning without challenging the day to a weeping match."

And, as usual, my parents drifted off into their charmed world, their happy involvement with each other.

¶

DURING MY STAY AT THE VICARAGE LAST SEPTEMBER, when my father was recovering from his heart attack, Jane came up for the second weekend. Because she had seemed so glad to get rid of me in London, I was wary of her. But she was surprisingly cheerful. We walked a lot in the countryside around the village. It was cold and damp, and the air slowly labelled her white cheeks with two pink dots. She gripped my hand and I gripped hers, and with nervous happiness I glanced at her often to see that she was indeed happy, taking my signs from the firmness of her chin and the always sensitive needle of her ponytail. I used to look sideways in this way at Jane, so as to know how to act, what to say.

We walked in the relentless northern rain, along the road between Durham and Sundershall, and I looked through Jane's eyes and saw again the high hills, where cloud-shaped sheep moved, and the lower fields, which were full of cows. As the cows sighted us, they pricked a swaying wander over the sucking mud, came to the fence and snorted faint figures of steam. Their mooing noises buzzed deep down in their unemotional throats. We dripped at the cows and they dripped back at us, and then we walked a little more, noticing the birds that jumped onto the fence, the starlings and jetty rooks so abundant in the north, each high-strung, jerking movement resembling the separated frames of a film. At dusk, on the telephone lines, the starlings armied.

The rain ceaselessly fell, a million little surrenders of water,
and the hills and fields surged green. Sometimes a car went
past us, lashing water to the side.

We had been instructed by my mother to pay a visit to
Max's parents, Colin and Belinda Thurlow. The order was
characteristic; I think that my parents considered that the
Thurlows, whom I very much disliked, were somehow good
for me. Peter thought that Colin's abrasiveness fortified
me somehow. And they also liked to show Jane off to the
Thurlows, I think. On my own I was no match for Max's
great success as a journalist. Max the great columnist at *The
Times*, Max the opinion-maker. Perhaps my parents were
ashamed of my wasted years. But with Jane by my side, I was
at least a significant married man, with an advantage over
the still-bachelor Max. Jane was evidence that I had clearly
made *some* use of all the hours and days of my wilderness
twenties.

Colin and Belinda teach at Durham University, though
Colin is now emeritus. Belinda is an historian, of leftish
and once Marxist slant, and her older husband a classicist
who writes under the forbidding initials C.R.M. Thurlow.
When they first arrived in Sundershall, in the summer of
1973, Mother promised me that I would gain a friend: the
Thurlows had a thirteen-year-old son, exactly my age. But
Max was allowed out to play only rarely, as if ordinary life
were a dubious party from which children had to be swiftly
collected. Dear Max, bespectacled and tall, with a slight
stoop even as a teenager, was studying for a scholarship to
the day school I was already attending in Durham, and
seemed to be almost imprisoned in his bedroom. When,
rarely, he was released, he generally brought with him a
schoolbook, which he read if the excitements flagged. But

Max certainly enjoyed smoking, which we did at the top of Pilgrim's Path, underneath the large, spreading, Atlas-like oak tree. He became a junior scholar of cigarettes, erudite on the different strengths of Gitanes and Dunhills.

The Thurlows live in a pretty Georgian house lit with bright honeysuckle, which covers the dark red bricks in seasonal distractions. Other than the vicarage, it is the only large house in Sundershall, and is known as "The Oratory." The household at The Oratory seemed strange to me when I was young. Colin and Belinda were remote, cold, pedantically involved in their "work." There was none of the Bunting geniality at the Thurlowses'. I remember how Max used to open the door (whispering in my ear that he had "some new fags"), and as he did so, two study doors on either side of the hall opened. From one side appeared Belinda's head, and from the other Colin's nose. Belinda, seeing that it was only me, and Colin, apparently merely smelling my presence, then withdrew. The Oratory is very plain inside. I once peered into Colin's study during the winter and was shocked to see plastic sheeting nailed to the windows, presumably to keep out draughts. Through these sheets the garden looked submarine. The corridors are freezing, in all weathers, and in the downstairs bathroom a bar of green medicinal soap, with a magnet embedded in it as if it were a grenade, clings stingily to a metal holder which extends from the wall. Thanks to its magnet, it seems, the bar of soap lasts years.

I especially dislike Colin. His ears are large and on fire with a tiny network of veins, which also cover his nose and cheeks. In some men these veins suggest a life of drink and wasteful pleasure. In Professor Thurlow's case they suggest a lifetime of studying minute connections and branches of knowledge; the veins are like little paths of rewarded endeav-our; it is as if a map of diligence covers his face. In happier days, my mother used to imitate Colin Thurlow's quick, uncertain smile; she made me and Father laugh when she reproduced some of his sayings, such as "Driving a motor car is intellectual suicide, of course," and his peculiar com-plaint about "the girls who serve at Marks and Spencer—really the lowest of the low, intellectually speaking." Belinda Thurlow lacks her husband's pedantry and malice. (She also drives the family car.) She has a bad back and often leaves the room to "have a lie down." She wears shapeless denim dresses with large storage-pockets, giving her the air of an intellectual poacher. Belinda is Max's saviour; it can only be from his mother that he gets his sweetness.

Jane and I were led into the frigid drawing room. Be-linda left, and returned, wheeling an ugly silvered trolley before her. It bore a white plastic Thermos flask and a plate of white sandwiches, which were organized in four batches of four sandwiches each. An ambassador of each batch was impaled with a little coloured flag on the end of a cocktail stick. "We don't have you and Jane here very often, so we pulled the stops out," she said. "Now, you see, this enables me to keep the fillings separate in my mind. The blue flag is anchovy paste, white is cucumber, green is tinned salmon, and red is gooseberry jam." She poured tea from the Thermos. It fumed in the wintry air. "These cups keep the heat much better," she said, as she handed us large plas-tic mugs.

I looked at the electric fire, at the tangerine grin of its single coiled bar, and wondered if it would be rude if Jane and I left within half an hour. I prepared myself externally

by "setting" my face. It was during the first or second year of
our marriage, while I was working hardest on the Ph.D.,
that I contracted my habit of "setting" my face to resemble
an appropriate emotional state—humble in post offices (because the staff are always so sullen), generous in shops, distracted at the university (to impress the students), arrogant
in buses, confident with my parents, genial with Jane, sober
with Max's parents, and so on. It came about, I think, because I spent all day at home and had no one to show my face
to until I blundered out onto the busy London street—and
suddenly, people were looking at me, staring at me, and I
had to appear correct. That is also why I began the trick of
the solemn little cough. I can't recall how that started. I
think it was originally to hide a moment of social awkwardness. But then I began to give little coughs not to hide an
awkwardness but simply to seem serious and preoccupied.
There is something grave and quite contained about a man
giving a little cough with his fist held to his mouth, in the
classical way. Sitting there in the Thurlowses' house, I made
my face look serious and distinguished, with an analytical
squint and pursed Bunting lips.

Colin Thurlow asked about Max. The Thurlows do not
have a television, and Colin, at least, does not read a newspaper. He disapproves of newspapers. So I had to report on
Max's success in the media without making it sound as if it
was actually occurring in the media. I thought a pompous
patina might help.

"Is Max hard at work on his exposés?" asked Colin,
stretching out the last word.

"Max prospers. He's a most venerable figure now—at
only thirty," I said, with proper gravity.

"Aha," said Colin. He always said "Aha" in a flat, verifying way, as one might when copying down a number. Even when I told him a funny or strange story, his expression would not change. He would study the room in general and calmly say "Aha."

"What does eighteen ninety-six mean to you?" Colin asked me.

"Now, Colin," said Belinda, "you've been riding this hobby horse so hard it's broken its back."

"Eighteen ninety-six," said Colin, taking my silence to be ignorance, "is the date of the founding of the *Daily Mail*. I dare say one could do worse than date a certain civilizational decline from that moment. The tabloidization of our intellectual discourse." Colin always acted like an inspector from a rarer country.

"But Max doesn't work for the *Daily Mail*," said Jane. It was the first time she had spoken in the drawing room. "He's a columnist for a serious paper. It's *The Times*." Colin stared at Jane, as if astounded that a woman other than his wife would oppose him.

"He's a pundit!" said Belinda brightly, with what sounded like a curious, evenly balanced mixture of pride and disdain.

"He's a 'pundit,' as were, in their way, Voltaire, Heine, Carlyle, Orwell, Sartre, and on," I protested.

"I think he had the brains to be an excellent classicist," said Colin, ignoring me. "It's a great shame that he did not carry on into the academy . . . like you."

Like me . . . This was surely calculated irony on Colin's part. But Belinda wanted to change the subject.

"Isn't it sad about Mrs. Millington having to sell Vaughan House," she said.

"Oh, Max and I loved that house when we were little.

The red bricks, and the ivy—the river. Who'll buy it?" I asked.

"It's already bought. With all contents. Philip Zealy. You know him."

"Philip Zealy? That crook. My God." Everyone in Durham knew Zealy; he had a local car dealership, which had expanded into an empire. His latest experiment was a financial services company: credit, brokerage, loans, mortgages. He was based in Newcastle but chose to live in Durham. A familiar sight of my childhood on billboards and local television advertisements, he was universally thought of as shady and disreputable, thanks to a local government scheme in which he had profited. The ringleaders went to prison; Zealy somehow escaped charges.

"That's him. It's a Cornish name," said Belinda to Jane—"no, my dear, Cornish," she repeated, anticipating her husband's correction. "But he isn't living in it, apparently. Expect the worst. He'll break it up into flats or knock it down for profit."

"Mrs. Millington had six Pekineses, and all of them had extraordinary names," I said to Jane. "One of them was called B.D., for 'brain damage.'"

"What were the others?" asked Jane.

"Horatio, Albino, Salmon, and—oh, I'm getting old, I forget now," said Belinda. Our conversation was clearly becoming too warm, too feminine, too much of a conversation, to please Colin, who was staring at the window, waiting for a natural break to announce itself. Once again I marvelled that Max, so sane and dependable and cheerful, had grown up with these parents.

"How is that Ph.D. of yours progressing?" asked Colin. Enquiry had been inevitable.

"It's nearly finished," I said. "Really close to the end now."

"Aha." The verifying stare. "You know that I don't have one? A questionable supplement. It's largely for people who like letters after their name." While you, I thought, like letters in front of your name.

"And how is Birkbeck?" Colin asked.

"It's University College, actually."

"University College. Indeed. A cut above, a cut above. No wonder you wanted to correct me so fast."

My thesis is on the influence of the Epicureans on early modern English thought. Colin Thurlow told me that he did not "like" the Epicureans.

"Why not?" I asked.

"They were rather juvenile. They may seem mature about death, but if you study it you'll see that they were juvenile about it. Terrified of it. Emotion posing as rationality."

We got away as fast as we could. I told Jane how, when Max and I were small, we had heard Colin talking to my father at the dinner table. From the cigarette smoke drifted the phrase, in Colin's precise accent: ". . . the Kyrie is recited ninefold in that rite, I believe." Max and I laughed for weeks about the word "ninefold," which we had never heard before.

On the Saturday night of Jane's weekend in Sundershall, I offered to cook supper for all of us. Father, who had been oddly invisible all day, stayed in his study; Mother and Jane, I remember, laughed at my grand manner in the kitchen: Jane stole pieces of food from the counter. I like to play at being rather magnificent when cooking; half the pleasure is in disobeying all the rules of the recipes and refusing to measure anything as precisely as instructed. I threw around clouds of herbs and roughly upended the newly opened wine bottle into the casserole so that I could hear that delicious steady choking noise as expensive wine blunders in tides into the pot. Of course, I have to be careful to be not *too* blasé. Jane, who knows nothing about cooking, used to enjoy suspending her adulthood in the kitchen. Her favourite trick was to give my arm a nudge while I was spooning or shaking something into a pot; she had no idea that I was really keeping a secret tally of weights and measurements—that, in effect, I was measuring my own carelessness. To her it was just another area of Thomas's anarchy, but one which, unlike bill paying or accepting invitations, did not affect her.

I produced an aromatic coq au vin (made with some pricey wine I had bought in Durham and a few interestingly different spices) for my parents, who were at their best, high-spirited and genial. My father was exceptionally jaunty, and told Jane, when he emerged from his study, about his day. His bald head shone.

"Jane, Jane, my dear. Your presence in this house is the single star in the unrelieved blackness of my day."

"Oh, Peter, it can't have been that bad," said Jane, enjoying the old man's attention.

"I have passed the day in utterly monkish solitude. There was no one at all at the early communion this morning, not a solitary fig, so I had to administer communion to myself, swill down the wine like a Neapolitan, and resist the exceedingly strong temptation to skip great chunks of the liturgy. Then I went home, had breakfast—alone, because my esteemed wife had been too greedy to wait for me and you sluggards were still in bed—read the morning paper, changed into civvies, and spent most of the rest of the day writing a book review for Jim Earley at the *Theological Review*."

"You should have been resting, dearest," said Sarah.

Peter looked meaningfully at me; it was my cue to ask him about the book.

"What was the book?" I asked.

"A shallow study of the resurrection, but it did allow me to invent a rather good joke, though I say it myself." Again, my cue.

"Yeah?" I asked, stirring the casserole, and watching my strong, healthy father, impish and commanding. I tried to find any suggestion of weakness, of recent frailty, and failed.

"Yes, I said that the author was certainly right that although the resurrection is the hardest miracle in which to believe, it is nevertheless the central one, the only one really, and most faithful Christians in this country do in fact believe that Jesus rose again."

"I don't get it—"

"I'm not finished. I then added that there is a certain modishly unbelieving Anglican bishop, 'who shall remain nameless,' that was how I put it, who obviously does not believe in the great triumph of the resurrection and who 'seems to think that when they took Jesus down from the Cross he just ran down the other side of the hill and disappeared.' That's what I wrote. What do you think?" He looked at me hopefully.

"Not bad at all, Dad."

"Oh good, you like it."

At the table, Mother asked Jane about her teaching, and about future concerts. I couldn't help noticing that my parents seemed almost afraid of Jane, respectful of her talents and accomplishments.

"I haven't been able to practise hard in the last two years, because of my heavy teaching load," Jane said, and looked at me briefly, dazzlingly, with her dense, filled eyes. As usual, I had to look at the rest of her face to check that she was not angry. She was not; and yet I felt that she mentioned the teaching reproachfully, since had I not been essentially unemployed she would not have needed to support me. I felt my parents looking at me, felt some kind of hard rise of energy, and became irritated.

"I'm not going to apologize, if that's what you want," I said, cursing myself for having so baldly shown my hand.

"What on earth are you talking about?" said Jane. At which point my mother, whether designedly or not I don't know, seemed to choke on her food, and said:

"This is a *very* strange coq au vin. Is that a caper on my fork? What on earth have you put in it, Tommy?"

"Made by a very strange chef," said Father, and we all laughed.

After supper, at Peter's suggestion, Jane played for us. The usual apologies were made—how often I have heard them—for the poverty of the English upright piano in the sitting room. ("No one ever plays it in this family, you see.") As so often, Jane seemed to be lifting her hands to calm the instrument, soothing and stroking it. I identified with the piano. The black and white keys went up and down, madly disagreeing with one another, yet from this curious enclosure came beauty and loveliness and harmony, and Jane was their provider. I envied her this unworldly ability to bring flocks of sound from sheets dotted with abstract black collisions. She played a Chopin mazurka, slightly primly seated in the way that had excited me when I first saw her, her bottom softly quenched by the soft seat, which made me want to be that seat, and she moved her long thin arms, and the bright repeating Polish music filled the room, the notes quickly running, but running a little stiffly, with pointed joints, as if a barrel organ were turning the sound, a street music, a people's peg-leg dance, full of clanging joy—I could imagine them throwing out their legs and kicking the air—and all this raised by English Jane, primly seated.

When she plays, she raises her head and closes her eyes, and seems to leave the world a little, to be alone with her notes in almost religious silence. I have sometimes to struggle with selfish resentment—resentment that she is so free, that she can so easily slip out of reality, that she cannot take me with her, that she seems almost to be at prayer (which as a secularist I am bound to disapprove of). We do indeed differ on religious matters, though Jane is so mystical that we have never really argued about the subject. She pities me a little, I think, for having no God to believe in. But if Jane does believe in God, then, as far as I can tell, He is really little more than a bearded old patron of music, a male Saint Cecilia. "A note," she once said to me, "is an extraordinary thing. It wasn't created by humans. Humans reproduce it; they borrow it and lend it to each other, by using instruments." I objected that the instruments were created by humans, not by God.

"Yes, certainly," said Jane. "But you can't tell me that harmony is created by humans; how could it be? It's like logic in maths. We don't decide that two plus two equals four, we come upon that, it's already made—isn't it?"

"Yes, the ancient world talked about the music of the world—they felt it lay in the arrangement of the celestial spheres, that kind of thing. You know how keen I am on Schopenhauer—"

"I certainly do. How much was that book you bought on him last week? Thirty pounds?" Jane was teasing me, smiling broadly.

"It'll earn its keep, believe me . . . Well, Schopenhauer has this mad but really quite likable theory that divisions in music correspond to the divisions between the organic and mineral worlds. He says something to the effect that a chord with a wide gap between soprano and bass sounds good because it parallels the gap between the animate world and the inanimate realms. Though I should add that I could never quite work out if he was thereby saying that the bass voice belongs to the mineral kingdom and the soprano to the animal."

"That sounds very silly." Jane stuck out her chin.

"Well, don't blame me, blame Schopenhauer. But look, there are plenty of things which obviously haven't been created by humans—the sea, for instance, or most human and animal instincts—and this knowledge, this knowledge that they exist outside our creation and control doesn't necessarily compel us to posit God as their author. Well, not *me* at least."

But Jane had lost interest.

"Tom, you're speaking your language again. I can't stand it when you 'go philosophical.' You know I can't, I can't argue it logically. All I can say is that I feel when I am utterly suffused in music, immersed in it, so responsive to it that, that . . . well, in some silly way I want to change colour like a chameleon does, and become the colour of music—when *that* happens I go through the music as if it is a cloud, and, yes, I believe, I believe. I can't *not* believe; nor could Bach or Handel or Bruckner or Elgar, and many others."

I told her my father's joke about the chameleon who finds himself on a tartan picnic rug and is so confused by the challenge of mimicry that he explodes.

"That's me," I said. "While you're turning the colour of music I'm exploding! By the way, what does this something, this musical God, look like?"

Jane seemed genuinely surprised by the question.

"Look like? He doesn't look like anything. He sounds, He-She sounds like music."

Actually, although I think of Jane as excessively law abiding, she and I are both rebels in our way, I against inherited religion, and she against inherited indifference. Her parents are certainly not spiritual or musical. They live in a beautiful old house in Wiltshire. We used to go there fairly often when Jane and I were together. Jane insists that her parents have no money, though they were always able to summon a few thousand—out of the question for my parents—when we got into difficulties. Her father, Humphrey Sheridan, had been a lawyer and then in his fifties had some kind of nervous "collapse," and took early retirement. I wondered when I first met him if it had had anything to do with alcohol, since he was always inviting me to join him for a drink on the pretext that "it must be six o'clock *some*where in the world." Her mother, Julia, is vague, amusingly snobbish, and intelligently frustrated—she reads a novel a day, she says, and has no one to talk to.

I remember how nervous I was when Jane first took me to Wiltshire. She told me that her mother disliked or disapproved of most of her daughter's friends, and always communicated her disapproval in the same subtly oblique form:

by using the word "touching." As soon as she told Jane that she had found one of her daughter's friends "rather *touching*, darling," Jane knew that it was all over. "I used to wait in terror for that word 'touching,' and Mummy knew of course exactly what she was doing."

For whatever reason, Julia Sheridan did not find me "touching"—though presumably she now does—and Humphrey seemed quite taken with me. He asked me about my work, and when he discovered that I spent all my time at home on my Ph.D., he broke into laughter, which made the ice cubes in his gin-and-tonic chatter, and warmly said, "How *very* dolly! Welcome to the club. The ticklish thing is getting some poor bugger to *pay* for us to do nothing at all." I laughed with him, though I was hurt and felt naked in front of Jane, who had heard her father. I coughed in embarrassment—this cough representing, perhaps, a forerunner of the "artificial" cough.

One of the Sheridans had inherited a Bechstein grand, which neither could play. Jane started thumping out notes when she was three or four, and her parents always supported her, with a sluggish upper-class amazement at their daughter's brilliance. (There is a brother, Hugo, six years older, who is also intelligent, a lawyer like his father, but stolid and conventional, not very close to Jane.) In the English way, they made their support sound like benign disapproval, something wrested from them. Humphrey said to me: "Of course, Jane's music is jolly deep water, pretty much beyond me and Julia, though Julia had a good voice when I met her. We put Jane on a musical fast track, sort of Ascot Gold Cup, just letting her vamoose through, after Miss Ison, her piano teacher, called us in and said Jane was special and should go to an actual music school. Ison was a ferocious old bruiser. We bloody well did what we were told to do, or she'd rap you on the knuckles."

They had watched Jane's progress with secret pride of course, though success of any kind was looked upon with faint social amusement, and very successful strangers were talked about proprietorially, as if they were all part of the larger aristocratic family. At one of our visits, Jane put on a record; it was Daniel Barenboim playing Beethoven. Julia Sheridan wandered in, picked up the record sleeve, and said vaguely, "Oh yes, dear. Barenboim, we see his name in the papers. He's doing *frightfully* well, isn't he?" This way of looking at the world, as if it all belonged to them, was quite novel to me, and I wondered how far the sense of ownership might stretch. Was Beethoven considered to have "done *frightfully* well"? And if Beethoven had only done frightfully well, what of poor Jane (not to mention poor Thomas Bunting)?

But the Sheridans, petrified by the old bruiser Miss Ison, did indeed send Jane to a music college, where she prospered under the tuition of a formidable Armenian, who for a while forced her to play standing up, at a distance from the keyboard, to make her touch lighter and to wean her off the loud pedal. During the term-time, while Jane was away, her parents lowered the piano top and returned their silver-framed family photographs; and in the holidays, when Jane came home to the half-timbered house, the photographs were removed and put in a box, and the top was raised, and Jane played and played, while her parents strayed in and out of the drawing room and sometimes stood by her, staring encouragingly at the inexplicable sheets of music. Her mother, who was moody and somewhat "sensitive," would come in when Jane was crashing out titanic Beethoven, and complainingly say, "It is awfully *loud*, darling." Then, when the music, following its own form, suddenly became pianissimo for a few minutes, Julia would smile and say, "Thank you, darling, that's *much* better," as if Jane and Beethoven were willingly conspiring to ease Julia's nerves.

It was during that visit to Humphrey and Julia Sheridan that I first thought of marriage. In fact, though, I never asked Jane to marry me; she hinted at it one wonderful evening, about two weeks after the trip to Wiltshire, and I found myself happy to be the recipient rather than the actor. I remember it well. Jane was in a buoyant mood and suggested that we have supper somewhere pleasant. We went to L'Escargot (she was paying, of course). It was a warm summer night, mid-June, and crowds were shuffling along the pavements as if they were chained together at the ankles; I felt as if I was being multiply pickpocketed; but there was no sense of menace—quite the opposite, it was the usual clumsy English attempt to mimic Italian or Spanish street-life. The English version involves crowds of people squatting on pavements outside roaring pubs.

"They think they're in Rome, so they're having a great time," I said, as we picked our way over the stationary drinkers. "They don't have to go back to Neasden or Kilburn until eleven p.m." I was still trying to impress Jane in those days, and I affected an occasionally snobbish tone, while subtly "improving" my accent as I spoke.

"Let's *go* to Rome, darling," said Jane. And then, shyly: "On our honeymoon."

I ignored her—though her words had set off a great excitement inside me—and continued:

"Up in the north, in Durham or Newcastle, the men and women don't get together like this. The lads go around in packs, looking like they want to beat you up, and the lasses go around in packs, looking like committees of prostitutes on the move."

"Tommy, you're very naughty! Do that northern accent for me again." In those days, I found Jane's pearly, upper-class diction quite erotic. Her chin was jutting forward.

I drew a breath, and then bellowed, Newcastle-style:

"How! You looking at my bird? Cos' if you look at my bird one mair time I'll knack ya face in!"

Drinkers gazed up at me from the pavement. Jane seemed delighted. "Then what happens, Tommy? You can't leave me in the lurch."

"Then what happens is that you cravenly apologize, you say that you weren't looking at the bloke's girlfriend at all, it was the furthest thing from your mind. But you lose anyway, because he says: 'What's wrong with me bird, then? Funny, last time I looked there was nowt wrong with her. Mind you, praps I *missed* summat. Praps there's summat *wrong* with her? But I divvent see owt *wrong* with her.' And so it goes, with ever-threatening irony. The trick is to make sure that he doesn't bring his mates into it. De-escalation is the name of the game."

"How *do* you de-escalate? You know I had such a pro-tected, completely musical upbringing that I barely ever went into a pub. By the time I was free enough—"

"Free?"

"Yes, free from the endless musical imprisonment, the music school, the relentless practising, all that. By the time I was more relaxed I didn't feel like going to pubs anyway. I was too old. I was twenty-one."

"An old woman."

I used to tease Jane about her six years' superiority over me. She would sometimes joke that she was "a woman in a hurry," and I would calm her down with wise sayings from the Epicureans.

"You de-escalate, by the way, by offering to buy everyone drinks, or by introducing your own girlfriend to them. The latter technique is foolproof. Never fails."

"Girlfriends, girlfriends!" Jane squeezed my hand as we walked down the street. "I don't want to hear about them. I'll edit them out of your photograph like Lenin did."

"Stalin." I kissed her. "As long as I can do the same with your boyfriends."

We had a fine dinner. I would have liked to have shared the bill, of course—that was the only shadow, really. I remember that at one point in that dinner Jane suggested that I tended to see the world as a matter of strategies, techniques, tricks.

"You're always going on about the 'trick' of things. The trick of this, the trick of that. Why do you need all these tricks?"

"Because the world is a tricky place, I suppose, and one must match it, evil for evil." I spoke quite glibly.

"You don't really believe that, do you?" I loved Jane for her inability to treat anything lightly.

"Yes, certainly. I think that adult life, that adulthood, is all struggle. The reason we so love, so cherish our childhoods, is that they represent life before this struggle of adulthood. I have a theory, actually, which I'd like to write about some day, that Adam and Eve deliberately got themselves booted out of Eden because they had not experienced childhood. Perhaps they thought that beyond Eden's gates was childhood itself. How wrong they were."

"You're mad, darling. How would they want childhood if they had never known it? You go in for the strangest spec-ulations. Is *that* what you do all day?" Jane would never have dragged herself into a project like my BAG. Far too sensible and direct.

"Well," she continued, "what *are* your tricks? Hang on a minute, I have to deal with this *awful* music." This was not the first time I had witnessed Jane's absolute inability to eat while music is playing. She drew on all her reserves of haughtiness and calmly waved the waiter over with her long, professional fingers. "I'm awfully sorry, but I'm a musician, a concert pianist, and I am trained to *listen* to music. Now, I can either listen and not eat, or eat and not listen. But I can't do both. I know it's already quiet, but *might* there be a way for you to turn it down? I'd be *so* grateful." And she gazed at the waiter with her dense eyes, and her ponytail swayed, and of course he complied.

"Now, darling, tell me about your tricks." I am not ashamed to admit that it has always been the greatest joy to hear that word "darling" from Jane's lips. It was spoken fast with a rather short 'a' and an almost Indian lilt—"daling." In my family, my mother called both me and my father "dear" and "dearest" and "love," but never "darling."

"Which tricks are you interested in? Well, here's one. If an argument seems to be getting out of hand, say at a dinner party, it almost always works to point to the chin of your in-terlocutor and say, 'By the way, you have a little piece of food on your chin.' For some reason it takes the wind out of people's sails utterly. The palaver they get into with wiping their chins! 'Have I got rid of it now?' 'No, you've just moved it to the right.' 'Have I got it *now*?' 'Not quite, it's still hanging on.' 'Now?' 'Yes, now you have.' And all the while there's nothing on the poor person's chin at all. Once you are finished with all that, it rarely seems worth continuing the argument, and you can get up and go to the loo. It's all about knowing when to break the moment. Once the right interruption has been launched, the hostile encounter often collapses like a tent that's been blown over. But you have to be the controller of the wind, that's what's crucial."

"The controller of the wind, I like that." Jane's eyes were very bright. We had ordered champagne, and it was making our blood fizz. "That's your mode, isn't it—being the controller? Controlling sticky situations?"

"I play them like a piano," I joked, with mock assurance.

"Marriage wouldn't be a trick, would it?" asked Jane, again shyly.

"No, it wouldn't." We were silent for a minute. "Am I hearing what I think I am hearing?"

"You might be."

"Shouldn't it be the other way around?"

"Well, make it so, then."

We were married three months later. Max was my best man. Roger and his choir sang at least eight anthems—really, they gave a concert briefly interrupted by the triviality of our vows. It was held in Wiltshire. How well I recall shaving that morning in the little local hotel, with my parents coughing and stirring on the other side of the bathroom wall: my hands shook, even though there were three hours to go. Clear, breezy, lightly warm, barely blue English September day. High hedgerows. Everything prettier than in the north.

I remember sitting with Max, waiting for Jane to enter the church; with my hand I was keeping my right leg stuck to the church floor in case it started shaking with nervousness. Trumpets and drums sounded at the back of the church: friends of Roger. The medieval sound of the instruments made Jane seem like a great queen and Max and I humble ambassadors representing a new republic. Jane advanced on her father's arm, gently talking to him in that quietly theatrical way one sees on stage. Only I recognized the tiny hesitation of the left foot. What was she saying to her father, what was she saying? "I am afraid"? "I love him"? "I love you and Mummy"? "I have waited for ever to do this"? A fine grey veil obscured her face like a layer of expensive dust. But then she stopped next to me and raised that curtain and turned to me and smiled a calm, grateful smile. Into her hair chains of wild flowers had been sown.

The local vicar married us—the Reverend Hugh Fillimore, dressed from head to toe in black. Black suit, black priest's stock, salty black Oxfords on his feet. He smoked a black pipe and had glasses seemingly made out of the same substance as his pipe. He seemed to have been carbonized long ago in some awful prehistoric conflagration. Remarkably, his amiable, ambling, vacant address never once mentioned our marriage. Not once! It was all about "the importance of having heroes—intellectual, spiritual, moral. Now," he burbled on, standing in the exquisite carved pulpit, "enough abstraction. You all probably want to know who my heroes really are. All right, I shall oblige. My intellectual hero is Martin Luther. I don't think that needs further justification. My spiritual hero—well, there are so awfully many, but I will nominate Father Brown, in the marvellous old Chesterton stories. And my moral hero: Winston Churchill. Plenty wrong with Churchill, and actually the other day I was dipping into one of the recent revisionist biographies, but in the end he just can't really be dented. Toenails of clay, I'd say, at the worst. Now, of course, Christ should be our greatest hero, but from time to time when our faith feels faint we do need worldly models, too! And that's why I've dealt with the subject today."

We spent the night in a country hotel. We were too late for dinner, but room service sent up smoked salmon sandwiches and a big Stilton cheese, veiny with blue fogs. Jane ran the bath, took off her dress, looked tiny in her punitive panty hose. Behind her in the bathroom the big taps were orchestrating volumes of steam.

"I am famished. God these sandwiches are good. Darling, you were a miracle," she said.

"No, no, it was you. I did nothing."

"Well, we both did it. And tomorrow Rome!"

"Poor us. Let's toast Uncle Karl." Karl was paying for our honeymoon.

"Uncle Karl."

"Uncle Karl."

I touched Jane's anxious thin back, and then the calmer swell of the hips.

"Would it be a bad omen if we skipped our canonical marital obligations tonight? I am utterly exhausted," I said.

Jane laughed. "Despite your unfamiliarity with baths, might I be able to persuade you to join me in the water?"

"Oh, I should think so."

"And we can see what happens from there."

"You bet. We can take it from the top, as they say in music, no?"

"That's in *pop* music, Tommy. Though I must say I'd never thought of that phrase in a sexual light before."

Probably, now that Jane and I are separated, our friends have said to each other, "I always thought it was a bad omen that the vicar gave that bizarre address—you know, you remember, the one in which he never mentioned Thomas and Jane." But at the time it seemed only amusing.

10

S I SAID, all seemed well between us last September when Jane was in Sundershall, which made her behaviour on my return to London the more mysterious. She seemed uninterested in talking to me; even stranger, she stopped fighting those elements of my temperament that she had recently been resisting. She said nothing about my dirty dressing gown, my slovenly side of the bedroom, the Ph.D., the BAG. Over the next two months she seemed to shrink inside herself. She began to grow impatient with my drifting and apparently leisurely ways, and at breakfast would announce coldly, "I will be incommunicado until lunchtime," sticking her chin out and up as she did so. I would hear her start practising while I was still enjoying my morning coffee and cigarette (I am my father's son). It used to be that Jane, smelling my first cigarette of the day, occasionally cried out, "Fee fie fo fum, I smell the fug of an Englishman," which I loved to hear, and came into the kitchen to kiss me. I would be sitting in the paisley dressing gown, a scarf round my neck for warmth, and reading some or other edifying book. And then she would slick her lips with lipstick and munch them together, and rush out of the flat to Trinity, tossing "I love you, darling" behind her. But in the last few months of our marriage I seemed only to anger her, and she marched off every morning to the piano. Sometimes I walked to the edge of our tiny sitting room and, standing behind her, watched the knitting wings of her thin back, and turned away.

Jane and I didn't separate until last Christmas, but I date the real end of our marriage from September—from the moment I left London to visit my afflicted father. Why was Jane so pleased to have me out of the flat and two hundred miles away in the north of England? It's true that just before my mother called to tell me about Father's heart attack, I revealed to Jane for the first time the existence of the BAG, and mentioned that I was becoming increasingly interested in it. I told her that I felt correspondingly faint-hearted about the Ph.D. I didn't tell her that I had been working on the BAG almost exclusively for the last nine months; I merely said that it was "absorbing all my thought." I hoped for sympathy. What I got was a kind of fear. Jane looked truly terrified! She watched me as if I were threatening her.

"What's wrong with you?" I asked her. "You look very alarmed. I just said that this project has been absorbing my mind. It's a mental distraction, that's all. It hasn't got in the way of the Ph.D., which I will *certainly* finish by the end of this year."

"Tom, is there any way, any way at all that you could combine the Book, what did you call it?"

"The Book Against God, or some title like that," I said shyly.

"Well, is there any way you could combine this Book Against God with your work on the Ph.D.?" Jane continued to look alarmed.

"But you're treating this as if I have been working for months and months on the Book Against God! It's just a mental distraction, I'm telling you. It's something that I can see getting in the *way* of the Ph.D. in the months to come. A potential *risk*, that's all. And to answer your question, no, there's no chance of combining them, even if I wanted to. The Ph.D. is very very focused and the other is very very broad."

"But you just said to me that you were feeling faint-hearted about the Ph.D. You said that. That was the word you used."

"Yes, a figure of speech. I don't really feel fainthearted at all. It's just that sometimes it's a bit hard for me to concentrate on it, and this last month—well, for the whole bloody month they've been taking up the road outside, as you know, and it's quite hard to apply myself when they get going with the drills and everything. The windows almost rattle! And then I get easily distracted by thinking about this new Book Against God. And I haven't felt very well in the last week, as you also know. Bad headaches. Very bad indeed, actually. But I really have been working quite hard on the Ph.D."

"I'm sorry about the headaches. Tom, you've been working on the Ph.D. for how long now?"

"Well, six years I suppose."

"Seven in fact, I think."

"Seven, all right. Yes, seven."

"And we've known each other for nearly five of those years. And your promises have come and gone like the seasons. Your Ph.D. has already seen Mrs. Thatcher off, and it'll probably see Mrs. Thatcher's successor off, too. For all I know you'll still be at it when a Labour government gets in."

"When universal socialism is declared in our land and the lamb lies down with the lion," I murmured.

"I'm glad you find it funny. But if you can't finish the Ph.D., if you know that you will never finish it, then for *God's sake* get rid of it, and do something with your life. With *our* life. You know, darling, it's not, it's not . . . very *manly* to have you sitting round all day in your pajamas. I'm sorry."

I thought that a very low blow. But I was silent.

"I'm sorry, but that is how I feel," she continued. "That is how you make me feel."

Despite appearances, all this was said quite lightly, and I didn't trouble myself too much. By taking a light tone, I forced Jane to moderate her gravity. And then two days later I was called by my mother, and events in Sundershall took precedence. I wish now that I had attended to that strange look of pure panic that consumed Jane's face when I told her about the BAG. Pure panic! In that fear lay everything that was to come. I suppose she felt she had suddenly been given powers of prophecy; she could see that the BAG was not going to go away. And in all likelihood, she didn't believe me when I said that I had not been working on it. Obviously, she couldn't have known about the "four notebooks," but she probably had a good idea of what I had been up to. I know this now, but chose not to know it then.

When I think of the last few months of our marriage, I see Jane in my mind's eye, always angry with me, and always practising the piano. I haven't denied that I was difficult to live with, not least because my need to work on the Ph.D. (or BAG) meant that I was always at home filling the place with cigarette smoke. But this happy life had worked as long as Jane went out to Trinity. My understanding was that she practised there precisely so that we wouldn't be together all day in Islington. Suddenly, however, she deliberately stopped practising at Trinity, and began to insist on playing the piano at home. After my return from Sundershall, Jane somehow transformed herself into someone who went out only to teach—three afternoons a week. I suppose that while

I was in the north she had got used to staying at home and playing the Steinway baby grand that filled our sitting room. And once I had returned, she was not going to adjust her regime. She wanted to stay at home.

A strange exchange seemed to take place in our marriage. She would not say anything about my dirtiness, my dressing gown (which she once tried to throw out of our bathroom window), my unchanged clothes, the beard clouding my face, the anarchy of books by my bedside, and the indirection of my reading. But in return, she just ignored me, and instead practised and practised on that damn piano until the sound of those nodding felt hammers drove *me* out of the house. And I should say that it was a certain kind of practising that was making it impossible for me to work. Complicated music I can shut out of my mind; it means little to me. Certainly, I understood Jane's need for hard work last September and October; she was practising for an important concert with a well-known string ensemble, and she was very anxious about it. But she seemed to be repeating what sounded like a rather easy passage on the piano, playing it once, twice, three times, then again and again for what must have been an hour, with such fearless will and fierce commitment that to hear it almost made me weep with frustration at my own weakness. "Commit a sin twice and it will not seem a sin," goes a Russian saying. But what about four hundred and forty times? Will it not seem a sin then? I felt that Jane's endless repetitions at the piano were a way of punishing me for my lack of application, for my inability precisely to repeat and repeat and repeat, to "stick at it."

When it comes to music, my powers of "neutralizing" are ineffective. I discovered the neutralizing technique while flying to Rome on our honeymoon. I'm a nervous and infrequent flier, especially jittery when the plane meets air turbulence. But this time I was walking back to my seat from the lavatory when the plane violently dropped and I tripped and fell halfway to the floor. As I stood up and continued to my seat, I realized that I was not nervous. This was surely, I reflected (becoming "philosophical," as Jane would have it), because I had been turbulent at the same time as the plane and had cancelled out the plane's turbulence by equalling it. Of course, there's no need actually to fall on the floor: once seated, as the plane continued to shake and dip, I experimented by gently rocking in my flimsy seat from side to side, and I found I was unaware that the plane was moving at all, because I was rocking with it.

I've expanded this "neutralizing" principle elsewhere: I smoke a cigarette in smoky rooms, if I can; I eat food if I have indigestion. A real success was scored with my insomnia—until recently, while I have been writing the last stages of this account. Instead of trying to think sleepy or lulling thoughts, I deliberately set my mind ablaze with random nagging contemplations. Now, the logical response to Jane's piano playing would have been to "neutralize" it by making music of my own, perhaps by humming something. But I have a terrible voice, and can't keep a tune anyway, and unlike smoking, thinking, eating, or moving, singing does not feel like a natural activity to me. So I lay on the bed and tried to read, as the music sounded around me, and I tried not to let my feelings blacken. And then I took my books and went out, to find a library or quiet café.

11

AX CALLED ME as soon as I got back to London from see-ing my father. He adored Father—who adored him in return—and he wanted to hear my impression of his health. So I took a cab to Ladbroke Grove, despite Jane's insistence that we couldn't now afford such luxuries.

He was not wearing his spectacles when he opened the door to me, and his reduced eyes made me squint. Max "looks like a man in three acts," as Peter used to describe him. His head is rather narrow, his shoulders of average width, and his pelvis quite broad. The heavy, broad-based body suited him when, as a teenager, he liked to pose as the real sceptic, the slayer of fraudulent emotion and slack thought. On Pilgrim's Path, during meetings of our grandly named Pitmatic Philosophical Society, Max used to narrow his bespectacled eyes as he lit a Dunhill, and seemed to smother untruths by slumping over them. I can still see him in my mind, seventeen years old, heavily sagging under the oak tree and saying to me, "Is that *true*? Can you *verify* it?"

Just as Colin and Belinda think fit to serve tea from a Thermos, so Max, who resembles his parents more than he knows, presents the strangest food at his flat. Naturally, the only alcohol he had available, when I arrived, was a deformed plastic flagon of ouzo and a bottle of Domecq amontillado. I sat in his kitchen as he blundered good-naturedly among his cupboards, emerging at last with a plate of crackers and a huge tube of Primula cheese spread, lain alongside the crackers with apparent dignity like a sceptre.

"Stop, stop! Why don't we just cut our losses and go round the corner to the pub?"

"Why?" asked Max, in obvious bewilderment. I took pity on him, and gently lied.

"I need whisky, that's why. I've been in Sundershall—army rations as far as drink goes."

"That's fine, then. I need cigarettes." Max used to drink alcohol when we were younger; now he feeds mainly off coffee and Coke. I sometimes think that the only thing Max is worldly about is tobacco; he is still loyal to Dunhills. The broad packet, rosette-red on the outside with icon-gold innards, so that the box always glows like a medal, obviously still pleases him.

We walked down Max's street and turned onto Ladbroke Grove, which was mad with people, most of them menacing.

"It's a while since I've been here," I said.

"The atmosphere is always . . . basically a race riot just beginning or ending."

"Max, are you quoting yourself?"

"Not . . . yet," he said brightly.

Max speaks frustratingly slowly. It's not halting speech, because he has such a clear idea of where he is going; he is simply being very careful with language. I used to love his earnest, slightly showy silences—he is a terrible exhibitionist in his quiet way—when we were teenagers: Max, measuring out words as he measured out everything, sagely, intelligently. But nowadays his portly intermissions seem controlling, a way of keeping his audience in the theatre. I have to struggle neither to complete his sentences nor to bridle at his reticent authority.

"This is an amazingly grim place," I shouted—we were entering a crowded pub. Even to a smoker it seemed deadly: the thick air was a hanging traffic of grey, produced, it seemed, by every single human in the room.

"Why?" asked Max, blinking.

"Well, is there anyone in this pub not smoking? It's like the entire French nation on a night out."

"I've never noticed," said Max. "It's where I get my cigarettes, that's all. But, Tom, you don't like pubs anyway. You've grown pub-phobic. Living with Karl for all those years . . . did that to you. They're too proletarian for you, too easy. The juvenility of beer is offensive to you, you only like bottles with . . . years on them."

"I do like pubs," I said, as we made our way to the only free table, "I just don't like beer."

"Well, today was a column day for me and I have earned my pint."

"What was it about today?"

"Boring stuff. A piece about how we're no longer inventive as a nation. Blah, blah. You've read it a hundred times, by . . . diverse hands." Max pushed his spectacles back up his nose, a gesture I am fond of.

"It's not boring to me," I said. Was Max really shy, or did his reticence contain a kind of condescension? Would he have swallowed the fruit of his efforts so swiftly with fellow journalists? Perhaps behind this apparent modesty lay the ghost of my "failures"—not only the unfinished Ph.D., but the unwritten obituaries. He was trying to spare me the exhibition of his success.

"I am capable of following an argument," I said. Max blinked at me, became uneasy.

"I wasn't . . . I wasn't implying that you weren't a worthy audience. But the piece itself is ordinary. Two hours flat . . . is how long it took me."

Max was in several ways more "philosophical" than I was as a teenager. But at Oxford (then dominated by logicians) he found philosophy unexpectedly difficult. He used to ask me for help, and I largely wrote his big end-of-term essay on Aristotle (which humblingly received a B minus). To the delight of his horrid father he switched to classics. After Oxford, he decided that he wanted to be "in the real world," and became a reporter for a newspaper in Bristol, followed quickly by a similar job in London, at *The Times*. One week, he offered to write a column in place of the star columnist, who was on holiday, and the editor liked the piece so much he was given his own space. I still have a copy of that first column. The news of Max's precocious success—at a time when I was still living at Uncle Karl's and just starting on the Ph.D.—spread fast, and it was in fact my mother who phoned me to tell me that I should go out and buy *The Times*. I was excited as if for myself, without any stirring of envy. I remember wondering why I was not at all envious. I concluded that I felt happy because Max was succeeding for both of us. A locket of the purest provincial atavism broke in my hand and released an intoxication; it was Sundershall Max, pitmatic Max, who was appearing in *The Times*.

And there was his name opposite the venerable letters page. The date was October 13th, 1984. Max was twenty-four. He was much less conservative than he is now, and his article was quite a fierce attack on Mrs. Thatcher, and on the speech she had just delivered at the Conservative Party Conference in Brighton, where the IRA had sent her an inconvenient, hotel-collapsing gift. Mrs. Thatcher was undeterred by the IRA bomb, of course, and pressed on with her

speech, which was largely about the Yorkshire and Notting-
hamshire miners, who had been on strike for seven months,
protesting pit closures. Some of the miners had dared to return to work, and these few, this happy band, were cheered
on by the Iron Lady: "They are lions! Men and women like
that are what we are proud to call the best of British."

The subtlety of Max's article lay not in his attack on Mrs.
Thatcher, whom he faulted for the "almost cinematic lurid-
ity of her political vision (in the land of the blind, the lady
wearing 3-D spectacles will be queen)," but for the way he
suggested that such was the natural inertia of British life, the
future of the coal industry would be exactly the same whether
the miners went on strike or not. This inertia he blamed on
an age-old tussle between "anger" and "melancholy." Max
seized on Mrs. Thatcher's phrase "the best of British," and
asked what "British" really meant. To Stendhal, wrote Max,
a Briton was "only fully alive when he was angry." But as far
as de Quincey was concerned, wrote Max, the British were
essentially "melancholic." Both de Quincey and Stendhal
were right, Max said. He argued that English history had always oscillated between acts of anger and ideas of melancholy; and that sometimes these opposing tendencies acted
against each other at the same time or in the same person.
And this is how we British like it, he said. It means that
nothing gets done, which is what we want. But along had
come Mrs. Thatcher, an "angry" woman, determined to
wreck that slothful balance.

Since that first explosive success, Max has written steadily,
once a week. I have cut out many of his columns, because for
a long time I thought about writing an analysis of what I did
and didn't like about them. He sounds, at times, inauthen-
tic, aping the confidence of older men. And I think he

writes too much. The pundit should not become a hack. Max's fluency, his amazing capacity to write *something* every week, is a danger. His recent work has seemed especially routine to me. But Max's readers obviously don't agree with me, to judge from his burgeoning popularity. And certainly I should not be trusted on this matter. Not only because of what Jane told me last Christmas about him, but because of a general sad feeling I have that Max is no longer playing on my side.

But in the pub, last September, Max was sweetly—or diplomatically—modest.

"Look, Tom, I don't want to grizzle on about myself," he said. "And surprisingly enough your dad is much more interesting to me than my latest column. Which you can read tomorrow anyway."

"Oh, Dad's fine, of course."

"Did he seem changed? Is he weaker? How is your mum?"

"Yes. No. Fine. To each question respectively."

"What's wrong with you? Anyone would think that . . . it was *your* heart that had gone into arrest."

"You're quite right," I said. I couldn't say to Max what I wanted to, that his reverential respect for my parents had always irritated me. I should have been more understanding. His parents, after all, were Colin and Belinda Thurlow. It was no surprise that he had transferred his affections from them to Peter and Sarah Bunting.

"But he did seem changed?"

"Yes. Thinner, older, I suppose. But only to the trained eye. I doubt most people would notice anything significant."

"Well," said Max, "I'm pretty . . . *au fait* with the way he looks and speaks."

"Max, you were last in Sundershall about a year ago. Or was it two years? I forget."

"But every time I go I drop in to see your parents."

"As I was made to do this time, to *your* parents."

"I didn't know that! Why didn't you say? How was . . . the Crassus of the North?" Max sometimes called his father Crassus, after a figure of the same name in Pliny ("*not* the famous Crassus," Max told me), who was apparently celebrated in the ancient world for never having laughed.

"Your parents were grilling me about your column."

"As if they care." Max pushed his spectacles back up his nose, then ducked into his gravy-coloured beer. His eyes, just above the raised rim of the glass, bore magnifiedly on me.

"Oh, they care all right," I said. "I think they're proud of you actually. But too proud to admit their pride. They might even be secretly reading you for all I know."

"Mum once told me that Dad had confessed to reading me very occasionally in the periodicals room of the university library."

"So there you are."

"No, Tom, they can be intermittently proud and still totally opposed to what I do. Apart from the fact that I'm a journalist, nowadays they also don't like the . . . progress of my politics. Last time I was there, Dad and I argued about the function of newspapers, while Mum and I argued about Thatcher and the liberation of the Eastern bloc. So I stay away, and I think, actually, that my columns are the better, the bolder, for my knowing that they are entirely unread in Sundershall. Absence . . . makes the . . . art grow stronger, I suppose."

"You're not unread in the vicarage. My parents are always going on about you. *The Times* is their paper."

"Sorry."

"Don't be sorry. Well, do be sorry for one thing. I wish you hadn't mentioned those obituaries to them. Dad turned it into a joke to use against me, and it just enabled him and Mum to sharpen the comparison they already like to make between us." I did find it hard to forgive Max for wantonly spreading the news about my failed assignments.

"Oh, I didn't think those obituaries meant so much to you, or else you would have written them, right?" Max was being inscrutable.

"Well, they didn't mean very much. It was journalism, I could have written them in a flash."

Again Max looked at me with his magnified eyes.

"I don't mean it like that, you know I don't. I meant that I could have written them without any difficulty. It's simply that I have very little time at the moment. Very little time! I have to get this Ph.D. finished."

"Fine. Fine. I know you have to complete the Ph.D. Certainly I wouldn't have mentioned them if I had thought that . . . the powers-that-be in the vicarage would use them against you. So what was your dad's joke?"

"He said that it was a good thing that the obituaries were still unwritten, since obviously my not writing them was keeping the subjects alive. Very droll."

Max laughed at this, and exclaimed: "I do love your dad!"

"I wish I *had* written those obituaries. Hegley will have recommissioned them now."

"I can check if you want," said Max eagerly.

"Forget it. It's very nice of you. Truly. And, yes, I could have done with the money. You bet. Jane and I had another row last night. We're going to have to start economizing. You should approve, Max. We'll have to learn how to be good monetarists."

"Well, yes, Thatcher's monetarism was a good thing, but as far as personal finances go I think that one should always try not to spend less but to earn more instead."

"Oh, thanks for the advice. What if I am one of those people who earns less while spending more? Is there a name for that?"

"Yes, there is. Monetary laxist, that's what you are."

"What?"

"In economics, there's a term, 'monetary laxist'—for people who are lax with the . . . monetary flow. I like the sound of it. Vaguely . . . medicinal."

I felt a familiar surge of warmth for Max, as his slow, clever words, spaced by exhalations of smoke, sounded across the table.

"It's no laughing matter. Right now, Jane and I are always at each other's throats. She blames me for not bringing in any money. The burden for earning is entirely on her."

"You can appreciate her position, then? It's very difficult for her. I bet she'd love to give up the teaching and just play."

"What's she been saying to you?" I asked quickly.

"Nothing at all," said Max. "Nothing at all." I thought he said this a bit too certainly.

We both drank, and then had little to say to each other. After a while I began again:

"You know I told you about this other project I have in mind?" Now I was the one speaking slowly.

"Yes, it's the . . . bag you're currently into."

"The bag . . . You're teasing me."

"Could be."

"Well, Jane has no appreciation of it, I'm sure. That's why we are arguing at the moment."

"Have you mentioned it to her?"

"Yes, just before I went north."

"What did you tell her it was about?"

"I didn't really tell her anything. I said to her that it was something I was thinking about, when in fact I've been filling notebooks with it for months. I had to have *some* explanation for what I've been doing."

"So how do you expect her to . . . appreciate it if she doesn't know anything about it? I can't 'appreciate' . . . poltergeists, or Bombay."

"You wouldn't appreciate it, either, probably," I grumbled into my drink.

"That's a non sequitur."

"Pitmatic!" I said, smiling at Max.

"I'm sure I would appreciate it if you deigned to show any of it to me."

"Actually—I have a few pages with me. I brought them." I suddenly felt very shy. I removed four folded pages from my jacket pocket. They were about Kierkegaard. Max looked very pleased, and said:

"This is the first thing you have shown me since—when?—I can't remember. Can I read them now?" He started to read, and to give him time I went to the lavatory. The filthy blocked urinal displayed my bubbling piss for me. Behind me, in a cubicle, a man said again and again to himself with great vehemence, "Bollocks! Bollocks! That's complete bollocks!" When I returned, Max exclaimed:

"It's all about Jane, not about Kierkegaard."

"What d'you mean?"

"Here, and here, and throughout."

"Oh God, I meant to cut out the references to Jane be-fore I gave the passage to you."

"Keep them in," said Max.

"For whom? It doesn't have any readers."

"I can think of one reader—in the . . . medieval sense."

"You've lost me . . . Oh . . . bloody hell that's a nasty joke." I laughed.

"Not at all. Isn't God your intended reader?"

"But I don't believe in Him."

"Yes you do," said Max. "Yes you do."

"No I don't. Why are you so anxious to prove that I do? You're not secretly scurrying to church yourself, are you? If you have revelations to make, please be gentle with me."

"No," replied Max. "I'm not going to church. But I think as I get older that no one is really ever an *atheist*. Every-one believes."

"Oh, I see," I said sarcastically, "it's sort of unavoidable, rather the way that mysteriously I always seem to have a re-cent cut or bruise somewhere on my shins. I don't know where the hell I got it, I don't remember bumping into any-thing, I'm not in any pain, but always there's this scab on my shins. Religion is like this. Is that what you mean?"

"The scab of religion! Tom, I can see you getting worked up. Your voice has risen. You don't need to. I'm not about to . . . fall on my knees. I'm just probably moving towards the idea that since religion is a human creation, and its form is man's, then . . . everything in it is at least as true as we are."

"Ha. I never did believe in your atheism. You're a closet Christian."

"No . . . neither closet nor Christian. But I don't think that religion is . . . a machinery of propositions, to be argued with, fought with, and disproved. It's a way of life, a series of habits. Practices rather than knowledge, facts of existence. If a peasant woman kisses an icon, you can't say that she is wrong to do this. It's like farming. People have always gathered the harvest in a certain way, and this can never be . . . wrong, even if newer and quicker methods are invented which supersede it. Or like music. You can like or dislike a piece of music but you can't call it *wrong*. It is not only . . . pointless to argue with this, it is . . . meaningless to argue with it. Am I right?"

"Why meaningless?"

"Because the desire to pray, like gathering the harvest, is a need, a hunger, not an idea. You can argue with an idea, but you can't argue with a hunger. Nor . . . should you."

"I reject almost every word of what you just said."

"Well, you would, or you wouldn't be writing a Book Against God." Max smiled.

"It's nonsense. First of all, music, when I last looked, has not caused centuries of wars. Nor has farming. At least, not as a timeless business of cultivation and harvesting. But religion has. Ergo, this hunger, this 'need' you talk about, contains ideas about which people have cared enough to go to war. The peasant who kisses an icon before embarking on a journey does so because her tradition tells her that to do so will guarantee her divine protection and blessing, as a man might nowadays cross himself before his plane takes off into the air. How come that isn't a proposition? In your scheme," I continued, "how would one ever be converted, as Paul was, and how would one ever lose one's faith, as I did? As *we* did! To find or lose a faith is to find or lose belief in a series of propositions and guarantees, laid out by Jesus and the Gospel writers."

"It's not a contract! Anyway, there we're a bit different," said Max. "I . . . never had a faith to lose."

"Well, neither did I, really."

"That's not true. You had something, then you lost it. At fourteen or fifteen. I remember you telling me about it. Most of all you had your parents' faith, and that . . . had to be fought."

"Oh, I'm not fighting *their* faith. Definitely not."

"No? Oh, this is getting good. We haven't done this for a while. What are you . . . staring at?" asked Max.

"There's a large fly sauntering across the table. Christ, look at it!"

"Tom, it's a . . . fly. A fly."

"You know how I feel about insects."

"A fly, Tom, a fly."

"I will have to liquidate it. It's disgusting." I slapped the table with the beermat; the fly veered away, then cheekily landed once again on the table, pausing to sharpen its front legs. I tried again with the beermat. Again the fly evaded me and returned.

"I can't sit here with that insect," I said. Part of me sincerely meant what I was saying—I do loathe insects very much—and part of me was quite happy to use my hatred of insects as a way of ending our discussion.

"This is a phobia you are going to . . . have to control," said Max.

"Indeed, that's what Jane says. But in the meantime, let's go, shall we?"

Max was right: it was a joy to be arguing with him again, as we used to. But our meeting left me a little suspicious.

Max seemed to be crossing over to the other side, joining the group of people we used to call, when we were boys, "the God-talkers." And when I look back at our conversation a year later, I notice how cleverly he avoided the real subject: Jane.

12

THESE ARE THE PAGES Max read in the pub. I have followed Max's advice, and retained all references to Jane,
to our marriage, and the Islington flat, where I originally
wrote this passage:

Kierkegaard was an awful prig, how could he not be; his
name essentially means "churchyard" in Danish. He is always
amassing all the qualities that make Christianity hateful—
its cruelty, asceticism, the impossible challenge of imitating Christ—and then shouting out: And this is *exactly* why
you must follow Christ! For instance, he writes that Christianity is rooted in the concept of sin, and this strikes even
him as too severe. But, too bad, he says. Christianity *is* severe. Socrates thought of sin as ignorance of the good; but
Kierkegaard thinks this was too generous of Socrates. Christianity, he says, knows that we sin in two ways: we sin willfully; and secondly we are all inheritors of original sin. The
Churchyard admits that original sin is a hateful idea—"the
Christian doctrine of sin is nothing but insolent disrespect
of man, accusation upon accusation"—and writes that "a
man sitting in a glass case is not so constrained as is each human in his transparency before God." These are beautiful
words, and over the years I have often thought of this poor
man in the glass case being watched by God, which merges
in my mind with something I read about Momus, the god
of ridicule, who wished that a glass case could be installed

in the breast of man so that his heart could be seen (a vile image!). Yes, these are beautiful words, suffused with anger *against* God, against the disrespect of the idea of sin, against the awful glassy transparency of our relationship with God.

And what does Kierkegaard do, of course, but, like a man eating black beetles or sheeps' testicles and then stubbornly pronouncing them *delicious*, turns and says: But this is *exactly* why we must be Christians!

But nothing is worse than the passage entitled "The Edifying in the Thought That Against God We Are Always in the Wrong," at the end of *Either/Or*, which surely represents The Churchyard's own horrible thoughts. Kierkegaard says that we are always more loved by God than we can possibly love Him, and this (combined with the fact that we are always sinful) means that "against God we are always in the wrong." We should *want* this wrongness, he says, it is edifying. His analogy is with ordinary love. If I really love my wife, and she does me a wrong, says The Churchyard, I will be unhappy because I am suddenly made to be in the right and she in the wrong. In fact, if I *really* love her, I will want to exchange places with her, so that suddenly she is made to be in the right and I in the wrong.

It's true that when Jane sometimes makes a verbal error (the other night she made "hoi polloi" sound like the elite), or puts a philosopher in the wrong century, I have a momentary urge to correct her, which then passes and is replaced with a stronger desire to say nothing at all, as if the error were my mistake. Kierkegaard may be right about this: perhaps because I love her I do not want to be in the right against Jane, which is painful, but rather in the wrong against her, which is less painful. I'm writing this in Islington, while lying on our bed. Looking at the bed, at the two sides, hers and mine, I ask myself: Why is it that Jane's side is always fragrant, cool, creaseless, as if she has hardly slept there, while my side seems to have been monstrously inhabited in the night, with trapped smells, crushed pillows, and sheets cast with hairs? How delicious it is to lean over onto her side, and breathe into her perfumed pillow. Yes, yes, I think, the Dane is very wise, one wants to change places with the person one loves, because one is in the wrong and she is so often in the right. One longs to *be* right.

But that isn't what Kierkegaard says. He argues that I should want to exchange places with Jane not because I am in the wrong and want to be with her in the right, but because I should *want* to be in the *wrong* against her. He envisages an ideal world in which, if Jane said, "Spinoza was German, wasn't he?" I, feeling horribly in the right, would not only *not* correct her, but would take the mistake on *as my own*, and murmur in reply, "My mistake, my mistake." And she would do likewise if I claimed that Berlioz was Spanish.

That is what our relation with God should be like. With this great difference, says Kierkegaard: we should not think, "God is always right, *therefore* I am always in the wrong." Instead, we should think, "I am always in the wrong, *therefore* God is always in the right." He loves us more than we can ever love Him, and we do not deserve that love and we must rejoice in the gorgeous injustice of it, the swollenness of this top-heavy fraction, and simply say to ourselves again and again, "Against God we are always in the wrong."

Doesn't Kierkegaard's "love" sound rather like hate? He is exactly like Simone Weil in this regard. Couldn't we substitute "hate" for every use of "love" in Kierkegaard's (or Weil's) work, and get a more accurate picture of the world? God *hates* us more than we can *hate* Him, and we do not deserve that *hate*, and therefore against God we are always in the wrong. Kierkegaard wants us to go about muttering, "My mistake, my mistake," while God lets His earthquakes and Holocausts and famines rage, all the while saying whatever nonsense God feels He wants to say: "Plato was English," perhaps, or "the Holocaust never happened, I, the Almighty, great Jehovah, deny it." (Yes, God would have a *very* good reason to be the first Holocaust-denier.) Kierkegaard's idea of our relations with God reminds me of a story told by Cicero and several other classical authors, one of those exemplary stories offered as a model of Stoical self-control. Archytas, the owner of a vineyard, discovered that slaves on his estate had behaved offensively and disobediently, and then, realizing that he was feeling too wound up and violent towards them, stopped himself doing anything, except to say mildly, as he walked by them, "You're lucky I'm angry with you."

Well, that's our relationship with God in brief, isn't it? Archytas's idea of "luck" is not far from Kierkegaard's, is it? We are "lucky" that God is angry with us, "lucky" that He made us, and even when we have not behaved badly in the vineyard and have done nothing bad at all, we should still bow and scrape, and murmur, like my father's poor parishioners going down on their knees, "My mistake, my mistake, I am lucky that You are angry with me"—all because Adam, who was anyway created by this hateful tyrant and might not have wanted to be created, this poor Adam, ate the luckless apple. Oh when will humans murder this devilish concept of God? For is God really any more dead now than when

Nietzsche told us He was a hundred or so years ago? Until that final day, that real day of murder, of cancellation, of blissful clearing, the holiday of life, an emptied sabbath of repose—until that moment, I propose instead an edifying inversion of Kierkegaard: "the edifying in the thought that against *us* God is always in the wrong."

13

HY SHOULD I BELIEVE in Jane's promise of reconciliation? How many times has she deigned to see me since
the end of the Harrods job? Three times. Three times in
as many months. And now September has just become
October, and whatever kindly momentum there was has
completely gone. This weekend I got into a panic and phoned
Roger to ask his advice. I thought he might be willing to
intercede for me, put in a good word (even tell a white lie
on my behalf). He is very close to Jane, has known her since
music college. But first of all, Roger typically enrolled me
in physical labour. He is always moving something somewhere—a harpsichord, or fifty folders of sheet music, or
a thousand LPs, or clumps of human beings, usually carless
members of his choir. Would I be "a brick," he asked, and
help him take six boxes of fliers about a forthcoming concert from the printers to his flat? "This concert's crucial,"
he said, very fast. "We have to take on the Tallis Scholars
and beat the bastards at their own game." So we spent the
morning crossing London, in a cab filled with boxes. And
then Roger said he had to "dash off" to pick something else
up, and I was left alone in his chilly flat for two hours. At
three o'clock he came racing back, poached in sweat, and
voluble.

"Please forgive me. It's been one of those days. Oh
Christ, the bloody time, it's three, how can you bear to even
look at me? Sorry sorry."

"Roger, calm down. I've been having a perfectly happy time here working my way through your bookshelves."

"Wasn't it Max who once pointed at your bookshelves, Tom, and declaimed, 'Thomas, *these* are your real friends!' I think it was."

"Yes indeed. I often think the equivalent about you when I watch your choir."

"Ha! Speaking of which, why don't we call it a day and go and hear the choir sing Evensong at Westminster?"

The choir certainly make a pretty sound; we've been before. And I had not yet had a chance to mention Jane to Roger. So we crossed London again, heading for Westminster, Roger talking the entire time. Cathedrals in big cities confuse me; I am used to Durham, to the climb up a quiet cobbled street crowded with buildings, and then the cathedral in front of you, and the great shock of the open space around the building. But Westminster Abbey exists amid the proud circular business of Parliament Square. The contrast was with the cool darkness inside, which seemed a perpetual dawn. Sitting in the unfulfilled shadow, with Roger whispering about "the terrible acoustics," I enjoyed resembling a penitent while my head was thriving with secret blasphemies. And here suddenly were the canons and archdeacons processing up the nave, one behind the other. As they moved past, the fluttering hems of their cassocks condescended to the stone of the cathedral floor. They dropped their heads with loud modesty; *they* were "setting" their faces, I thought. At Durham, pious Canon Percy, an old friend of my father's, used to hold his hands in front of him, pressed together and made to point forward like an obedient fish. When he turned left to go into his carved stall, Canon Percy bent the fish of his hands left, too.

Behind the priests walked the choir of the Abbey—the little boys first, and then the grown men, the whole group resembling a pious growth-chart which had blushingly omitted adolescence. From innocence to experience, without any botched transition. Then the precentor began to intone: "O Lord, make clean our hearts within us." During the service, they sang Psalm 123, not one of my favourites. "Have mercy upon us, O Lord, have mercy upon us: for we are utterly despised." I enjoyed the correspondence of so many different voices and types: a sickly bass, who sucked clicking lozenges during the prayers; a pompous alto, who sang in an angry flutter and who, possibly to contradict the effeminacy of his occupation, had grown an adventurous beard; a young tenor, handsome except for his long neck and enormous Adam's apple: it was hard not to watch its wooden struggles, which lent him the effect of a man trying to swallow a large peg. The boys stood in front of the men. I awarded them personalities: the saint, the bully, the early masturbator, the blond one whose mother envied his looks, the one who couldn't sing, the weakling whose parents visited his school each weekend, bringing underpants and fruitcake. And conducting them was the Master of Choristers, a delicate-looking fellow who was no doubt secretly laughed at by the boys for his determination, during rehearsals, to pronounce "ensemble" with a French accent.

Of course, it was hard to hear any music, because Roger maintained a racing commentary throughout the service. Whenever the boys strained for a high note, Roger winced and theatrically whistled through his teeth. He rattled the service sheet and jabbed at it with his finger.

"Why do these choirs do all this Victorian drivel? It's shameful nonsense," he said, into my left ear. "We have a great English heritage from the Tudor and Elizabethan period just sitting there—just sitting there!—and these choirmasters roll out Harold Darke and Herbert Howells and Wesley and Sumsion and Balfour Gardiner, though I will say that the famous Balfour Gardiner chord—the famous diminished seventh, or perhaps infamous diminished seventh—well, that's a pretty marvellous chord. That one chord—that one chord—is worth more than the whole of Hitler's career."

Hitler, of course, was not Hitler, but the famous and disliked conductor with whom Roger was obsessed.

"Roger," I whispered, "what on earth are you talking about? Sumsion? Darke?"

"You see that's my point, that is my point! Their very names denote their mediocrity. They are English church composers from the beginning of the century. A term I dislike massively. Church composer! No such thing. They're no bloody good at all. And meanwhile, Tallis, Byrd, Gibbons, Purcell are ignored—in favour of Naylor's *Vox Dicentis.*"

"Well, hang on"—it was useless to hope for silence from Roger—"you're no one to talk about names. All your music friends, I mean the professional ones, the ones who are in the public eye and always on the radio, seem to have been named by some kind of marketing committee of the English Tourist Board."

"Not me."

"Well, Roger Trelawnay is pretty English. And how about all those 'authentic instruments' people? Ralph Barley, and Christopher Robinson, and Jeremy Darbyshire, and that weird continuo player, Simon Peacock, or whatever his name is."

"Steven Peacock."

"Well, you get my point. These guys seem to have been named in order to make a point about English authenticity! Don't they all play things like the sackbut and the hautboy and the lute? At least four of them were playing at our wedding. I'm waiting for the day when you make a record with some-one called Adam Albion on viola. Just to be done with it."

In the corner of my eye, I saw a pale old verger approach us. He walked evenly down the aisle, as if on velvet wheels, and stopped at our pew. Curiously, he said nothing, but merely stood watching us, perhaps with the ambition of looking menacing. Then he gently wheeled off.

"Have you got the message?" whispered Roger.

"I think it was aimed at you, you're the one who's doing all the talking."

As the service ended, and the choir began to process, the organ sounded—beautiful, that silver dapple of complicated breath through a thousand mouths. At the close of his piece, the organist slowed down as the final cadence approached. It seems sometimes, doesn't it, that organists enjoy holding on to the moment of portended resolution just before the final major chord. And then, finally, came the last chord, more satisfying even than its dragged prophecy had suggested. One, two, three, four, five seconds, and still the organist kept his fingers and feet pressed down, as if he had died on the job. The building was filled with sound—the mineral jangling of the small pipes, and the dragonish gargle of the large ones. And after the chord had finished, there was a ghostly echo in the building, one, two, three, four, five seconds—the memory of the chord equal in body to the actual event.

Roger and I stayed sitting while the building emptied. I sensed my moment, my opening.

"Those musicians at our wedding . . . It wasn't so long ago, the wedding, but it feels as if it was in another era," I said, leadingly.

"Hmm. Our choir wasn't in its best voice that day."

"Well, that might be said of all of us," I said, again with deliberate wistfulness.

"Yeah, but I mean it. Our best baritone wasn't there, and Mandy Sullivan, you know, our largeish soprano, brilliant voice, huge breasts, had a nasty cold and was singing at about sixty percent capacity."

"It was a funny day. Very happy. Everything seemed possible then—I mean between Jane and me. Everything seemed rosy. Even the Ph.D."

"We mangled the Tallis at your wedding. *O nata lux.* With Mandy below par we just couldn't do it justice. What an anthem, though! My god, what an anthem. It's a curious fact that between Purcell and Elgar, a period of more than two centuries, English music produced nothing of the slightest quality. Nothing. That's why I object to these choirs singing Sumsion and Darke. It all went wrong at the Reformation, if you ask me. All went wrong in 1536, when Hugh Latimer removed all the feast days from the ritual year. No more St. Anne's Day, no more St. Cuthbert's, St. Swithin's, Holy Cross Day, etcetera. Decimated the Sarum Calendar."

It seemed impossible to persuade Roger into the hospitality of dialogue. He was lost in music, which had also claimed Jane at times. My only hope was to be brutally direct.

"Roger, why do you think that Jane persists in ignoring me? Look, she had every right to abandon me last Christmas. I don't know what she told you, but she had every right. We had a fierce argument, secrets were betrayed, and she felt that she'd had enough. But that was a long time ago now. Getting on for a year ago. And I thought that in May, I thought that when my own father died, sheer human decency might . . . Well, as you may know, at the funeral she said that if I really proved to her that I had reformed, she would have me back. She said we should meet every so often for lunch and so on, and I would prove to her that I was a changed man. Those were her words. But she never sees me, so how can I prove to her that I am reformed? Do I have to go round and break into her fucking flat?"

"Well, getting all angry about it won't help," said Roger peacefully, through his hectic dentition.

"Angry?"

"Yes, angry. Give it time. Jane's got a big concert coming up, her biggest, actually. Wigmore Hall. She must be tiptop for that. She's doing the bloody *Hammerklavier*! Now, that one's not for the fainthearted, dear me no. Not for the emotionally distracted. What you can do for her is give her a bit of space, so she can really prepare for it, that's all."

Roger, incorrigibly unmarried, made our lapsed marriage sound like something that Nicholson, who is Jane's agent, might draw up—a legal form, apportioning hours for visiting and piano playing and so on. I realized that Roger was the worst person to consult on these matters. He had lived alone for years in his icy flat in Camden, dominated by a grand piano and a harpsichord. These vast wings of polished wood made all nonmusical movement difficult.

Roger was almost entirely undomesticated; though who am I to talk?

"Look, Tom, I'm having a music party—you remember the old music evenings I used to have—in a week's time. I've invited everyone, including Jane. And Max will come, too, and that totally unmusical girlfriend of his, Fiona."

"Oh yes, Fiona Raymond. Jane and I met her first in Sundershall last Christmas. Actually we met her the day before Jane and I had our tremendous argument and she went running off back to London. Haven't seen much of Fiona lately. Nor of Max, either."

"Yep, *totally* unmusical. Now, I wasn't thinking of it in these terms, but why don't you come along and put your toe in the waters, as it were? If you can't get to see Jane the normal way, then ambush her. I promise to tell her at the last possible moment that you are coming."

Roger was trying to be helpful, in his way, and I accepted his kindness. We parted outside, at the great door of the Abbey. He had somewhere to be, and was already half an hour late. I had nowhere to be, and stood for several minutes smoking a cigarette and watching the traffic in Parliament Square. From behind me, through the high door, two files of little choirboys, dressed in black capes and wearing black mortarboards with purple tassels, emerged and crocodiled past, on their way back to school. They looked indistinguishable from the black-caped choirboys at Durham. Whenever I went home I used to go to hear the choir sing, and I always thought there was something horrible yet almost funny in watching those cheerful little boys singing words of such ungraspable maturity, about David going up to his chamber and weeping after the slaying of Absalom, or the beautiful words from Revelation, my favourite in the Bible: "And God shall wipe away all tears from their eyes; and there shall be no more death, neither sorrow, nor crying, neither shall there be any more pain: for the former things are passed away." But it was hard not to complain, too, when the boys at Westminster Abbey sang those words from Psalm 123, "Have mercy upon us, have mercy upon us: for we are utterly despised." Were they despised? Twenty minutes later, the same children might be kicking a football around in the schoolyard, or arguing like refugees over a five-pence piece. I remember leaving the cathedral at Durham once, and coming upon a group of six choristers, juniors in jackets and regulation short trousers. They were surrounding a boy, whose outstretched hand they seemed to be holding. A fight, I thought. But they were counting his money. "It's twenty-four pence," said one. Another said gravely, "It's not enough. But we can go window-shopping." I couldn't help smiling as the little group set off for town, with twenty-four pence in hand, probably breaking school rules, walking and running, the backs of their jackets swaying naively, their step made particular by the uneven cobbles in the Cathedral Close.

Are we utterly despised? I don't feel at all despised. Do we need to beg for mercy? But what sins have those little boys committed? Whose hearts are unclean? Not mine, certainly not my late father's parishioners'. In Sundershall, when Father was alive, the old ladies of the village knelt on their dry knees and confessed their sins. Muriel Spedding in her dead shoes, and shyly intransigent Susan Perez-Temple, and Miss Ogilvie with her three canes. And they were joined by Terry Upsher, whose capless head was covered in thin, immature hair. Sometimes I sat behind him, and his strong neck seemed to be giving off a confused pulse. And I remember Terry's father: dourly old Mr. Upsher sat and loudly he used to speak, because of his deafness; his smoker's voice—his miner's voice—came out in a burned croak, as if a scar were speaking. In the Nicene Creed he pronounced "apostolic" with a curious heavy stress on the second syllable rather than the third, and threw everyone out of step, like a lame pallbearer. It was easy to do this because there were so few worshippers . . .

Now, I ask you, what sins have these people committed? What sins? They kneel and intone their confessions—"we have sinned through ignorance, through weakness, through our own deliberate fault"—but what has any of them done in the week since last Sunday's cringing absolution? A snobbery here, malice there, blowing the car horn at a slow tourist in the next village, a fold of desire, an argument with the sister about how long she could come to stay, a furtive refusal to shut the door properly of the local shop because of something said by the shopkeeper four years ago. But all this is no more than the daily seed of life, blown all over the land from human to human. *This* is the bread of life, this unimportant failure to be perfect. I remember exactly when the strange thought first occurred to me that if these people did not believe in this God they would not be asking Him to forgive them in the first place. I was thirteen. Nothing was the same again. An extraordinary liberation, frightening at first—and then not frightening at all, because whether I decided God existed or not I still left the church and ate Sunday lunch (beef, pork, lamb) and watched the rain fall in the garden.

Most people are not happy, after all, I decided. *I* was happy, I *am* happy, but in the largest scheme my small single happiness is quite unimportant. No, underneath each soul is a bowl of tears, whose level rises and rises in a lifetime. In some cases, the bowl does not overflow, so that you hardly know it is there. Others are swamped by grief. But you can't say that anyone is really happy. If anyone is, then the sensation is fleeting, and sparkles away. How much stronger, more distinct, more lasting, is the sensation of unhappiness.

14

I DON'T THINK QUITE AS FEVERISHLY NOW, of course. Those teenage years were a terrible time of self-absorption. That period in my life was akin to the moment when one is passing low over land in a plane, and the sun is shining, and every so often a roof or a car or a lake glints sharply, and it is hard not to think that they are glinting because you are passing over them, that you are making them glint and that they are glinting at you. Of course, your passage is having not the slightest effect, is it? In my adolescence the most arbitrary occurrences seemed to conceal secret messages, meant only for me. And my thinking about God was like this.

One day, in my teens, I did try to talk to my father about these matters, about sin and pain. As ever, Peter was evasive, cheerful.

"Surely," I said "original sin is just . . . just an unfair idea? All those nasty threats about how the wages of sin are death."

"Yes, it is unfair, Tommy, and somewhere Augustine grinds on about how each child inherits the sin of his parents' copulation. How's *that* for unfair?" I instantly knew that "unfair" was the wrong word, a schoolboy word, and that Father would worry it to gentle oblivion.

"But why are you agreeing with me?" I asked anxiously.

"Well, original sin is no more unfair than anything else, is it? Inheritance cannot be fair. It's rather unfair that I inherited my grandfather's baldness and my father's high blood pressure. It's unfair that I might die tomorrow, or that I was born at all. But this doesn't make it untrue."

"But why," I persisted, feeling myself lost—it was exactly like sports at school, as the athletes began to lap me on the racetrack—"why should anything *be* unfair, if God made the world? He's love, you always say. Love isn't unfair, is it?"

"Oh dear. You *are* melancholy at the moment. 'Shades of the prison-house begin to close upon the growing boy,' eh? Why should anything exist at all? Don't tell me you don't want to exist, Tommy! Or are you sitting up there in that locked bedroom of yours reading Mr. Beckett?"

Peter turned somewhat to my mother, and said, brightly, "Actually, the wages of sin *are* death, and I can illustrate this quite well. I came across this the other day. About six centuries ago, in Durham, some of the noblemen wanted to kill the bishop, who had become difficult. So they hired two thugs, real sons of Belial, to do the deed. And do you know what the payment was for these two murderers? They got to keep the fine clothes of the dead bishop! It struck me that this is a literal example of how in their case the wages of sin really *were* death. These chaps were paid by the corpse! I might use that sometime." He laughed and gently patted my hand. I looked away.

I felt imprisoned by my father in those days. Ah, he was so sure that I would "see the light." But not if I put huge drapes up against the windows! That was where the lying began, you see. My instinct was to hide myself, to hide my thoughts about God. A lie was necessary to protect the truth, that was obvious, as clothes hid the truth of the body. If my parents asked me whether I prayed to God, I would say that I did, and I felt that in lying about this I renewed my private truth. I began to think of truth as mine alone, and I could almost visualize it in my bedroom, protected by a locked door. My lies were saving the truth. At first, I only lied defensively, to give myself cover, and only about my lack of religious faith. But really, once you started, there were so many truths to protect that there were hardly enough lies to cover them. I liked smoking cigarettes with Max, and obviously it was necessary that I should tell my parents that I did not; moreover, it was necessary to tell them that in fact I loathed tobacco, that a single puff revolted me. It was the same with wine and gin, which Max and I were stealing from his parents.

Around this time, a friend of my parents, Canon Palliser, asked me, when we were alone, what I was studying for my O-level exams. Into the list of these subjects, I inserted Greek, which I had never studied. This was new. A lie wholly gratuitous. I felt a rush of sheer joy. The purest lie, because before there was even a truth to protect, I was, as it were, anticipating truth's protection, truth's needs. It was a kind of chivalry towards truth! You took the lie to the enemy, preemptively, so that you were not *forced* to lie.

That curious ecstasy I felt when I lied was the ecstasy of freedom. I became unknowable, unaccountable at the moment I lied. The difficulty was that I was always tempted into further risk. For it's not truth that is bottomless, but untruth. Around this time I woke up one night in my bedroom, needing to urinate. I could barely be bothered to rise and walk to the bathroom. A shame that there was not some kind of commode, I thought. Seeing a half-empty glass on my bedside table, I finished the water, and then, impulsively, urinated into the glass. It filled with my warm waste. The sensible thing would be to empty the glass at once in the lavatory, or hide it under the bed. Instead, I carefully placed it back on the table, knowing that in the morning Mother—and sometimes Father—would enter the room, draw back the curtains, and wish me good morning. In the mornings, my mother enjoyed a moment of tenderness with me. She would move indulgently about the room, picking up dirty laundry and water glasses and teacups, fondly complaining about the untidiness and telling me that she and "Daddy" had already had breakfast but that I should take my time. It was quite different with Father. When he came to wake me up, he would stand at the door, and ask: "Interested?" This was the cue for me to say, sleepily, "Yes," at which point he announced the news headlines he had heard on his little transistor radio while shaving: "More strikes today. No trains." He borrowed the habit from his army training just before the outbreak of war. The staff sergeant used to waken the soldiers with the latest news he had heard from London in the officers' mess. Father loved to tell the story of the day the Pope died, and how the sergeant, having announced the information, turned to the only Catholic soldier in the room, still asleep under blankets, and said, in robustly sympathetic tones, "Sorry, O'Brien," and marched out.

I knew that my father would never notice the glass, but that my mother would stand next to the table, and I placed it there in the hope that she might see it. What joy for me to look at her, and deny that it was what it resembled, to express complete ignorance of its origins, to lie to her face. But she did not notice the glass, nor on four subsequent mornings—I repeated the nightly filling—and I got bored, and ended my game.

15

TWO WEEKS HAVE PASSED SINCE my meeting with Roger. One good week followed by one awful one. In the good week, which started well with Roger's invitation to his music evening, I made some progress on my Ph.D., and did excellent work on the BAG, and thought as little about Jane and my late father as possible. And then it all came crashing down. First of all, I saw Jane, of course, at Roger's, and that threw me out for several days. I can't blame Jane; this was my ambush. Indeed, hubris sent me to Roger's place. I was hopeful, and started entertaining fantasies of reconciliation. I knew how optimistic I was when I found myself taking a bath in my Finchley Road bathroom, washing my hair and then rubbing a bit of old sunscreen into my skin to give it gloss. I have never been conventionally very clean, and currently I have little incentive. Jane used to order me to bathe and assured me that the rest of the civilized world would look upon me with horror if it knew how truly filthy I was. But she only responded like this near the beginning of our relationship, once I had told her that I was no fan of the bath or shower; in other words, I seemed unclean to her only when I told her, not in fact. For I did not—I *do* not—smell; I was never actually very dirty while we were married. Those very civilized creatures who wash so thoroughly every day—what on earth are they washing? Do their legs and stomachs sweat? I hardly ever sweat (except when I am lying) and I've found that a quick wash of the torso suffices for sev-

eral days. There's a case to be made that washing is not especially philosophical. My BAG has several entries about washing. Plotinus preferred massages to bathing. Saint Jerome
argued that those who have been washed in the water of
Christ do not need to bathe. In fact, the secret of staying
clean while not washing lies only in one thing: the daily
changing of underwear. The soldiers of Napoleon who put
on clean underwear before a battle—in the expectation of
death they wanted to be clean for their Maker—had it right,
though naturally my adaptation is a secular one.

Anyway, my skin glowed impressively when I turned up
at Roger's in Camden. Jane was already there. I could see
her in the kitchen; her back was turned to me. There were
strangers wandering about. One of them was introduced to
me as Joshua Smithers, a composer. He seemed very peculiar. His whole body was violent. His hair seemed to have
been torn from his head—or perhaps from someone else's—
and stuck roughly back on; it pointed forward from his
brow, aiming at the world. Like Roger, Joshua spoke very
fast, and as he did so he jerked his arms. He blocked my path
to the kitchen, and started telling me about how little he
liked jazz. "Completely fraudulent." Perhaps he thought I was
a jazz musician. Then he solemnly informed me that "the
greatest twentieth-century composer" was Percy Grainger,
who wrote *In an English Country Garden.* I looked around him.
Jane was talking to Max and his girlfriend, Fiona Raymond,
still with her back to me. There was something offensive
about this turned back. Surely she knew I was there. By way
of escaping Joshua's exclusive attentions, I asked him if he
knew Jane. She turned at her name, and looked straight at
me, and I am ashamed to say that I became a fool in her
presence. Those dark eyes made me null. I was aware of my

face reddening, and then I felt my whole body warming. I began to plan how, without raising her suspicion that I was lying, I might give her the impression that the Ph.D. was finished. Jane said my name, fondly, easily, and then looked at my chest, and said, "Tommy dear, you've spilt something on your shirt." And with scandalous composure, she dipped a cloth under the kitchen tap, approached me, and pressed at the spot, which was just above my left nipple. I watched my dark chest hairs become visible through the wet white shirt. I smelt her familiar perfume, and felt a kind of rage. How dare she deal with me in this wifely, familiar way. Was it so easy for her, then? I wanted to grab her thin, precious, talented wrists, and break them into bits. But all I said was, "You see, I'm useless without you, I can't go anywhere," which sounded self-pitying. And she replied, "Oh, you're doing fine. You smell nice, by the way."

It took me half an hour to forgive Jane for her flippancy—for her plain ordinariness. The difference between my anxiety and her calmness was horrible to contemplate. It was insulting. And why had Max not greeted me when I first saw him? Fiona had come up to me and asked me how I was, but Max had wandered off to get a drink. Since Father's funeral, Max had been newly distant.

I moped in a corner of the room while Roger and Joshua put different pieces of music on the record player. Jane sat on the floor, very close to one of the loudspeakers, as usual; I refused to look at her. The music meant little to me, so I closed my eyes and thought about what it provoked in me. Roger took control, speaking fast through his twisted teeth. Despite Roger's brilliant musical ear, and immense knowledge of early music, which he edits and writes about, we always had to dissuade him from relating everything back to his choir and its performance schedule. Joshua wanted to play some Berg. As he was fiddling with the record, Roger said:

"Hmm. Berg's no good for us, I'm afraid, he's anniversarially poor."

There was a silence.

"The choir. No good for us."

"What was that peculiar phrase?" Max asked.

"Anniversarially poor," said Roger.

"Yes? And?"

"You don't get it, do you? Not even Jane? Well, Berg—and Michael Praetorius, actually—both of them died at fifty. So you can only get two anniversary festivals from Berg per century. Whereas with Bach"—Roger was now spitting with animation—"you get four per century."

"I don't follow," said Max. "Please reconfigure your sentence." Everyone laughed. I was reminded of how Max and I used to "philosophize" as teenagers.

"Oh dear, you're still not with me because you don't run a choir. Look, with anniversary festivals, you are allowed to do concerts at a hundred years and at fifty years from birth or death—i.e., in units of fifty. So with Bach, who was born in 1685 and died in 1750, there was a celebration in 1950 to mark two hundred years since his death, and in 1985 there was one to mark three hundred years since his birth, and in 2000 we can have one to mark two hundred and fifty years since his death if we want—I *do,* actually—and in 2035 we will be able to mark three hundred and fifty years since his birth, and so on. But look at Berg. He's born in 1885, dies in 1935. You can celebrate a hundred years since his birth—1985. But if you try to celebrate a hundred and fifty years since his birth, you are celebrating in 2035—which just happens to be also a hundred years since his death. That's what

I mean, you only get two a century from Berg and Prae-torius—the fifty-year celebrations always overlap with the hundred-year celebrations of his birth or his death. So we lose out. Very inconsiderate of those two."

"I'm exhausted," said Max.

"But, Rog, you'll be lucky to be alive in 2050, so what's it to you?" asked Jane.

"I'm speaking conceptually, of course. I like playing around with these little puzzles in my head. Thought every-one did."

"Also," said Joshua, "how many times has your choir *ever* sung anything by Berg?"

"Well, but that's not the point, is it, Josh?" said Roger.

It appears that Joshua writes music which no one present seemed ever to have heard; and each piece he mentioned sounded, to me at least, more outlandish than the last: folk songs set in a parallel universe, a piece for string quartet and ukelele. His current project was an opera set in an aquarium to a libretto written by his grandmother. "Granny's very dear and dotty. She's created four major characters: Stingray, the baddy; Cod, a sort of holy fool type, always getting into scrapes; Coral, the goody; and Poseidon, who acts as a kind of chorus. As a literary text I think it's completely brilliant— *you* should read it, you know, Max, and write a column about it." When Roger put on a Bach fugue, Joshua lay on his back on Roger's old worn carpet, rolling with delight under the harpsichord, and crying out, "The bastard, the bastard! Listen to what he's doing, he can do anything he likes!"

I cheered up at this, and joined the conversation, which was becoming political. Everyone fell into natural humility before Max, who was considered to be an expert on political matters. When he talked about the European Union, people were quiet. The old Max, pitmatic Max, was in love with philosophy and metaphysics and theology, and knew how to keep the tedium of political discussion in its proper place. But as he has become more successful, more of a "pundit," to use his mother's phrase, he has become more and more worldly, at least on paper. Of course, his worldliness is a stunt. It is entirely derived from books. Remember that Max grew up without television. Newspapers did not enter The Oratory. The Thurlows never travelled. They starved life down to its academic minimum; life was a footnote to the great text of mental existence. He was educated, like me, in an unworldly provincial town. I remember how, years ago, Mother made me and Father laugh when she told us that she had just seen Professor Colin Thurlow, Professor Belinda Thurlow, and little bespectacled Max standing on the main bridge in Durham, "all determinedly and rather intellectually eating Mr. Whippy ice creams without the slightest sign of pleasure on any of their faces."

"Look, Roger," Max was saying, "ten years ago Britain was the fabled . . . sick man of Europe . . . you know, as Turkey was thought of in the nineteenth century. And there was no good reason for this. Remember the old saying about how Britain is a lump of coal surrounded by gas and oil and fish. We are a . . . rich nation but we were living then like . . . paupers. Not any more." Not you, at least, I thought to myself, as Max continued.

"And we have Thatcher to thank for that, whether you agree with all . . . her ideology." Max is forever writing about Mrs. Thatcher's great successes.

"Oh, come on, Max, she's not FDR," I said. "Where's her New Deal?"

"She's a revolutionary, and the British don't like . . . revolutionaries," said Max, indifferently, as if my objection barely merited a response.

"Oh yes?" I asked. "So what were Herzen and Kropotkin doing for so long in England?"

"That was, when I last consulted the matter, the . . . nineteenth century." Again, the curious indifference.

"Well, you said that the British don't like revolutionaries."

"I think Mrs. Thatcher's brought a new morale to this country. But I don't especially . . . want to argue with you about it," said Max.

"Who called it an argument?" I asked, smiling. "I'm just putting a little pressure on you."

"Fine, but the . . . quality of the pressure is what counts." Max said this while letting great clouds of smoke escape from his mouth. His languid emissions irritated me enormously.

"What the hell does that mean?" I said.

"It means that I don't 'put pressure' on you when you want to talk about . . . the Epicureans or God or . . . whatever." I think that his "whatever" meant Jane.

"Oh no?"

"And I'm not sure you know anything about this."

"Boys, boys, stop it, this isn't going anywhere," said Fiona Raymond. "Roger wants to put another piece of music on."

It was Max's amiability which ensured that, when we were teenagers, our Pitmatic Philosophical Society met weekly and never suffered a cross word. We founded it (Max and I were its only members) in part to fight what we called "the God-talkers," adults who were either explicitly or implicitly propagandizing for God. Sometimes, as in the case of

Canon Palliser, the propaganda was open and transparent. Sometimes, as with my parents, the instruction was careful, subtle, evasive—but all the more potent for its snakelike slithering. After all, how did Mr. Duffy tell us to write our essays? He stood at the front of the class and bellowed at us: "Children, start your essays with a bit of a bang. Bacon began his essay on gardens, 'The Lord God Almighty first planted a garden.' Try to emulate him."

But I thought: Who is "him?" Were we to emulate Bacon, or, really, Him? I became convinced that Mr. Duffy was secretly trying to put the idea of God in my mind. Max agreed with me. So we established our Society, which was dedicated to the frank discussion of atheism, amorality, and decadence. We met behind the oak tree on Pilgrim's Path. We brought cigarettes, alcohol when we could get it, and a feeble cassette recorder, from whose toyish loudspeaker we coaxed an illusory depth, as Led Zeppelin (denounced by Colin Thurlow as "satanic") and Pink Floyd flimsily corrupted a cubic centimetre of air. Dear Max, pitmatic Max. Sitting in Roger's flat that night, pitmatic Max seemed to have completely disappeared.

I approached Max and drew him aside. "What the hell was that all about?" I asked.

"Don't overreact. I am . . . *allowed* to be sharp with you, you know."

"I don't deserve it," I said. I thought to myself: With what I know about you and Jane, it is I who should be sharp with you.

"Tom . . . isn't it time you stopped . . . feeling so sorry for yourself?"

"Not you, too. Not the two of you together. Against me. I should call my work the Book Against Tom."

"I'm on your side—but no, no, why does it have to be a . . . question of sides? Those are your terms, and they are . . . ridiculous. It's not about sides at all. Whatever anger Jane has towards you is not mine."

"Ah, so you *do* have some anger towards me," I said.

"No, I just want you to stop moping in your bedsit and doing nothing—painting yourself with . . . tar and rolling in a great big bag of . . . feathers."

"You know nothing about this. And *you*, who for so long have been telling me to keep going with the Ph.D., to put in another six months, another year, to get it done at all costs."

"Tom, pull yourself together, for goodness sake. Your father is dead. Didn't you say to me several times that you felt Peter was always . . . breathing over your Ph.D.?"

"Yes, I suppose so."

"So, feel released. Finish the Ph.D. Or if that's over, if you can't finish the thesis, then write the Book Against God, and write it with . . . a sense of freedom, with a sense of new life." I couldn't stand being given "advice" by Max, and when he added that since Peter was dead I should no longer think of the Book Against God as my own little secret, my own "private crime"—those were his words—I was deeply offended, and I walked away from him while he was still talking. "Be a baby, then," I heard him say behind me.

I went to sit next to Jane on the carpet. "You don't have any cause to be mean to him, you know," said Jane, looking down between her knees. "You're not blaming *him*, are you? Surely you've got over all that?"

"No, no. Max is forgiven—for *that*, at least," I said.

"It didn't sound like it just now. It sounded as if both of you are furious with one another."

"I forgive Max. Look, I sympathize with him for being in love with you."

"You have nothing to forgive," said Jane. "As I said to you at Christmas, take a long hard look at Fiona. Max *has a girlfriend.* He has no interest in me."

"Okay, but then he should forgive *me*," I said. "For whatever I've done—which is what, exactly? What have I done to Max?"

"I think Max is angry with you for the same reason that I am—your behaviour at the funeral."

"You know, my *father had just died.* Is that so hard to under-stand?"

But Jane was lost in her own thoughts.

"That you mentioned our marriage in your speech in church. That you mentioned us. In that *awful* speech. Oh, Tommy, that was terrible."

"I'm sorry. I'm sorry. But what about your side of the bargain? What about the promised period of probation? You've seen me exactly three times since the end of July. It's October now!"

I felt my desperation made me seem foolish and emotional, and my reproaches made me seem weak and hectoring.

"Jane, I know you have this big concert coming. Roger told me about it."

"Are you blaming my music again for getting between us?"

"No, I mean it. I'm not being sarcastic. Roger said that it's the biggest concert yet. I'll be there, you know, cheering you on. If you want me to come." I felt tears in my eyes, and hung my head. "Janey, I'm very sorry for everything. I know how utterly useless I am, I know how awful I was to live with, but I can't seem to pull myself out and up. I can't seem to."

Inclining her body towards me, so that I felt the outline of her warmth, Jane said:

"Are you all right, Tommy? You know we all care about you." The words fell like instantly evaporating rain.

"Oh good, it's nice to know that you *all* care about me," I said, with excessive bitterness.

"You're being unpleasant again."

"And you are being less than sensitive."

"This isn't the place for—*this.*"

We carried on like this for a minute or so more, but the evening was ruined. So much for my optimism, so much for the sunscreen! I left the flat early, just as Joshua Smithers began defending, to Roger, some minor work by Mendelssohn, and walked home, up Adelaide Road to noisy Swiss Cottage.

16

AS IF JANE AND MAX HAD NOT PUNISHED me sufficiently, the next day my bank card was taken by the machine in the wall, because my account is overdrawn. I couldn't face asking Uncle Karl for money, and I have to pay back the money I borrowed from Philip Zealy, so that afternoon I bought the *Evening Standard* and responded to an advertisement for telesales operators. They wanted me there the next morning, in Hatfield.

Without knowing it, I had chosen a car magazine; their glass tower was near the station. There was a group of us waiting at reception, where we were met by a middle-aged man who called himself Rob. He was a big fellow, with short, load-bearing legs. He pulled his jacket tight, creating a masculine bustle as the jacket's single flap stuck out in a prim salute over his backside. Rob explained that we were to phone people who had advertised the sale of a car in another magazine or newspaper, ask them if they had had any success, and, if not, persuade them to re-advertise in his magazine.

He led us upstairs to the selling room, a huge windowless pasture full of nodding humans—nodding, because all of them were on the phone, and all of them talking and moving up and down as they spoke. There was the universal proud blandness of all office noise, and as I heard that awful continuity I thanked my stars that I have for so many years avoided this form of drudgery—for so long I have been what Psalm 81 calls "delivered from the pots." Well, we were shown to bare plastic desks, handed sheets of telephone numbers attached to names and models of cars, and told to "get on with it." At each successful sale, or "take," we should raise our hand. Every minute or so a hand went up in the room, at which fat Rob rose from his chair at the front and walked with short, Japanese steps to a blackboard, where he adjusted a running total—of advertisements sold that day, I presumed.

I made £27 in two hours, which wasn't bad, but quite apart from the humiliation of the work, I suffered an attack of nerves while having to walk through the room to the lavatory, and this attack was far, far worse than even the job itself. Simply put, I found that my legs were beginning to seize up as I tried to make my way to the bathroom. The desks were all facing me, I had to walk against the visual tide, as it were, and I felt that all eyes were turned my way, even though reason told me that no one in the room had the slightest interest in my passage.

In a second, the horrors of adolescence returned. I vividly remember the moment, in my fourteenth year, at which I became self-conscious. I was late for school assembly, and had to walk into the hall while several hundred boys and girls watched me. I realized that for the first time I felt very awkward being watched, and my legs began to freeze, and I barely made it in one piece to my seat. Should I try to look as if I was not being watched, or try to look as if I knew I *was* being watched?

I can laugh about it now, but how terrible was that hurtle into self-consciousness; it was like a second birth. After that

morning, whenever I went into assembly I became sure that
everyone was looking at me; I imagined they could even hear
me swallowing, and so I tried to control my flow of saliva. A
terrible dryness and pressure would build in my throat, and
then the only way to swallow without being heard was to give
a little cough (the forerunner of the later "artificial"
cough). For several months I seemed to have no personality
at all, except the one I daily built. Writing this, I am reminded of that grand line from one of the Psalms: "Except
the Lord build the house, they labour in vain that build it."
But as soon as I write this down, I am also reminded, less
happily, of what Jesus says to Nicodemus: "Except a man be
born again, he cannot see the kingdom of God." Well, this
agony was *my* second birth. I became anxious about speaking
in public; when asked to read aloud from a schoolbook by
one of my teachers, I bit into my pen and flooded my mouth
with ink, and then ran from the classroom, as if to clean my
mouth. My nose seemed to be getting larger than the rest of
my face; or rather, my nose seemed to be becoming adult
faster than my mouth or chin. In fact this was just the familiar way that adolescent faces, whose parts are enlarging at
unequal speeds, sometimes resemble parodies of stretched
heads by Picasso. But I was horrified, and for a while at
nighttime, once I had said goodnight to my parents, I would
strap up my nose with tape and elastic bands, to try to arrest
its growth.

I became the victim of involuntary erections. Surely
everyone could see the bulge in my trousers blooming like a
flower in time-lapse photography. Now, as an adult, when I
remember those erections, I think of one of my school-
teachers, Mr. Conners, showing our class photographic
slides of ancient statues. When the fertility god appeared,

with its penis crudely extended, Mr. Conners dealt with the subject forthrightly, took a breath, and said: "Note the engorged phallus." He had clearly prepared the phrase; of course it failed, there were the usual laughs in the darkness. After I had mentioned it to her once, Mr. Conners's phrase became a happy refrain between Jane and me. On those mornings when the usual male helplessness was stiffly facing her, Jane would sometimes look at my springing penis, and say, "Note the engorged phallus!"

Desperate, I wrote away to an American company that was advertising in one of my mother's magazines. They sent me a self-hypnosis cassette, which promised "Self-Confidence." My parents teased me for this extravagance, which cost all my pocket money. You were supposed to fall asleep to the sound of a man's soothing words. At night (my nose taped up), I put on plush headphones, rested my head against the pillow, and drifted off on waves of Californian generosity. The man's voice sounded bearded, somehow. Very gentle and bearded and muffled. He told me that I was a "valuable person," that I should think well of myself, and could be brought into a new life if only I filled myself with self-esteem. It is hard to say if these words did me any good, because I was always asleep within two minutes. For all I know, the tape ended after two minutes, or suddenly turned into a vicious attack: "You are selfish, self-absorbed, utterly nugatory. You think that listening to this pathetic American tape will help. Think again, you little nonentity . . ." and so on!

A second birth, a second birth. The Greeks should have said: "Call no man happy who is born *again*." And I'm not just talking about very shy and obviously damaged people, like Samuel Spedding, Muriel Spedding's son who still lives in Sundershall, even though he is over fifty. Poor Sam Spedding, whom Max and I used to tease when we were boys. He was so shy that when you phoned him and asked, "Is that Sam Spedding?" he answered, in a very quiet voice, "It is, actually," as if slightly amazed that he existed at all.

17

SO THE TELESALES JOB brought me very little, and I was still without a bank card. It was humiliating to have to search for lost pennies underneath my armchair cushion just to have enough to buy a sandwich. After four days of living on bread and jam I decided to phone Uncle Karl and arrange dinner at his house in Chelsea. We both knew the begging drill; we had done it before.

I have loved Chelsea ever since I first went there for Uncle Karl's wedding party, at the age of thirteen. The tall, Victorian apartment buildings impart a childlike, fairy-tale feeling, like walking in a forest of wardrobes. From these buildings, with magical speed, richly dressed ladies emerge, as if all they do inside is put on and take off expensive clothes. Inside, Karl's house is how I imagine all Chelsea houses to be: an enormous drawing room looking onto the rich street, a primitive and unused kitchen, a lovely bathroom on the second floor with curling, telephonic taps and hoses. Sofas in jungly chintzes (birds of paradise), thickly lined curtains heavy enough to wrap a corpse in, immovable furniture, beautiful old carpets worn in places down to little lyres of parallel strings, and on the dining-room table heavy silver cutlery, tarnished as if it has been drowned in ancestral lakes for a century.

Uncle Karl has done a very good job of impersonating an aristocrat. I've always felt close to him. First, we are both subject to delusions of grandeur. He knows very well that in my dreams I would come from a distinguished family, would be able to tell you what the Buntings were doing during the Reformation, or at least the Counter-Reformation; and knows well that, things being less than ideal, I am barely able to tell you what the Buntings were doing during the Industrial Revolution. (Schoolteaching, as far as I can make out.) Second, and consequently, we both love fine things—food, fabrics, furniture. And, third, we are twins in thought—he a secular Jew, I a secular Christian. He generally dealt with my parents' Christianity by treating it as a form of madness, of an admittedly benign, English kind. As far as he is concerned, religion is something invented by the priests, the rabbis, the mullahs, an enormous international caravan spreading war and hatred and inquisition across the sands of the world. Briefly a lawyer before going into art dealing, he once said, in lawyerly fashion, that the New Testament, if indeed a final testament, had been "so badly drafted that it had given rise to two thousand years of vicious litigation," a *mot* so *bon* that I have copied it into my BAG.

Father told me about Karl's life when I was a teenager. He came to England in 1939, when he was eight. His parents put him on a train in Berlin, and he never saw them again. At Harwich, he was among a group of Jewish children who were "viewed" and "selected" by English parents, in a manner that now seems to me a strange inversion of the famous sixth-century story told to us as schoolchildren, of how Pope Gregory came upon a group of English slave-children for sale in Rome, and, struck by their fair hair and blue eyes, asked which land they came from, and then requested that Christ's word be taken to this benighted country.

Karl was "selected" by a wealthy London family who, unimaginably, sent him away to a boys' boarding school for a proper English education. Karl never talks about these early childhood experiences and I never ask, but my father told me that Karl stood every day with the other boys after breakfast, waiting for letters from their parents to be handed to them. For six months there were letters from Germany, and then there were none, though Karl could not stop hoping and quietly wept in the lavatories after these morning sessions. The picture stayed in my mind, and returns to me often when I see Uncle Karl: I imagine the little boy, darker than his fair-haired English schoolmates, dressed in grey short trousers . . . and then the headmaster, breakfast-warmed, stinking of pipe tobacco, reading out the English surnames from the envelopes: "Carter, Warburton, Hall-church, Sim, Drury-Lowe, Wheeler, Scrase-Dickinson," each of them solidly shouting out "Yes sir!" and going up to receive a letter and wandering off down a corridor still heavy with food smells.

Not surprisingly, Karl ran away from school, was picked up and returned, ran away again, and eventually the charity in charge of the refugee children reassigned him to a poorer but much happier family in rural Yorkshire. There were three brothers and one sister, and they welcomed him and played with him in their large garden. The father was a taciturn farmer—so they all ate comparatively well during the war—but the mother, whom Karl always called "Mamie," was a warm and loquacious woman, kind but firm, given to non sequiturs and illogical statements. Karl did speak of these years in Yorkshire, he seemed to date his English life from this change, and he had a favourite example of Mamie's way of talking. Near the end of the war, he told me, when he was thirteen or fourteen, Mamie overheard one of her sons calling the Germans "Nazi bastards." The children, including Karl, liked to imitate dogfights between the RAF and the Luftwaffe, running around in the garden, their arms outstretched, their mouths savagely tut-tutting imaginary bullets from wing-mounted guns, and in the course of one of these games, in which the Germans always lost, one of the boys shouted, "Kill the Nazi bastards!"

Mamie immediately stopped the game and asked her son to repeat what he had said. Haltingly he did so, adding in defence: "That's what everyone's calling them now."

"Well," said Mamie, "that may be, but not in this house. As long as this is a free country, nobody's using that kind of language here about the Germans."

Karl loves telling this story, as an example of English "decency"; I have heard it three or four times. He starts laughing before he has finished it, so that strangers often mishear it.

Karl did well at school, quickly becoming fluent in English (though never losing a slight formality of speech), and in 1949, exempted from National Service because of his background, he went to university at Durham, where a year later he met my father, who had arrived as a young lecturer in theology, and who had his own war stories to tell. The two men became very close friends. My father, I believe, somewhat adopted Karl. Peter was thirty, wanted a child—something my mother once told me suggests that my parents tried for a long time to produce me—and there suddenly was Karl, eleven years younger than Peter Bunting, vulnerable, trailing his past. Apparently Karl was often at my parents' house in those years before my birth, a pretty old house near the cathedral with four stone steps which are depressed in the middle like saddles and a red front door hemmed by a bruised brass strip.

Karl, by the way, does not look especially worldly, except that his clothes are quietly expensive, with subtle cross-stitching and discreet herringbone patterns and silk threads—the sort of wasteful and lavish attention to texture, barely visible to the distant eye, that puts me in mind of life as seen under an electron microscope. But his body is unsybaritic: he is very thin and bony, broad-shouldered, so that his clothes, despite their fineness, hang from him rather. His skin is sallow, and becomes even darker just under his handsome eyes, where there are creases and little ridges. As a child I was fascinated by these dark drains underneath Uncle Karl's eyes; it seemed to my fanciful imagination that the skin there was stained with a kind of rust, a rust which might creep up on any of us if we neglected to wipe away our tears with a proper thick handkerchief.

At our dinner in Chelsea, Karl was wearing a rich, prickly tweed jacket, like a hair shirt worn inside out, and a fine tie patterned with blue digital dots. He stood in the doorway with his usual calm, ironic air. And standing right behind him in the hall was—Jane. It was an immense shock, but I struggled not to show it.

"Jane," I said, "again! How nice. We mustn't make a habit of this." Karl had been naughty, if typically generous; inviting Jane without telling me was clearly part of his campaign to reunite us. Karl laughed as soon as he saw me.

"Oh, God, that beard will have to go, Tom. You look almost Hasidic, you know." Every so often I neglect to shave; Jane knows this and corrected Karl.

"It's not a beard, Karl, it's an absence of shaving. It just means that Tom has run out of blades." She gave my beard an affectionate stroke. Her hand was warm and delicate. She wore a short green suede skirt, which I had not seen before, and which looked very good. This time I was strengthened by her earlier flippancy at Roger's and felt myself the match for it. This time I was not going to display my weakness, I was not going to let her know how much I needed her. I "set" my face to the appropriate mask.

We had a pleasant dinner, actually, but it was shadowed by my knowledge that once it was over I would need to ask Karl for money. At the table, we talked about my mother. Karl was concerned about her and said that he would try to visit her over Christmas. I complained, a little gracelessly, that she was continually phoning me.

"But you cannot fail to know, Tom, that she loves you and is concerned about your future? That is all. Just as Peter was—and, yes, I know that you and Peter had some problems. Several problems, perhaps! How I miss dear Peter . . . Sarah wants just the utter best for you, like any parent."

I couldn't help saying, helplessly, "But what *is* the best for me? What should I do?"

Jane said briskly, "Come on, Tom, we've been through this."

"Not with Uncle Karl, not with him."

"As soon as you abandon your laudable commitment to higher thought," said Karl, "I would love to help you on your way. But I suspect that what you want is to sit in a room on your own, reading during the day and earning no money at all, and then, no doubt, oysters and champagne at night at the Ritz."

"That sounds fine to me," I said. "Plato by day and Alcibiades by night."

"You remember, Jane, I spent those two years in Nice?" said Karl. "There was a beach outside the town I liked to swim from, I went there on Sundays. After their church visiting, the old Frenchmen, who were pure and freshly confessed from their church, real old Provençal types dressed in dark suits and white shirts, stopped at the beach on their way home to ogle the girls who were not wearing their bikini tops. Even on Sunday they were not very godly. Tom, you remind me of these men—I can't for the *life* of me think why."

Do I want incompatible things? In fact, it's a better description of Karl, who is a considerable connoisseur of women. My parents often talked about "Karl and women" with the same kind of resignation that they talked about Durham weather. Karl married two more times after his famous wedding party in London, and is currently separated from his third wife, Antonia, whom I liked very much. I miss seeing Antonia in Karl's flat. In each case, the issue has been his inability to refrain from extramarital activity.

I let Jane leave us early, so that she wouldn't see me begging for money. Buoyed by the success of the evening, we warmly agreed to "do this again," a repulsive charade in which we spoke to each other like mere lunching acquaintances. "I'll phone you," said Jane, as she kissed me with those lips.

Karl and I had brandy in his drawing room. A delicate ludic Klee looked down at us from above the marble mantelpiece.

"She won't phone me."

"You are too young to go through this, you realize," said Karl.

I looked quizzically at him.

"Separation, divorce, ex-wives. Accept this from a specialist."

"It was very sweet of you to invite Jane tonight. Thank you. Quite a shock." I shook my head.

"Clausewitz's most important principle. The element of surprise. He says it is the foundation of all undertakings."

"I don't think it'll work, even on our tiny battlefield. I'm supposed to be winning her back, that was the arrangement, but she never sees me."

"What were the terms?" Karl asked this like a lawyer, matter-of-factly and without any surprise.

"Oh, the usual. I have to be a better human being, and so on." I laughed nervously. I didn't want to tell Karl about the lying, about the real cause of our separation. I cherished his respect too much.

"Well, Tommy, I will do all I can. I will speak to her."

"Thank you."

"I would be doing nothing more than repaying you," he said gently, with fondness in his eyes.

"Oh, that."

It was true that I liked Antonia so much, and loved Karl so deeply, that when the familiar and expected news came from my parents—"Uncle Karl's in the marital soup again"— I did all I could to convince Antonia of his immense goodness. She and I spent most of the summer of 1988 on park benches throughout London talking about Karl's overpowering "sexual needs." I hadn't known that Antonia had told him.

"As I say, I will do everything that is in my power."

I gently bent the conversation towards my bedsit on the Finchley Road. I would have Karl round for dinner, I said, except that it was too horrible where I was living, and Jane's flat was no longer available to me. Now we were back on familiar terrain. We both knew the rules, and followed them. How awful *is* this place? asked Karl, and I made it sound a bit better than it was, in order to seem nobly stoical, the op-

posite of a beggar. At which point, Karl said, "Now don't
obscure things from me, Tommy. If it is not a viable place to
inhabit, you can always come back here. I have assured your
mother this." And I, restless in my seat, with mixed feelings
about the knowledge that Karl and Mother were discussing
me, said that I didn't need to stay with Karl, but I *was* wor-
rying a bit about the rent. "Well, why did you not say so?"
said Karl, thus releasing both of us from further discussion.
The cheque, I know, will appear in the post in a few days'
time, posed to look like a stray thought, a wisp of generosity
unrelated in any way to our conversation last night. It will be
for vastly more than it ought to be. And it will be the third
such cheque I have taken from Uncle Karl since the funeral.
Commit a sin twice and it will not seem a sin . . .

18

BUT NOW I MUST explain the terrible events of last Christmas, and how Jane and I came to separate. After my September visit, I didn't return to Sundershall until the day of the annual Christmas Gathering. (My mother has always called parties "gatherings"; it's a way of making them sound less secular. Her strict and ascetic parents used the same word for all social events and she can't abandon the habit.) Last year's Gathering was momentous, because I inadvertently confessed my atheism to my father.

Jane and I drove up for the Christmas week. Uncle Karl was due in three days' time. We arrived late, an hour before the party, to find my parents running around, preparing things. Or rather, my mother running around. Every two or three minutes she came into the sitting room, but she seemed really to want to move from room to room talking to herself. Father, who had surely done nothing to help in the preparation, strode in and stood by the fire, smoking a small cigar and striving to mimic his wife's frowning, in the interests of harmony. Whenever Mother disappeared, his face had its usual easy and genial aspect; as soon as she appeared in the room, he busied his face to match hers, and studied the fire as if he were in charge of it. Amused, I sat and watched this performance. He looked very well.

One of the villagers, Mary Surtees, looked in, and Peter stood to attention and said, "Jane, you remember Mary, don't you? She is Our Lady of the Waters tonight—she'll be slaving away at the washing up." Then Mother entered.

"Dearest, I'm not fooled by you," she said, with a laugh. "What have you lost in there, a ring?"

"Eh?" said Peter.

"You seem terribly concerned about the fire. Have you lost something in it?"

Peter went after Sarah, feebly offering to help, and then returned to the sitting room.

"Everything all right?" he asked us both.

"Oh yes. I need a drink, though," I said.

"Ha! You've brought a little bit of London with you to our modest village party," said Father, with a satisfaction that immediately set me on edge.

"How come?"

"You've passed my test. I've noticed that the more so-phisticated a society, the more people say that they 'need' things, which is always in inverse proportion to their *actual* needs. Whereas up here, in our humble little village, our people say they want things when they really *need* them." I was annoyed by Father. I suspected him of preparing this obser-vation in advance; it sounded almost memorized. I felt that his observation was doing double duty for him: while subtly criticizing me, he also wanted my approval, wanted to sound "philosophical" with me—not just the clever parish priest who should really have retired by now but the owner of a "proper mind." And why the sarcasm of "our humble little village"?

"Is that so?" I said heavily. "Well, Dad, if it makes me seem purer, I can tell you that when I entered the room I only *wanted* a drink. But now, thanks to you, I really *need*

one." I said this cruelly. Father's face went red, and seemed
to swell into sadness.

"Oh, Tom—" he said, while I poured myself a punitively
large scotch, and ignoring my father, asked Jane what she
wanted. The bell went. Excusing myself, I went to the door.
It was Colin and Belinda Thurlow, rawly punctual as ever.
Behind them appeared Timothy Biffen, who was a younger
colleague of my father's in the theology department when
Peter taught at the university. Timothy is in his late fifties,
but is boyish with thick hair. His habit of wearing summer
clothes throughout the year—thin open-necked shirts, light
linen trousers, flippant and airy shoes—gives him an eager,
frivolous aspect, almost like that of an unsuccessful playboy,
quite at odds with his intellectual reputation, which is fero-
ciously abstract and theoretical. Peter liked him, had liked
him when Timothy first arrived at the university, "with the
ink still drying on his utterly incomprehensible Ph.D.," as
he put it once. Father was interested in him because he was
the only member of the theology department about whose
religious beliefs one could not be certain. "I think he doesn't
believe. But he wriggles like a puppy. Impossible to pin the
fellow down. One day he's hot, the next he's cold."

I feel at ease with him, because Timothy, playing up to
his reputation as a secularist surrounded by believers, adopts
a somewhat risqué manner with me—he likes to discuss religious matters in a deliberately "brutal" and chilly way, as if
he accords their claims no real respect. This made him a
pleasant sight to me, as he took off his cold coat to reveal the
customary light clothes underneath.

Mother appeared, welcomed the Thurlows and Timothy, and then whispered to me that Terry Upsher was sitting

in the kitchen and that I should go with Jane to pay our respects of the season. "Just for a second. That would be polite."

I had not talked to Terry when I was last there in September. Under a strong light in the kitchen his dark temples seemed littered with grey hairs, and his rough chin with white spikes. He was standing at the sink.

"Mary cannat stick the washing, so I'm doing it. She's got hands that are that precious she won't put them in the water," he said mockingly, in his high quaver.

"Sherrup," said Mary. "You're a proper blather you are. You asked yourself over so's you could get your hands on a proper meal for once." And as she spoke, she seemed to be preparing his supper, putting various foods onto a dinner plate.

"Don't witness her," said Terry to me, "she's the one what's blathering."

In all the years I had known Terry, I had never thought of him as the possessor of sexual desire at all. He had for so long been effectively married to his deaf old father. That Terry might be chasing the plain and always very single Mary Surtees, and that this was bringing both of them pleasure, made me oddly depressed.

I introduced Jane again. She had met Terry before, but her presence made me awkward. She has very little experience of anyone outside her social class. Faced with Terry, she tended to speak more loudly, as if he were an uncomprehending foreigner.

"How long you up, then?" asked Mary.

"Just a week this time," I said. "How've you been, Terry?"

"Middlin," he said. "I've had pains in the arm, well,

ever since me da died, and that was twenty-three months
ago, and Dr. Khan . . . well, the part of it is, the doctor
thought the arm was hurting me so much through stress,
and he said I should have a holiday."

"It's a good idea," I said.

"I can tell you that *doctor* should find himself a holiday.
Eee, vision him doing *my* job, vision him doing this garden
at the vicarage, or any of them gardens, his hands are cod-
soft. Stress! I said to Mary his head should be checked."

"He's coloured, mind," added Mary, from the sink.

"Mary hinny," said Terry sarcastically, "now, you're
s'posed to say he's with the ethnic minorities or they'll come
and get you in your bed."

"Well, that doesn't make him more white, does it?
D'you think a doctor who isn't English can understand us
prop'ly? They don't have medicines like us."

For some reason, made uncomfortable by the turn of
the conversation, but also wanting to be part of it, and eager
to please, I said:

"They don't have medicines like us, but they certainly
have lots of stress! Millions of people shouting all day at each
other, hot weather and all that. The Third World, isn't it?"

Mary giggled and Terry loudly grunted and said, again:
"Stress! It dries me up hearing that. By the way, I'm
building a shed for yor da, he asked us last week. Proper
thrushed wood." The front door bell rang.

"What does he want a shed for? In the garden? I haven't
heard anything about it."

"I divvent kna. He said he wanted to store books down
there."

"Don't be silly," said Mary. "Books!"

"Actually, it seems quite likely," I said.

"See," said Terry to Mary. "It's definite, the books."

"Gerron and leave us alone."

The oven was filling the room with a woolly heat; I would have loved to have put my head on the table and slept while Terry and Mary talked around me, it would have been a falling into the easy gentle bake of childhood. But I felt that Jane and I were intruding on them, and that our absence would be noticed. I said goodbye, Mary brightly said, "Tara now!" and we returned to the sitting room. As we walked along the hall, Jane pulled me aside, and whispered:

"Why did you do that?"

"Do what?"

"Why did you encourage that racism and *ignorance* by lying like that?"

"How was I lying?"

"You don't think like that, so why play along with them?"

"Look," I said, "it's complicated. I always have played along with them, as you put it, it's how I've survived here, how I've grown up here. I've needed to fit in, I've needed a bit of camouflage. When I was little I used to put on a Durham accent when I got on the bus and asked for my ticket—you know that, I've told you that many times. Otherwise I would have been attacked." Jane surprised me by strongly gripping me.

"Oh, Tommy, *please* don't hide yourself, darling—from me or from anyone else."

"I'm not hiding myself. This *is* myself." We were teetering on the brink of an argument.

"God, I hope not," said Jane, giving me a kiss, and closing the hostility. "All right, are you ready?"

"I am."

We went into the sitting room, which was now full:
Muriel Spedding had arrived, Mr. Norrington was there,
Miss Ogilvie, the Thurlows and Tim Biffen of course,
and Susan Perez-Temple, and Canon Palliser, and several
others.

A discussion was in progress. The theme seemed to be
town versus country, corruption versus simplicity. Father
had obviously mentioned again his little distinction between
wanting and needing.

"London, of course, is hardly British anymore," he was
saying, with his usual confidence. "It's a European city, its
corruptions are Continental, except perhaps around King's
Cross—which will, ah, remain forever England." He pursed
his lips.

"But there's a difference between country and town
just between Sundershall and going into Durham," said a
woman called Marian Rance. "I can sense it immediately
when I go in to do my big groceries."

"Oh, really, I meant a country and city division in the
classical sense—north and south, that kind of thing. Sundershall is still remote enough from London that some of the
villagers, as you well know, Marian, have never been to London," said Peter.

"But, Peter, there are perfectly rational economic arguments for that," said Belinda Thurlow.

"Yes," said Marian firmly, ignoring Belinda and pressing down on her argument with Peter, "but you don't need
to go to London to get a sense of this corruption. As I say,
just the ten miles into Durham is quite sufficient. That awful bus station."

"Don't get me started on the bus station," said Susan.

"Well," said Peter in defeat, "you may be right, but it's really the gap between the capital city and the rural provinces that is the *classical* division—eh, Colin?"

But before Colin could speak, Marian said, "Well I wouldn't know anything about that," in a tone of slight affront, as if Peter himself, by mentioning London so persistently, had become an example of that corruption.

As Colin began to speak, Timothy Biffen approached me. Quietly, he said, "Who is that bloody woman? She's like the cook in Proust who always thinks of the *monde* as the *demimonde*. Bloody hell." Timothy liked to drop swear words into his conversation, but when he said "bloody" or "bugger" or "shit" he did so with a fatal hesitation, surrounding the word with slightly more attention than it deserved.

"It would take a long time to tell you," I said.

"How's the Ph.D. coming on?"

"That, too, would take a long time to tell you." We moved towards the drinks trolley. I could see, at the top of Timothy's open-necked shirt, that his chest was hairless. The skin was like taut dirty cloth, indeed it was barely distinguishable from the thin grey shirt.

"Frankly, I'd welcome a bit more corruption up here—beginning with our esteemed theology department," said Timothy.

"Oh yes?"

"It's full of little shits who think that there are only certain legitimate subjects, certain ways of dealing with them—Incarnation, Paul, the Hard Sayings, Logos, blah. I'm trying to get a little funding so that I can spend a few months in France to work on my Pierre Bayle book, and every time I bring it up they all put on their mitres and chasubles, as it were, and go into session, and then, bang, I'm turned down again. Why don't they see that I have very little interest in the bloody Letter to Titus," he said bitterly, as if speaking to himself.

Instead of discussing Timothy's book, I said, surprising myself, "You know, my father has always thought very highly of you, and always used to talk you up to me when I was younger."

"He was a bloody lifesaver when I first arrived and everyone thought I was a Marxist."

We both looked at Peter, who was on the other side of the room, talking to Jane and the Thurlows. One of his hands was on my mother's shoulder, the other held a wineglass. He was a picture of genial energy. His bald head was glowing. I saw his round, clean face, with its little loyal ears— seemingly tightly pinned to his head—and his smooth young cheeks, and at that moment I thought, "He will live for a long time." And a sudden urge for honesty, for honest encounter, came over me. I had a strong desire to say to Timothy, "You know, my father can't tell if you believe in God or not." Instead, I said,

"What Dad likes is the fact that you can't be pinned down. On belief . . ."

"Likes?"

"Well, it interests him, I think."

"It interests me quite a bit, too," said Timothy. "I'm not surprised that *he* is interested; he's quite wily himself, isn't he?"

I felt an inexplicable desperation, as I stood beside Timothy and looked at my handsome, "wily" father across the room. It was suddenly important that I knew what Timothy believed and did not believe, important that he spoke directly to me, passionately even.

"You're not wily, are you?" I asked anxiously. "I mean, you're not playing games? It's a matter of the utmost importance, life-or-death, to you as for anyone else?" I felt my hand shaking a little. Timothy looked with alarm for a second, and then breezily said,

"Oh, you know, it's as Pascal has it—impossible to believe in God, impossible not to."

"But that won't do, in the end, will it? We have to *decide*, no?" I asked, with a tremor in my voice. Timothy paused, and then in very even, calm, academic tones, said:

"The extremity with which you pose the question—either/or, yes or no, for or against—assumes that one can *know*, that one either believes or doesn't because of some certainty, a certainty founded either on inner knowledge—i.e., faith—or some kind of external suggestion, i.e., some kind of vision or visitation, a miracle, or what as you know were in the medieval dispensation called 'proofs' of God. Since you ask, I don't have that kind of certainty one way or another. I've never had a vision, and I don't hear God's still, small voice in my breast. Formal proofs, of course, like the ontological proof, are pretty silly nowadays, hardly anyone intellectually decent is working in *that* field. So I suppose I do envy the certainty of a Newman, say, who thought that when he died he would see God face-to-face and also his nearest and dearest. On the other hand, I can't possibly say to you that because of this paucity of proof or suggestion that I don't think God exists, or that 'I don't believe'—whatever that word 'believe' means. Even Newman, to return to him, lamented God's absence, His invisibility in the world, what he called 'the tokens, so faint and broken, of a superintending design.' We all have to live with these faint and broken tokens, and, unlike Newman, just *because* of their faintness and brokenness I can't commit myself to your kind of language of certainty. I can't even *speak* it, because if I do I am committing an intellectual lie." He stopped, looked across the room, and then at me, and said, much more kindly, "Your father, by the way, if it's a consolation, is probably much less wily than he seems, and more conventional. I think he's a pretty solid believer. I'm sure Peter would say, 'I know that my Redeemer liveth.'"

I was moved by Timothy's confession, and certainly moved by his unexpected kindness. I poured myself another large drink, and then turned to him, with my back to the room, and said, quietly, insistently:

"I can't help being certain! I don't believe that a God exists who created the world we live in. And if you ask me for 'proof' of this certainty, for how I *know* this, what do I do but ask you to look at the world. There's the proof! A place of horror and pain and utter senseless longevity for millions and millions."

"Well, but it's not a proof. And the world isn't horrid for *you*," said Timothy, again with an alarmed look on his face.

"Not for me—not yet. Not much," I said. I lowered my voice as my mother came towards us. But she was on her way to the kitchen.

"Timothy, give Tom a *deadline* for his Ph.D., won't you," she said with a light laugh as she left the room.

"But my small happiness and small unhappiness—that's all irrelevant," I continued. My mother's joke was best ignored.

"Yes, but if instead of cosmically including the globe in your gaze, you start with your life, you might find that you don't have this certainty about God's nonexistence anymore. You might say to yourself: 'I am healthy, happy, purposeful, loved. And I was undeniably created by someone or something.' That's quite a good start. And, by the way, exactly how is your atheism saving people from starvation in Africa or rescuing children from Romanian orphanages?"

"Well, but how is religion helping them? I'm surprised at you. You know perfectly well that I don't have to prove that atheism can alleviate pain. I simply have to show that the existence of pain is not compatible with the idea of God. Atheism isn't a practice, it's a principle."

"Or, more precisely, it's a belief," said Tim, with a smirk.

"Okay, it's a belief, a rival belief. And I believe that this world vandalizes the face of God. I don't believe that any God worthy of worship or comprehension made this world." As I said this, I looked directly at my father, who, I could tell, was being lectured to by Colin Thurlow. Though the words I was speaking to Timothy described the very abyss that separated me from my father, the sight of him stoically suffering Colin, something we had all done, brought forth a surge of fellow feeling.

"What interests me is your certainty," said Tim. "It's one thing to say that the world is a horrid place—if indeed it is— but it's another to say, 'Ergo God doesn't exist.' I'm not sure you can make that leap. I mean, if you suddenly lived in a world *without* any suffering, without any pain at all, would you then say to yourself, 'This is such a happy world that I am convinced that God *does* exist'? I don't think so. Arguments from design are always a bad idea, whether practised by believers or atheists, and that's what you're doing."

"I simply repeat that either God doesn't exist, or if He exists He is not a creator worthy of worship, love, or even comprehension," I said.

"Well, hang on a minute, if He exists, it's not up to you to decide if He is worthy of worship, love, or comprehension. You don't have any choice in the matter."

"If He exists," I continued, in a kind of rage, "He is a Satan. You mentioned Newman. He writes, doesn't he, 'if God exists, *since* God exists,' somewhere or other."

"Yeah. *Apologia.*"

"Well, I would say, inverting that: 'if God doesn't exist, *since* God doesn't exist.' In other words, even if He exists, I can't believe in Him and won't believe in Him—He doesn't exist for *me.*"

"Except that He palpably does exist for you," said Timothy, almost wearily, "because you can't stop talking about 'God.' You can't say 'He doesn't exist.' And you can't say 'He doesn't exist for me.' And I can't say the opposite—I mean, I can't know that God does exist. Neither of us can. Can you honestly say, hand on heart, that you know that the whole of religion is a colossal error? Can you look at our cathedral and just know that it simply represents an error, ancient ignorance, that it's just a big mistake?"

I was silent for a moment, and finished my drink. I thought of the cathedral, always watching the town, the grey trance of its hushed interior, the aspiring columns stout in their waists and bursting into fanned splendour as they met the ceiling, the long bare nave like a grey carpet, the patient, stony, everlasting, exact ambition of it. I hesitated, and Timothy, with a bland, victorious smile, said:

"A building Ruskin thought one of the wonders of the world, a city the medievalists likened to Jerusalem."

"You sound like Max. You remember Max Thurlow?"

"Oh, sure. Colin and Belinda's kid. To whom we should now bow down as *The Times*'s Voice of Unreason, right?"

"Max said something similar a few months ago to me. About how if religion has the form of the human, and is the product of humans, it can't be wrong. The cathedral is very noble, yes. I grew up with it, in a sense. But, look, there are many beautiful creations, beautiful representations, that arise out of beliefs subsequently known to be false or primitive. We all revere the Pyramids, but we don't believe in Isis, and in the primitive theological system disclosed by the hieroglyphics, do we? Or a better example, the medieval maps, with their information about sea monsters and vicious cannibals. No one would call these maps a mistake exactly, yet none of us now shares the worldview of the people who drew them."

"So," said Timothy calmly, as if he had just heard a paper delivered at a conference, "the cathedral *is*, after all, a beautiful mistake, a magnificent lie."

"Christ, yes, of course, if you insist. But, but . . ."

I had been conscious of someone standing directly behind me for half a minute or so. It was Peter, who looked at me for a second with despairing enormity, and then gathered himself into false pleasantness, and said:

"I'm loath to interrupt your architectural discussions, but Sarah has instructed me that supper is ready." So we moved into the hall, and then into the dining room, which was lively with the moving flames of many candles.

For the rest of the evening I had an image in my mind of my father's imploring eyes, glistening with what seemed like sadness. I had never seen him looking at me with such a strange look of pleading. I wasn't sure how much he had heard, but the last few minutes had constituted a greater confession than I had ever made to him. You see, I was pretty liberal with such speeches, as long as they were made

to people other than my father. Really, I'm quite addicted
to theological discussion, and like nothing better than the
argumentative wrestle over God. I think that the secularist's
duty is to proselytize, to take the flag over to enemy territory
and firmly plant it there. I want to be what a nineteenth-
century thinker called an athlete of reason. But my father
always made me feel, as it were, fat and short of breath, because he was himself a kind of athlete of reason while simultaneously a knight of faith. So we never had this kind of
discussion.

Towards the end of the party, I broke away and returned
to the kitchen. Mary could be heard rustling with something
in the pantry. Terry sat very still at the kitchen table, reading
a newspaper. I burst his silence. My words were thick; I felt
quite drunk.

"Terry, do you believe in God? I'm sorry . . ."

"Look out, now—"

"I was talking to Tim Biffen about it all, and my father."

"Depends a touch, doesn't it?"

"Depends—depends on what?"

"Just depends. Eee look out, I'll be had up if I start answering your questions."

"I believe," I said suddenly, the lie almost frothing in
my mouth.

"Well, it didn't do any good for me da, did it? *He* knew
he was shot to hell." Terry sounded suddenly bitter.

"What didn't? What didn't do any good?"

"Go on, I'll be had up."

Mother came in. "Dearest, the last guests are going.
Hello, Terry, did you enjoy your supper?" I followed her
out, said goodbye to the guests. We stood in the hall.

"All over for another year," said Father. "I say," he added quietly, but sparkling, "I think Terry has the hotpants for Mary."

"He spent hours in the kitchen while Mary fed him salmon like a prize cat," said Mother, laughing. "Mary may be a bit less keen."

19

WHAT A STRANGE TIME, that last Christmas before my father died. First the Gathering, then my poor behaviour on Christmas Eve . . .

Christmas Eve began well. Jane and I went to see Max, who was at home for two days over the holiday. We were both curious to meet his new girlfriend, who had come north with him, his first after a drought of two years. Max had told me about her on the phone. "Her name is . . . Fiona Raymond. The short version is—she's ten years older than us. She's written . . . comic novels, now she makes documentary films. Met her at a *Times* party. She's just back from Romania. You'll like her."

Even with their adult son home, the Thurlows seemed to be hard at work in their separate studies. Max opened the front door, and in the familiar way the study doors on either side opened almost simultaneously, as in a West End farce, or perhaps a masque representing dawn, and Colin and Belinda emerged. Max, always high-spirited, generally became buoyant and irresponsible when forced to spend time with his parents. "Christ, let's . . . get out of here," he whispered to me on the front step, and suddenly we were little boys again, and the running truancy of those days came back to me.

I set my face to the customary mask for Belinda and Colin—a slightly gloomy, scholarly sobriety, my eyes half-closed in an analytical squint, my mouth a little pursed in the Bunting style—and shook hands with them both. Colin was in an agony: his study door was open, and he kept on glancing at it with mournful indulgence. Obviously he was calculating how many minutes he had to sacrifice to the wasteful frivolity of human encounter. Fiona was introduced. Max was right, I did like her; she was blond, with rather dry, lined skin that seemed to have been written on. She had an appealing, open, frank manner, and a deep voice that made everyone think she smoked. "I don't, actually, but with Max around I don't need to."

We escaped Colin and Belinda, and drove down the wintry road to Vaughan House, Mrs. Millington's old place, now the treasure of Philip Zealy, the crooked businessman from Newcastle. The weather was cold and dead in that way that Christmas seems to reserve for itself. Everything I could see was drained of life; the grey bricks of the small houses were dead to colour, and lucid with cold: the tight sharp windows, the certain front doors, the black pavement, the river renewed by icy apprentice streams from the hills, all dead. We passed a wooden viewing bench, now alienated by the season. After a few minutes, we reached Vaughan House. It is very large, set well back from the road, and unusual for the area because built out of red brick rather than the local stone. A huge, undisciplined lawn stretches from the front of the house to the clear fast little river, the same one that comes sharp and novel from the hills, goes quickly through Sundershall, and then grows wide and mud-delayed as it reaches Durham. We stopped to gaze. I told Fiona and Jane that Max and I had always loved Vaughan House.

"The Pekineses," said Max.

"The Pekineses indeed, with the extraordinary names."

"It was always said that Mrs. Millington used to give

overnight guests a dog to take to bed, for warmth . . . Animal hot water bottles," said Max.

"Well, now it's Zealy's to do whatever he wants with it. I'm sure he'll put efficient heating in."

On a whim, we drove to Durham for lunch, where we ate at a very bad restaurant—"there being no other kind in Durham," as Max remarked. Fiona told us about her work. She had written six comic novels, superstitiously finishing each on her birthday, one a year. But she decided to stop writing when the reviewers began to write of each new book after her second that "this is not Fiona Raymond's best novel." This sentence had come up again and again.

"I got absolutely bloody sick of reading 'this is not her best novel, this is not her best novel.' I felt like shouting to reviewers at parties: 'Tell me which bloody novel was my best!' So there were two conclusions, then," she said, with pleasing crispness. "I once wrote a book that was my best—presumably my first—and I can't match it. Or I have not yet written that best book yet, and *that* is why no one ever mentions its title. For a while I believed the latter, and it got me up in the morning. Faint praise can be surprisingly energizing, it turns out! But slowly, oh, I don't know, over a period of a couple of years, I started to believe the former, and I got depressed about it all. I could see a dismal career stretching out for decades, books and books and books, with each one received in exactly the same way: 'This is not her best novel.' The books weren't the biggest thing for me, anyway."

"And since then . . ." said Max fondly, in a leading way.

"Yes, since then I've been doing this other thing—making documentaries, which I sort of slid into while I was doing my last book. That one was set in Monaco, and I did a short film about gambling."

"Fiona's come back from Romania with an extraordinary film," said Max. "About Romanian orphans. Terrible and harrowing. No one in the West knows the full extent of it. We all need to do . . . something, whatever we can, about this."

"I've seen some of that on the news. Awful. But you can count me out of that," I said. "I'm sure your film is brilliant, but I'm too weak for that kind of thing. Oh no, I couldn't bear it. Fortunately we don't have a video, so I may be spared it anyway."

After lunch we took Fiona, who had not visited Durham before, to the cathedral. The building rose up before us with black wings of stone. As we crossed the broad apron of grass in front of the cathedral, I reflected that the monks and masons who built it so long ago could not have foreseen a time when many or most of its visitors did not believe in God. Yet perhaps they did foresee that time; for what was the purpose of this sheer enormity except as a kind of insurance against the scepticism of futurity? Here we were, unbelievers at the end of the twentieth century, still bowing our heads before its size, and throughout Europe were these great flying buildings which had lasted longer than God, flying like the flags of countries that had disappeared.

Back at Sundershall, we tried to get Max and Fiona to come to dinner at the vicarage, but Max said that he was at home for such a short time that he should stay at The Oratory and "take the medicine in one . . . quick shot." They would come over later, though, after dinner. By the time Jane and I arrived at the vicarage Uncle Karl had arrived. Karl always came to stay for a week over Christmas; his regular visit was one of the indices of my childhood. When I was young, I didn't understand why he would not attend the

Christmas services. I used to slouch in the festive church, on Christmas morning, the place crowded with villagers. What a boyish feeling of anticipation and excitement: I liked the service, but I wanted it to end, I willed the hymns to their close, longed for the organ to cease its metal mimicry, urged on each prayer and waited for the divine moment at the end when Father opened the heavy dungeon-door of the church entrance and let the light, swelling all morning in the porch, fall into the church in spreading fathoms. I could not imagine, in those days, anyone in the world not having Christmas. Surely there was no child who was not getting Christmas presents, who was not going to run home over cold earth "hard as iron" to a lunch of turkey or goose and roast potatoes—and brussels sprouts, those funny tattered turbans of green leaves. Yet Uncle Karl was not beside me in church, Uncle Karl was not celebrating Christmas. What on earth was he doing at home, while everyone else was at church?

Now, of course, as an adult, I side with Uncle Karl, and would rather laze around the house in a secular maunder, helping myself to Christmas nuts and liqueurs, while everyone else crowds into church and imitates the credulous shepherds who, two thousand years ago, saw a great light in the sky and fell to their knees.

Karl used to drive up from London in a red MG with a creaking chassis, but this time he came in his latest car, a big blue Mercedes, whose twin exhausts reduced the massive engine to a siphoned tremble. It was a treat to see him, but he quickly disappeared with Peter, his real quarry. While Mother was cooking in the kitchen, and Jane was chatting with Father and Karl in the sitting room, I went upstairs to our

bedroom, on the pretext of "working on the Ph.D." Instead, I lay on the bed and started reading one of those religious apologists who get me so angry. They're all the same.
They admit that evil and suffering exist, that the existence of
evil and suffering may constitute a challenge to God's goodness and power—and then they just stop! Like Kierkegaard,
like Simone Weil, shaking on the very edge of blasphemy,
they stop the direction of their argument, in the same incomprehensible and apparently arbitrary way that a spider,
wandering across the ceiling, will stop moving at a certain
point for an hour or two, or even for good. And watching
the insect, we think: Why stop there?

Having correctly described a world of meaningless suffering, these thinkers assert: Well, God is love, God didn't
create anything except for love itself, and the means to love.
Therefore, affliction and suffering must also be forms of
love. It is a "privilege" to suffer. Ah yes, and here it comes:
the very image of affliction, Christ on the Cross, is also the
very image of God's love. God suffers, too, you see. He suffered on the Cross. He suffered, and suffers, with us.

From the bed, I could see that it was already dark, and
only four o'clock in the afternoon. Those awful end-of-
year days in Sundershall, jammed down into the very boots
of the year, where the light comes in rationed steps only, between nine in the morning and three in the afternoon—I
won't forget those days. Now I looked out of the window,
and saw that it was beginning to rain, and felt a sadness come
over me. And anger. The Cross, the Cross, how much we
hear about the Cross. Christ suffered with us on the Cross.
The Cross is at the heart of Christianity. The Cross is the
image of pain and of victory, of life and of eternal life. Well,

I reject the Cross; I stay clear of the Cross! I make a cross of my fingers, as the hero does in the Dracula movies, *at* the Cross, to make it wither and die.

But I should tell you about how I disgraced myself. Still thinking about these questions, and the doomed, grotesque effort to make suffering meaningful, I fell asleep, and woke to find Jane changing for supper. We went downstairs. Mother and Karl were in the sitting room. I looked hard at Uncle Karl, deep into his rusty eyes, and tried to imagine what he might have to say about the great God-given "privilege" of suffering.

"Tom, you're elsewhere," said Mother. "Might you get a drink for yourself and Jane, while I go and 'touch up,' as my mother-in-law used to say, the supper. Karl has a drink—"

"Karl always has a drink," I said, looking at him. "His task in life is to enact everyone else's secret aspiration: he drives a fast car, doesn't have to go to church at Christmastime, and flies to various European capitals at whim."

"Indeed," said Karl, "but lucky Karl is also unable to find a wife who will stay with him for more than three years. By the way, Peter is still out doing his rounds."

"On Christmas Eve?"

"He's taking some presents to the . . . Welbys, is that their name? A very poor family."

"You remember them, my love?" I said to Jane.

"Yes—Mr. Welby fell into a fire, or something." Jane, haughty, sounded like her mother at that moment, and looked like her, too, her face raised, her long nose dryly divining, and her dark hair, which was down tonight, flashingly acknowledging the electric light, a countless conformity of dark strands sealing her scalp in lustre.

"Welby, in fact, set light to his ear," I said. "He was drunk and was trying to have a fag in bed, and he burned his ear. Quite badly, because he didn't do anything about it for days."

"How many of these delightful facts do you know?" asked Karl.

"Quite a few. You know me, I collect them, like you collect East German and Russian stories. Welby burnt his ear; Tattersall, of course, knocked the pedestrian down; Seddon drowned in the river, that was alcohol again—he drowned on the night of his thirtieth wedding anniversary, which he had spent without his wife in The Stag's Head, a pretty depressing detail, I always think; and Louise Winters was fined for trying to sell captured squirrels as housepets. I can go on."

"Still, they *are* all God's good people, yes?" said Karl smiling slyly.

"Oh *yes*. Karl, do you have any new horrors from your Communist contacts?" Karl does a certain amount of business in Germany and Bulgaria, and had just started representing new Russian artists, the children of Mr. Gorbachev's *glasnost*, in the West. He likes collecting Communist jokes, anecdotes, scandals, and so on.

"I have something very good, which I heard the other day," said Karl, but at that moment my father walked into the sitting room, shining, pinkly stung by the cold—and cheerful, so cheerful. He was a vision of confidence and decency; the brilliant white priest's collar around his neck glowed like a fallen halo. His bald head was pipped with little drops of moisture.

"Everything all right? I got back just in time," he continued. "Now it's really coming down outside."

"I have calculated that of the fourteen Christmases I have spent here, only two have been entirely free of rain or snow," said Karl.

"Yes, it rains plenty here," Peter said. "But, you know, into every rain a little life must fall." His shrewd eyes looked around for approval. He went to stand near the fire, and installed himself like a policeman in Gilbert and Sullivan, his back to the flame, his arms behind him, and his legs planted wide. "Perhaps Jane will serenade us after supper, as you did so beautifully, my dear, in September."

"Oh, thank you, Peter, that's awfully sweet," said Jane. "It may go to my head, I've been living on a rather reduced diet of praise."

"My goodness, your husband does not appreciate you?" asked Karl, looking greedily at her. Well, I thought, when did Jane last praise me for anything at all? A month ago she was complaining that she had no time to practise, despite her endless practising, and now she was complaining that she got no praise.

"I'm not sure one deserves praise for *practising*," I said, charmlessly. The bell rang.

"That'll be Norrington," said Father. "Hope you chaps don't mind, I invited him to supper, he's all on his own at Christmas. Pastoral duty." This was bad news. Why had my parents spoiled the Christmas Eve dinner in this selfish way? Mr. Norrington—well, I have nothing against him especially. He is old, pompous, lonely, and fond of the phrase "apropos of nothing," which he uses as often as possible. He wears immensely thick glasses, and as a boy I had been interested in the thickness of those lenses, longing for the moment when he might remove them to reveal the weak failures, the tiny confessions, of his eyes. I was always supposed to feel sorry for Mr. Norrington because of his loneliness: Mother told me that he had seen *Brief Encounter*, his favourite film, eighteen times. He was in love with the actress Celia Johnson.

Norrington entered, shook hands, and in reply to Peter's offer of a drink, said, "A small glass of sherry wine, please," with great precision, and then sat down with his shoes perfectly aligned, as if he had taken them off before going to bed. I went to the kitchen to find a fresh bottle of whisky, and when I returned, Norrington was on his favourite subject, genealogy. "The crucial thing," he was telling Jane, "is the 1851 census. Lots of very nice material there. You can consult it in London at the PRO. You see, the Norringtons were originally from Shropshire. I can't prove it, but I'm pretty sure that our line of Norringtons is related to the Earl of Cavendish, via an illegitimate birth."

Over the years, in Sundershall, whenever an area of England was mentioned in Mr. Norrington's presence, he would say, with a strange coughing eagerness: "Now, I have a large number of relatives in that county . . . oh yes, Somerset"—or wherever was being discussed—"is absolutely full of Norringtons—yes, farmers"—and here he might correct himself—"farm *owners*, landowners." There he would sit, a small man surrounded by centuries of relatives in every corner of England.

Mother came in, waved us to the table, and on the way to the dining room I thought again about what I had been reading upstairs. "The sea is not less beautiful for our knowledge that ships are wrecked on it." This was one of the sentences I had read in the bedroom. The famous Jewish thinker I had been reading was trying to argue that beauty and suffering are entwined. You can't have the majesty of the natural world without the threat of danger; nature is not easy; freedom will entail shipwrecks. Certainly, it is hard to imagine a sea that still has all the large power of a sea while also being a place in which every swimmer and every sailor is always safe, a place that guarantees your safety. So beauty is freedom, and freedom is risk? You like swimming, and dipping down to the sand? Then you may also drown, for that is the natural property of wateriness. This was what the thinker was saying.

And suddenly, sitting at my parents' dinner table, at the old family table, I glimpsed something, and my mind was utterly alive with clarity. This moment lasted only a few seconds, but in those seconds I saw a new world: I saw a safe sea. It resembled a real sea—look, there are the unknown salty slums, many storeys deep, overcrowded with nether-life, the cloudy suspension of a million forms of existence! But it was an imaginary sea, because it was a safe sea. A sea on which I can sail, and on which at the slightest threat of storm, the skies suddenly clear and the boat continues on its happy way. A sea in which I can swim, and on which at the first moment of danger, an unseen hand lifts me up and places me on top of the water, as if on the surface of the Dead Sea. Oh, but my New Dead Sea, which threatens no human, is unimaginable, you will say; nature must follow its own laws of necessity. The kinds of supernatural tamperings I am imagining are impossible. Are they? But the Psalmist tells us: They that go down to the sea in ships, these see the works of the Lord, for he commandeth and raiseth the stormy wind, which lifteth up the waves thereof. And the Gospels tell us that Christ tampered twice with those laws, once when he walked on water, and once when he calmed a storm. Jesus *killed* the sea, made it Dead—and was the sea, in these divine instances, any less beautiful at the very moment

it became safe? So I invert the famous thinker, and I say: Is
the sea any less beautiful for our knowledge that ships are *safe*
on it?

At that moment, and only for a moment, I saw a world
in which the sea had no powers to drown us; and I saw a
kingdom where the skies were safe, and the stormy wind was
made mild, and the mountains did not erupt, and murder
had been abolished, and violence was defunct, and illness
was as rare as the unicorn, and where there shall be no more
death, neither sorrow nor crying, neither shall there be any
more pain, a kingdom where we shall be given beauty for
ashes, the oil of joy for mourning, the garment of praise for
the spirit of heaviness. The people inhabiting this kindly
world would not be human, not as we recognize the human.
They would not be free, not as we recognize the word. In
particular they would not be free to suffer; there could be
no Hitlers, no Stalins—but also no con men, no plausible
rogues, no jokers, no entertaining frauds, no brilliant cul-
pable politicians, for all these people cause suffering of
one kind or another. I saw a colourless kingdom, no doubt,
humans reduced to charitable prisoners, unfree robots. But
it is not *my* task, is it, to decide which world would be more
pleasant to live in—the suffering free world, or the painless
unfree world; it is not my task to choose between these
worlds at all. It is only my task, as a philosopher, as a human,
as an adult, as Thomas Bunting, to imagine such a world,
and *just by imagining it* to prove that the world we currently live
in did not need to be made the way it was made. If I could
imagine such a world, how much greater might God's imagining of it have been.

And do not tell me that the charitable prisoners in the
happy kingdom I am imagining are not happy because they

are not free. For the kingdom I have been describing is heaven—where the seas, if they exist, are utterly safe, where the wind is always mild, where there is no suffering and presumably no freedom, and "no more death, neither sorrow nor crying, neither shall there be any more pain." Who would dare to say that heaven is not a good or "beautiful" place to be? Heaven is all the proof we need that God already loves his charitable prisoners, and all the proof we need that God could have created a different world here on earth. God could have created heaven on earth! Why then did God create earth before heaven? Why the fallible rehearsal for perfection rather than perfection itself?

But my father's voice broke into my consciousness, and I discovered that he was saying grace, and that my head should be bowed to the plate. "For these and all Thy gifts, O Lord, we give Thee thanks." I don't remember much about the first course, except that Karl and my father were talking to each other a lot—rather exclusively, I thought. This didn't bother me too much; but I was chivalrously offended on behalf of Jane and my mother, who had to make do with the tedious Mr. Norrington.

Whenever my father and Karl met, they fell into easy reminiscence, and Father, conscious of the "nobility" of Karl's childhood and early suffering, tended slyly to promote his own moral dignity. On Christmas Eve this took the form of several stories about his wartime service. Karl, who is fiercely Anglophile, encouraged him to talk about English soldiers, especially eccentric officers. Peter did not boast; instead, he talked about other men as if they were completely unrelated to him, as if they had fought in a different army, and were a cause of vague wonderment in him. A clever strategy, I thought. It enabled him to praise all the more lavishly certain attributes which were then left to us, out of a spirit of fairness, to pin on him.

That evening Peter mentioned an ace RAF pilot. "His name was Rowland or Rowlands. He was as cool as a lamb throughout the most terrifying dogfights with the Germans, and once apparently brought his Spitfire down perfectly on a country road in Sussex—what the airboys used to call 'a real daisy-cutter,' if I remember correctly."

Of course he remembered correctly.

"Was he really a better pilot than everyone else?" asked Karl. "I mean by this, did he put down more Germans than his colleagues did?"

"No, no," said Peter, clearly enjoying himself. "It was his extraordinary coolness that made him famous. He didn't sweat; and the boys knew this because he changed his clothes far less frequently than the rest of them."

I thought that he sounded like my kind of hero.

"What became of him?" asked Karl. "You will now reveal to me that he went into Parliament after the war and became the most tedious imaginable Conservative back-bencher, as cool on committees as he had been in the cock-pit," said Karl, with his sweet, gentle smile.

"Ha, Karl, this is your vision of the English, this is what you secretly admire in them—German conformity! You *want* the poor fellow to have settled down and followed orders!"

Karl's smile widened, and his eyes glinted with pleasure.

"What actually happened, was that the chap was shot down, caught by the Germans, and put in a camp, fortu-nately with other British officers. He escaped once and was caught, and thankfully didn't try again, since the Krauts had a nasty habit, among several others, of losing their patience with escaped prisoners and shooting them—sometimes on

Hitler's orders. So he stayed put in prison for the rest of the war. His family was in the wine business, quite a famous and venerable merchant, actually. He entertained the other boys in prison by enacting imaginary wine tastings. They sat with their tin cups full of water, and had to perfectly describe a particular wine, and then he would tell them where—in occupied France, of course—their imagined wine came from."

Mother, Jane, and Mr. Norrington were now silent, and listening to Peter.

"Who liberated him, dearest? The Russians?" asked Sarah.

"No, the Americans, I think. I got all this secondhand years ago from old Bill Stapley, who knew him. You met Bill once, Karl, at the house in Durham. And to answer your question, after the war Rowland looked after the family firm for a while—and became rather a fine Christian, went on speaking tours and the like, and founded a charity."

I should have responded warmly to Father's reminiscences, but instead I felt that he should not have mentioned German camps in Karl's presence, in public; I felt that this revealed a bullying insouciance on his part. He should have shown more respect for Karl's suffering. Father and the theologians, they were in this together, I decided, judging the world from the citadel of their own strength, rather than joining the world in the shelter of its weakness. All of them deciding the tolerability of others' pain. The privilege of it! Horrid vanity, the martyr's vanity, the religionist's arrogance.

And sure enough, Norrington, the fool—though perhaps he knew nothing about Karl's origins—now wanted to discuss the godlessness of Nazism, the evil of the camps, and Peter seemed perfectly happy to join him. I was horridly embarrassed.

"Yes," Peter was saying confidently, "the two great engines of evil in this century, fascism and communism, were essentially godless, indeed set themselves against organized religion."

"Because without God, everything is permitted," said Mr. Norrington, with particular pompous pleasure.

"That's very stupid," I said, breathing fast, and looking at the tablecloth. "It's stupid because even with God, everything already and always *has* been permitted—oh, let's see, Crusades, executions, bloody wars, uprisings, monarchical totalitarianism, regicides, papal decadence, burnings at the stake, Inquisitions, revolutions, immoralities of every kind. All of this happened *with* God, so what was there left to be 'permitted *without* God'?"

"What was left to be permitted was precisely the Holocaust and Stalin's purges," said Peter quickly, looking at me glancingly. "Which was Mr. Norrington's point."

"I'm telling you," I said, into the stiffly silent company, "Mr. Norrington's point was stupid, and I'm very surprised that *you*, Dad, don't see that. As long ago as the Enlightenment, philosophers and historians were able to see as they surveyed world history that there was no necessary link between godliness and goodness. Some of them actually thought the link might go the *other* way, between godliness and cruelty. Gibbon thought this. And if you insist on using the Holocaust as your great example of godlessness, I have several points: first, Nazism wasn't resisted strongly enough, or at all in most cases, by the German churches—not to mention, of course, the Christian roots of anti-Semitism itself. And, second, if the Holocaust was godlessness run rampant, where the hell *was* God? Where had He suddenly gone? God did not 'die at Auschwitz,' as people like to say, because by this logic He *must* have already been dead, He must have died centuries before, during some other previous terrible atrocity. In this sense, the Holocaust isn't unique, and proves nothing, theologically. I really can't stand Mr. Norrington's pseudo-Dostoevskian line of argument, it's so fucking unempirical."

I couldn't look up into the frozen air. I was shaking, my head was pointed down at my plate. I heard my father screw the twist of his cigarette into the ashtray; it squeaked against the glass.

"I'm generally on Tom's side, as you know," said Karl, always the pacifier, "but I think in this case that we might say that the case remains unproven on both sides. If godliness does not entail good conduct, which may well be true, then godlessness can hardly be said to entail good conduct either. On the evidence of *this* century, the antireligious forces, which certainly made up the bulk of fascism and communism, don't come out of it very well."

"Actually, the divorce rate is higher among religious believers than it is among professed atheists," I said, but without bitterness, for Uncle Karl was trying to repair the atmosphere. "By the way, I apologize for any brusqueness towards you, Mr. Norrington. That was unforgivable. I get caught in the passion of ideas."

"You *are* a bit tired at the moment," said Jane.

"Tired?" said Peter coldly. "What on *earth* do you have to be tired about? What's detaining you at night? Your Ph.D.? The Epicureans?"

This was the point at which I left the table and went upstairs to our bedroom. Now, I feel only ashamed of the absurd speed with which I took offence. My dad had never heard me swear like that; it was deeply provoking, no doubt,

and he felt inclined to defend Mr. Norrington, I understand that now. But then I was in a righteous fury. So, I
thought, the news was out: my parents had no real faith in
my abilities, and never had done. My father classed me as a
juvenile because he, along with my mother, could not think
of me as an adult. And they thought this way because I hadn't
finished my stupid thesis, about which they were relentlessly
obsessed. If only they knew, I thought, of the existence of my
parallel work, my Book Against God. Then they would be
sorry, then they would be surprised, they might be shocked,
menaced, threatened, challenged, all this would be good for
them, it would shake them up a bit, they would see it as a
work of genius, of moral indignation but intellectual composure, with the most delicate and refined transits of language. But their interest is in each other, I thought—which
means, in fact, that their interest is in Peter Bunting, the
sun-priest, at whose court we all have to pay our respects.

Upstairs in the bedroom, I started writing in my BAG. I
think now that it was at this moment, without quite knowing
it, that I formally abandoned my Ph.D. and tipped myself
headfirst into the more serious business of planning a great
work of theologico-philosophical argument and commentary. But of course my parents would not be told about it
until it was an *accomplished* great work, something worthy of
intellectual scrutiny. Until then it would be my secret.

And now, of course, Father will never see my Book.

I was alone for a long time. I heard the front door open
and close several times, and the old bell was rung. Eventually, Jane came upstairs with Uncle Karl and Max and Fiona
Raymond. In that curious reversal that sometimes happens
in such situations, Jane and Karl looked sheepish, as if they
had taken on my guilty embarrassment and were about to

apologize for my misdemeanours. Max spoke. He was laughing, and despite my ill humour I found his mirth infectious. He took his glasses off, rubbed them, and said:

"Uh-oh. Right, Tom, it's no Christmas lunch for you. No . . . plum pudding. But this is the problem with Christmas. How long have you already been at home? It's far . . . safer to ration yourself to two or three days, like me."

"Look, I'm sorry," I said. "I'm afraid that you two were unwilling participants in an extramural class about the thoroughly intramural relations of the Bunting family."

"Oh love, what nonsense are you talking now?" said Jane.

"I mean that I'm sorry you had to watch me and my father circling around a very square hole."

Karl burst into laughter and said, "How *do* your students understand a word you say? Do they feel they are sitting at some shrine of The Great Riddler?"

"I don't have any students. Karl, I was angry for *you*," I said. "It was completely wrong and insensitive of my father, let alone Mr. Norrington, to be discussing the Holocaust, the camps, Nazism, and all that, in your presence. He showed you no respect."

"Tom, Tommy. Dear boy, Peter and I are old, old friends! He has known me from before you were born. Do you think we have *never* discussed my German childhood? Many times we have talked about Nazism. Peter has the greatest tact, the finest instincts, he is the only man alive who can tease me about being German, and even make a kind of joke or two about Hitler in my company. With honesty, I do not think of a thing that is wrong with Peter . . . well, except perhaps he has a weakness for going again and again to the doctor to get his ears syringed. But, you know, it is quite sweet of you to defend my honour."

"I wasn't defending your honour, as such, I was defending a principle."

"Don't be pompous, Tommy," said Jane.

"How did everything end?" I asked.

"We were all very nice to Mr. Norrington," said Jane. "Your father said that Christmas Day—what did he say, Karl?—has an almost magical power over warring parties, and that he fully expects reconciliation. Then Max and Fiona arrived and everyone cheered up."

"So you've been downstairs sucking up to the Buntings while I've been imprisoned in my turret up here?" I asked Max, mock-mournfully.

"Yep, that's about the measure of it," said Max.

"Maybe we should change places. You could come and spend Christmas Day here, and I could spend it at The Oratory."

"Oh no," said Max cheerfully, "I wouldn't wish that on anyone."

We heard my father's voice downstairs, and then the front door was opened and shut.

"That's Peter and Sarah going to the midnight mass," said Max. "So you can come downstairs, the coast is clear."

We got ourselves drinks, and Karl asked Jane if she might play him his favourite piece, the Bach aria "Sheep May Safely Graze." She needed to put up her hair, and searched for her elastic hair-ring. Then she reached behind her head, her elbows pointing towards us as if she were surrendering them, and I saw the ring slide on and suddenly she had harvested that hair into a single feathered sheaf, twisting her face as she did so, a gesture I loved, since it added a suggested strenuousness to a silky and weightless activity.

I liked the way, when she played this arrangement, that she picked the vocal melody out of the surrounding notes, as if the fingers responsible for playing that melody were indeed singing it. With enormous gentleness her fingers rescued from the surrounding mobility the walking lento of the tune.

We had happy, easy conversation. Max and I told stories about the village. We mentioned a man who had gone to prison for clumsily trying to blackmail a firm in Durham; and the time we drove our bikes over Susan Perez-Temple's kitchen garden; and the evening we tormented poor Sam Spedding by phoning him and hanging up. We got on to Max's parents.

"Do you remember," said Max excitedly, "when you lied to my dad about having got a poem into a literary . . . magazine? I couldn't . . . believe it. I was standing next to you, and almost bursting with laughter. You . . . invented the whole magazine, and . . . he believed you."

"Well, your father always made me uncomfortable, and so I had to secure some kind of internal victory over him," I said. "He always had a special way of looking at me, in fact he still does, which terrified me. You remember his first words to me, ever?"

"No."

"He said, 'You're a plausible rogue, aren't you?' Those were his first words. I was thirteen!"

"Colin is a psychological genius," murmured Karl.

"And at . . . the second or third meeting," said Max, still excited, "he asked you to list the seven wonders of the ancient world."

"Right, utterly humiliating, so I had to plan my revenge." But it was several years before I could put it into

action. I could see that Colin despised weakness and ignorance; clearly, I would have to be strong and knowledgeable.
And since, as a teenager, I wasn't naturally these things, I
would have to lie about them. Even Professor Thurlow
couldn't be more knowledgeable than me about a complete
fiction. I was sixteen, and at that time I was writing poems,
and sending them off to poetry magazines, often with letters
denouncing the poems that were running in these magazines—I had read somewhere that the way to catch an editor's
attention was to attack his choices.

"I forget now how your dad and I got onto poetry, but
anyway, he said to me that he had heard from you that I was
writing verse. And he sounded so dismissive that I decided
to invent a poetry magazine and ask him if he had heard of
it. I knew that he would hate to confess ignorance. Sure
enough, he said that he had heard of it! Well, I said, I just
got a letter from them yesterday telling me that I have had a
poem accepted. His face fell."

"Tommy is always so proud of his lies," said Jane to Fiona.

"Tom's moral sense has been . . . on sabbatical since
puberty," explained Max to the group.

"Actually, I'm much more embarrassed by the memory
of the poems I wrote than by my lie," I said. I wrote passionate philosophical poems, rhymed, often hazily antithe-
ological, and full of landscape. I tended to describe walking
up the hill and looking down at the village from Pilgrim's
Path:

And there, beneath me, lies "God's city,"
As the sun shines its electricity—
Bright wafer, which has turned but not harkened,
To the blood of our hearts, the pain of life sharpened!

Eventually, Max and Fiona went across the road to The Oratory, and Karl went off to his hotel in Durham (Karl always needed a double bedroom, and we had taken it), and Jane and I found ourselves in the strange position of being alone in the vicarage. I kissed her, and we continued upstairs. We made love fast, against the anticipated return of my parents. Sex had become a fairly infrequent activity in that last year of our marriage. By deciding to try to have a child, we had made sex veer from pleasure to function. Jane seemed always to be looking in her diary and announcing that "the next four days are the most fertile, the optimal window of the month," and informing me that we should have sex as often as possible in this brief opening. Frankly, it felt a bit forced. In the last months, whenever we had sex something always went wrong, and I drifted far away into my own thoughts, and we seemed, to me, like two separate entities masquerading at union—not unlike the old joke in which one man approaches another and says, "I like to walk alone," to which the other man replies, "So do I, so we can walk together." In this sense, Jane and I were walking together quite well.

As it happens, on Christmas Eve, as the rain continued to come down outside, we were very warm and intimate, tender on the bed, provoked by the thought of imminent interruption. I felt sentimental and kissed Jane so passionately that she whispered, "Less, darling, less," which only increased my desire. As she rose and fell on top of me, I remembered for a second my first lover, Rachel Worth. She was a friend of Max's, a fellow student of his at Oxford, and I took the bus there most weekends from London. Rachel and I were virgins, first-timers, both awkward. I remembered how we sat on the floor naked, like children at the

beach, trying to get it right, repeating the game until, suddenly, she was sitting on top of me, there was no gap between us, and I was inside her. "God!" Rachel said, and her
brown eyes were large. I felt unable to look at her, fearful of
the enormity and simplicity of the experience, and I think
we both thought: "Is this the beginning of adulthood? Is
this it?" Then we cried a little in each other's arms, and put
on music and danced around her freezing room in Mag-
dalen College overlooking the deer park. The deer moved
around on the grass in great separation, as if concentrating
on trying to ignore each other.

20

THE TERRIBLE THING I did on Christmas Eve did not really concern my behaviour with my father, but with Jane.

I had been telling one large lie for at least a year, and it had begun to master me. It is that I did not want to have a child, and was lying to Jane about it. I tried as often as possible to postpone sex during the announced "optimal window of the month" until the days after that time, when Jane was at her least fertile. More recently, my unwillingness to make a child with Jane had resulted in a kind of impotence. I would get some of the way with her, and then collapse before climax. Ever since our decision to "try for a baby," things had deteriorated. As soon as I became aware of having to concentrate on procreation, the "engorged phallus" steadily lost its rigidity.

On Christmas Eve, I did an especially bad thing. Remarkably, I had no difficulty in maintaining an erection. Excited by Jane's passion, I grew passionate myself, and maintained a rigidity that would have made old Mr. Conners very happy. Yet hearing Jane come before me, I decided to withhold my sperm and to fake a simultaneous orgasm. So afterwards, as Jane turned aside to sleep, doubtless feeling between her legs merely an illusory glue, and saying anxiously to me, "You *did* come, didn't you?" to which I whispered, "*God*, yes,"—I was rather ashamed.

I was ashamed to be so deceitfully denying Jane what she wanted. But I was, and am, sure that I did not and do

not want a child. At first, my motives were practical: I didn't
want a child *now*—why not delay the inevitable disruption for
as long as possible? I worried that I would be unable to
finish the Ph.D. once an infant was installed in my life. I
dreaded the constraints of paternity.

But these weren't the real reasons. My real objections
were metaphysical. What right do I have to bring life into the
world? To create a person who might, at some point in his
life, wish that he were dead? Who might complain—to me,
his father—that he had never asked to be born? True, we
cannot *ask* to be created; that would be like Baron Münch-
hausen tugging himself out of a bog by his own pigtail. So we
cannot complain that we were never consulted in the matter. But knowing this does not alter the truth that life, however enjoyable or pleasant, being imposed rather than
requested, is a sentence on us. That which seems uniquely
ours—our life—is not ours at all, since we were voteless at
conception.

Atheists and antireligious philosophers have often argued that though life is meaningless, we should not commit
suicide, since to do so is to surrender the necessary struggle
with the sentence of life. But I think this presumes too much
of life; suicide is no surrender of possession if we do not
possess our life anyway. If life is meaningless, then suicide is
meaningless too, and the reason not to do it is that to add
one meaninglessness to another meaninglessness is not a
solution but merely akin to a double negative in speech, a
blocked statement. Since we did not ask to be created, we
can never have been free enough for suicide to grow any
prestige of freedom. We cannot commit suicide—because we
are not alive; we cannot freely end—because we did not
freely begin.

Do I have the right to impose this sentence on someone else? Clearly not. Do I have the right to pass on my unhappiness? No.

And now, here I was, on Christmas Eve, in the middle of one of Jane's "optimal windows," and I did not come, but deliberately held back my sperm, and lied.

I told myself afterwards that I couldn't lie any longer. This lie could not continue, because I was not its master. This lie had mastered me, and would have to be confessed.

21

I GOT MYSELF through the Christmas Day festivities by quietly suffering my father. He greeted me cheerfully, as if nothing had happened the night before. It was an old trick of his, this Promethean regeneration of emotional tissue over-night. It was more complicated than denial, I think; he actu-ally killed disagreement, simply made it disappear. So I let him drive away the memory of the previous night, and I partook of the usual Christmas events: the service with the church full (Max and Fiona came, with Belinda but not Colin), lunch, and at three the television, briefly put on for the Queen's Christmas Address to the Nation. Yes, she was the same as usual, sitting in a bosomy room in Buckingham Palace. She was really no beauty, the queen; that broad lion-mouth, which she got from her father, with wide littoral of upper lip, was now giving her a royal-animal look, as if through sheer longevity she were becoming one of the heraldic beasts on her own crest. To read, she wore enormous square spec-tacles, each lens like a little television screen. Her baked hair had an unnatural streetlamp tinge. She spoke in a high voice about the Commonwealth, about a visit to India, about goodwill to all men, and wished "people of all faiths" a very happy Christmas—which struck me as illogical. The national anthem played, while an overhead shot tempted the masses with a vision of the mottled rooftops of the palace.

"Did that bother you?" I said, looking at both of my parents.

"What?" said my father.

"That she mentioned all faiths rather than one faith?" I saw that Mother was about to say something, but Peter broke in:

"Why would it?"

"Well, because one of her job titles is 'Defender of the Faith.' *The* faith. Anglicanism. She can hardly defend all faiths. And in fact, by definition, 'all faiths' cannot be defended by anyone."

"Oh, those other faiths can look after themselves pretty well," said Father very amiably, and I knew that he was refusing to take my challenge, which I had intended less as a strike against the queen than against the notion of many competing faiths. Peter, of course, wanted the last word. Looking around at Karl and Jane he said:

"You know the old joke about the Catholic who wished that the papal encyclical had been entitled *Cum grano salis,* 'with a grain of salt'? I take the queen's religious pronouncements, such as they are, *cum grano maximo salis.*" He looked at me with what I felt was arrogant finality, and added: "So should you." I felt Jane, tense, pressing against my leg, saw my mother with her head lowered, her customary position when my father and I were stalking each other like this, and I let it drop.

That evening, Jane and I quarrelled in our bedroom. I can't remember how it started. I do remember—I can see her in my mind—that she was wearing expensive sky-blue Jermyn Street pyjamas (bought by me as a gift), and reading Berlioz's *Memoirs.* At some moment I accused her of having stopped communicating with me.

"You don't think it could *possibly* be the other way around?" said Jane.

"No, I don't," I said firmly. "What do you think you do all day at the piano? Speak to me by vibration?"

"Why do you imagine I stay so long at the piano? Because at least the piano speaks back to me. At least I get a sound."

"That isn't fair, Janey. I long for you to come in to the kitchen or the bedroom and interrupt my reading and stop that damn practising. Every day I listen for that music to stop, so you might be on your way down the corridor. But it never stops, you go on and on."

"That 'damn practising,' as you put it, is everything to me, more than life!" said Jane with disdain. "And it pays our bills. You want *me* to come and minister to *you*. Never the other way around. It never crosses your mind that I might be lonely at the piano, that music is everything to me except that it is not my husband! When have you ever come through to interrupt me, when did you last ask me about a piece I was playing? And yet I have to buzz around you, I have to calm your anxieties, and deal with your family, and tell you that, yes, you can do your Ph.D., yes, you can continue with your stupid nonsense book about God, which will never be finished."

I said nothing.

"I'm sorry, Tom, I didn't mean that. I can't always help you, Tommy. I won't be able to do that. I need your help, too, I can't be the single strength doing double time for us, paying the bills and keeping the household in order and earning the salary, and replacing the toilet paper and thinking responsibly while you think irresponsibly. Do you even notice me? Do you even realize that money is finite? When did you last go shopping for anything? I mean, for groceries, not for expensive shoes. You know, I stand by the side of the washing machine holding one of your shirts and I think: What does he do for me? What does he *do*?"

We lay on our backs, and I took Jane's hand. There was a long silence. I thought that it might repair our intimacy if I confided in Jane, and so I told her that in the last few months I had been doing very little work on the Ph.D. and had instead been writing entries in my Book Against God. To my great surprise, perhaps tired from arguing, she was sympathetic, kindly even, and suggested that perhaps I could turn the BAG into something publishable and academically respectable. I think, now that I look back at that time, that Jane was protecting herself by refusing to become too involved in my wreckage. I can't say that she already knew what would happen, that she knew she would leave me. But she had her own important work, and she wasn't going to allow her concentration to be invaded, and so she refused to be drawn in too deeply, saying that of course she had "known all along" that I hadn't been doing my work (she was almost certainly lying, but I let it pass), that it was no surprise to her—and clearly, she said, I would get on with my thesis when I really wanted to, or had to.

This was a clever strategy on her part, because it forced me to become angry with myself, forced *me* to become the one disappointed with myself rather than let others become disappointed on my behalf. Jane forced me to reply to her that I *did* really want to get on with my work, that I really had to finish it, that now was the time, and if I could not finish it in the next few months I might as well abandon it, abandon teaching and consider another kind of employment. But again, Jane refused to be drawn; she had heard all this before. She merely replied that she believed me, believed *in* me.

Lulled by her softness, I decided that this was the moment to discuss the previous night, and the question of children. Could I tell her the truth? Could I? I suppose that I wanted Jane to be sorry for me, I wanted her to bring me round to the idea of children, or to say that she, too, had her worries and doubts, but that together we could manage it. Something to reassure me. So I began.

"Do you worry about having children?" I asked her.

"Of course."

"Do you fear it?"

"Yes, I have fears about us, about how we are."

"Is this a metaphysical fear? By 'us' you mean me," I said.

"I don't know what you mean by that phrase, 'metaphysical fear.' I mean that the responsibility frightens me, and it certainly ought to frighten *you*."

"No," I said firmly. "It doesn't frighten me. A child simply needs love and an absence of religion, and all will be well—to paraphrase Schopenhauer."

"Well, you can get Schopenhauer to breast-feed it then, and bathe it, and rock it to sleep."

"You leave it to me," I said, ironically, and gave Jane a smiling sidelong glance.

"I'd rather not, actually," she said, and she smiled, too.

It was now quite late. It had rained all evening, and had apparently just stopped; in exchange there was a liquid silence beyond the bedroom window. I felt tired, and very weak suddenly.

"Janey, I have something to confess." Jane was still.

"When don't you?" she murmured.

"Haven't we sort of drifted into trying to have a child?"

"No, Tom, if you remember we had long talks about this. And by the way, 'trying to have a child' is overdoing it. We've had sex successfully, at the optimal time, about three times in the last year. *Not* trying to have a child might be better."

"Why do you think that is?"

"Tom, darling, is *this* your confession? Do you think I'm so thick that I don't realize what your impotence has been about? I know you quite well! I know that, of all people, *you* would be anxious about having a child, and perhaps more than anxious—afraid, hesitant. If you could, you would put off every major adult responsibility forever. Unfortunately, this is one of those areas in which you are temporarily indispensable."

"So you've already intuited what I'm going to say."

"Well, darling, I don't know exactly what that is."

"I have a kind of horror at the thought of bringing a child into the world."

"Oh, grow up. Please, Tommy."

"And I have been sabotaging your attempts to conceive."

"Now you're being ridiculous. Sabotage is a big word for something you haven't been able to control. And what about last night, anyway? It went fine."

"Well, that's what I'm trying to tell you," I said.

"Trying to tell me?"

"I'm trying to tell you that it didn't go fine."

"Tom, you've utterly lost me."

"Last night didn't go fine," I said, sluggish in deceit, incapable of progressing beyond this foolish dance of repetitions.

"How, how?"

"Janey, it didn't go fine—are you forcing me to say the words?"

"Yes, because I can't follow you."

"Last night, I lied to you when I said that I had come. I withheld, I held it back—"

I could not speak. Slowly Jane went rigid, and turned to

look at me. I turned away. "Oh Tom, you aren't saying . . . you aren't saying that last night, that—look at me! So I was right when I asked you if you had come? . . . What is *wrong with you*?"

"I'm trying to be honest with you," I said. "I have a problem about the idea of a child." I went to embrace her, and she shook me off.

"Trying to be honest! You disgust me," she said quietly and slowly. "I have to go now, I can't stay."

"You can't go, it's the middle of the night, and we're here for two more days."

"I have to go now, don't you dare hold me back, I'm going now." She got out of bed and began putting on her clothes and saying again and again, as if reciting a mantra, "You don't exist, you don't exist, you don't exist."

"Stop saying that! You can't leave," I said. "What will I tell my parents?"

"Let me out of this house now. Let me out. I don't know you, you don't exist, you disgust me."

She sat down on the bed. The excitement diminished. "All right, I can't go now. This is the favour I will do to your parents. I will go tomorrow, though. It's up to you to come up with the appropriate lie for your parents. You've had lots of experience." Jane continued to sit on the bed.

"Why do you have to get away?" I asked, after a minute's silence.

"I can't breathe in your presence."

"Well, if that's your way of saying that you have been very peculiar and heartless with me since September, it's pretty feeble. Can't breathe! What is that?"

"Tom, you fool, don't you see that it isn't working? Jesus, Max can see this but my own husband can't."

"Max—Max?"

"Yes, Max can see it. Max took pity on me. He could see that I was totally neglected."

"*This* is news! Took pity? What the hell does that mean? When did he take pity?"

"Tom," said Jane. She stuck her chin out at me. "Calm down. Yes, if you want to know, I think Max is actually in love with me, though he's only hinted at it, and very obliquely."

"What do you mean by 'took pity'?"

"In September, when you were up here, Max and I had a drink in London, and we talked a bit about you and me. That's all. I found him very sympathetic. That's *all*," repeated Jane, as she saw me staring at her.

"September, September. I see, everything makes sense now. And don't tell me, you are really in love with Max. You probably *took pity* on him."

"Don't insult me. I can tell you with absolute truthfulness—which is more than you can ever muster—that I have never, ever found him attractive. And in case you didn't notice Fiona yesterday, Max is very happily involved with someone at the moment."

"Oh Christ, why are we even talking about Max! Max has nothing to do with this!" I shouted.

"Keep your voice down. I agree with you. I just said that your best friend is more perceptive than you are."

"Why do you think Max loves you?"

"I just do. Certain hints. In September he said something rather awkward, which I shan't share with you. I just have a certain sense."

"Which means, really, that you must love him."

"It does not. If you insist on inverting everything, then I'm sure you can prove that black is white and that you play the piano and I am a philosopher. Give me at least my honesty. If I say I don't love Max, do me the honour, give me the respect, of believing me."

"All right," I said grudgingly. "But you . . . *can't breathe* with me around."

"Not at the moment, no. Don't you see that your lies are repulsive to me. And *this* lie." As Jane spoke, she waved her hand across the bed, as if "this lie" were located there. "I can't even begin to think about what you are trying to do to our marriage with *this* lie. You must be trying to end our marriage. It's the only possible conclusion. You are killing our baby."

"Of course I'm not. Don't be hysterical. I can't defend my action. I don't know why I did it. But for once, I'm trying to be honest with you. Give me some credit for that."

"Credit—so if you are honest with me now, that somehow absolves you of the disgusting lie you are being honest about? I don't think so. It is *repellent* to me. I have to be alone, I have to be without you for a while. I don't trust you. You've thrown my trust into the bin."

The next day I told my parents that Jane had to get back to London to meet someone about a possible future concert. They were very disappointed and in return I said that I would stay up there a little longer. After lunch, Jane got into our car and calmly reversed (she has always been a methodical, safe driver). The car bristled away over the gravel—that luxurious substance that bears no impress, retains no memory of wear.

22

I DIDN'T STAY a few days. I stayed a few months at the vicarage, and I can't really say why. Was it some ancient instinct, some internal forewarning? Practically, the reason is that I had nowhere to go. Jane said that she didn't want me to return to Islington, and she owns the flat. She needed to be apart from me, she said. At first we spoke every night on the phone. I apologized repeatedly for my many lies. What hurt me most was not Jane's anger, but the sense I had that she was glad to have expunged me from her daily business. I kept on returning to the idea of Max, calmly, slowly, patiently analyzing our marital situation in some winebar in Islington. And after the drink, what happened then? What was the "awkward" declaration he made to Jane? Where did Jane and Max go after this awkwardness? To our flat? In my heart, I knew that Jane was telling the truth. She was not attracted to Max, and Max was far too decent, whatever his secret feelings, ever to act on them, at least as long as I was married. But in my need to work up a case against her, I tormented myself with the painful fantasy that perhaps Jane was not telling the truth, that something more than a sympathetic drink and a rushed awkwardness had taken place. She, for her part, told me that she had been "horribly hurt" by my action on Christmas Eve, and that the "wound" would take a long time to heal.

But after two weeks or so alone, she seemed refreshed by London, or so it seemed to my suspicious ears, and cured by distance from me. She was almost jovial. One evening she said:

"God, Tom, you'd be no use in a war." And I, mock-ruefully, said:

"No use at all? Not to anyone? What would I do in a war?"

"You'd steal bread for the underground resistance. You'd be a thief!"

After a month apart, we stopped speaking regularly. I found myself in easier spirits when not talking to Jane. My parents, unlike her, did not make me feel guilty for my poverty and my inability to earn anything. Once Christmas was over and Karl had left, I began to do some good work on the BAG, continuing the account I had started of my child-hood. As on paper so in reality: wifeless, I fell back into the old rhythms and dependencies of childhood. I moved from the guest bedroom to my old bedroom, and slept soundly in my single childhood bed, whose ropy innards now felt like the smoothest suspension. In the morning I stayed in bed reading (and once heard my father downstairs complain, "Ridiculous—it's like having a bally invalid in the house") and in the afternoon I worked on the BAG and then went for walks. In the evenings I looked into The Stag's Head. I like the atmosphere. In winter there was a cheery, jumpy fire in the grate, and the air seemed to be so dropleted with al-cohol that at any moment a spark might explode the room, which was usually amazingly quiet. Terry Upsher was there quite often, and I longed to ask him what he had meant when he had said that God had not done his father any good, but even Terry was silent in the pub, as if slightly awed, and I obeyed his silence. I sat at my table, felt the greasy, time-waxed wood under my fingers, and watched my cardboard beermat, softened by the wet glass, slowly surrender its integrity—like that of the humans in the room. Mr. Deddum stood behind his tall ale-levers, which now, to my adult, jaundiced eyes, looked less like toy soldiers than poles carved in the shape of women, with long slender necks and bottle waists and the little crescendos of the hips.

For a while I went every day to The Stag's Head, and spent quiet afternoons reading my philosophical heroes while Mr. Deddum's black labrador, Pin, lay at my feet sleeping. Her long gentle snout, the mouth closed raggedly as if loosely sewn, rested against my shoe. And I joined the simple, pastoral rhythms of my parents' lives. I heard them rise in the morning—Father first, promptly; Mother next, driftingly; I heard them chime plates and mugs at breakfast. Father went out on his "rounds," and then there was lunch, and Mother went in the car to get groceries, and Father retired to his study. As Jane's piano had driven me out of the house, so now the silence of those afternoons drove me out. That silence was terrible, as if everyone had died. Father sat in his room, and I sat in mine, and I felt stunned by our wordless proximity. The pressure was intolerable. That is when I would go walking, have a drink or two, and often come back to find Father listening to Elgar, and Mother reading in the sitting room. And then began the slow protocols of evening. Supper always seemed to amble into life, the bowls and plates appearing gradually on the table. Before supper, the radio was turned on for the news—how well I remember Peter standing next to the radio, his right hand on the kitchen counter, his handsome bald head held down, forlorn and solemn as if he were being rebuked by world events, while a cigarette trivially fumed in his fallen left hand.

I was not keen to join him for a cigarette because my parents had never known about my smoking, and I had never had the courage to tell them. Whenever I went home I simply stopped smoking for the length of my stay, a fact which has always amazed Max. Curiously, when staying with them I felt less like a smoker who was lying to them than like a virtuous nonsmoker. Whatever the cause, I quickly lost my addiction to tobacco when at home. My addiction to alcohol, however, increased. My parents were rather abstemious drinkers, and I felt constrained by their limits. My mother, in particular, perhaps because her parents were teetotal, treats alcohol as a kind of revolution-in-waiting that can be contained only by rational and enlightened administration. When Peter was alive she used to drink from her glass and say to him, slightly anxiously, "Oh, this is delicious wine, it has a wonderful taste!" in the manner of someone making concessions to the enemy. Peter was more relaxed, but he never indulged himself. One glass of anything visibly affected him.

So it was impossible for me to take as much of my parents' wine and spirits as I wanted to. Hence my return to The Stag's Head and hence my decision, since the pub was too expensive, to buy a bottle of Scotch and bring it to my bedroom. It would be useful for the silent afternoons.

One day, a hurtful package came in the post from London. Jane had sent my most recent credit card bills, bank statements, Inland Revenue letters, and the bill for the absurd charge card I had at the university bookshop. A note read: "I can't deal with this. It is *your* problem now." I was indebted to everyone. These were bills I had simply chosen not to open for months. I owed the Visa people almost £800, the bank £400, the Inland Revenue £700 (of the original £1,000 I had owed them, and on whose behalf I had told the lie about my father's death), and the university bookshop £120. Total: £2,020. But I had an idea about what to do. Philip Zealy's new financial services firm was advertising all over the place for just my kind of person. Add up your total debts, the advertisements said, and ask Zealy to pay them off, then help you to manage the debt into easy low monthly payments. I had to act. Zealy, the man, was a shady figure, no doubt about that. His broad face and fat nose, pitted like an orange skin, told you all you needed to know, and I had been watching that face stare at me from various venues for twenty years. But presumably, I said to myself, the firm is separate from the man. A contract would be issued, all would be above board. Surely he wouldn't be so popular if he did not deliver? I took my parents' car and drove to Durham. The Zealy office was in the town's marketplace.

A pleasant, professional young woman had me fill in a form. I admitted to my debts, and listed as many sources of income as I could think of (or invent), including private tuition, which I have never done. The woman went away, and returned with an older woman, who told me that, in addition to the management of my debts, Zealy would be able to lend me a sum of money, whose repayment could be added to my monthly payments. She had a soft Durham accent.

"I'm going to be a wee bit poky, and ask you right on—you could handle a bit of extra cash?" She said the last word as only a northerner can, making the hard "c" as hard as coal, and the soft "sh" as tough as steel.

"Yes, but could I afford your terms?"

"Well, pet, the terms would all be pursuant to you getting our approval of you in the first place, but looking at this form, I cannat see any *reel* problem. The secret is that we pay off your debts straight away, and then you pay us back over a reely long time. Prob'ly over two years. That chops them monthly payments right down."

"How much do you think the monthly payments would be?" I asked anxiously.

"Eee, pet, I haven't a clue!"

When I returned three days later, I learned that my debt had been approved, that I would take away a cheque for £1,000, and that I would pay the firm of Philip Zealy Ltd. (Financial), £226 a month for twenty-four months. Obviously, it was the purest usury, but it offered my only hope, and it put money in my pocket.

I hadn't wanted to tell my parents, but they came upon some of the bills Jane had sent, and to allay their alarm I told them it had all been taken in hand. They were horrified, of course, that I had gone to Zealy.

"He's a bloomin' moneylender, Tom," said my father. "He'll have your guts for garters."

I explained the terms.

"Why didn't you come to us, dearest?" said my mother. "We're not rich, but we might have been able to help. It's all so shabby, going to a firm like Zealy."

"I wouldn't dream of it. You know, there are thousands of perfectly happy customers, I presume, who have had their debts worked out by firms like Zealy's. It's almost banal."

"Ha! Almost banal! I like that," said Peter.

"Oh, Tom, this would only happen to you," said Sarah.

"No, it could have happened to anyone," I said.

"Yes, but it happened to *you*, darling," said Sarah.

"Mum, you're being illogical."

"She means that what happened to Oedipus could have happened to anyone, but it happened to Oedipus," said Peter. "We are all oedipal, no doubt, but only Oedipus was *warned* ahead of time that he would be oedipal."

Father looked at me with his big eyes. A smile seemed to

dance there, a tiny merry loiter, and I felt him to be irresistible, deeply lovable, for all that I disliked what he was saying. I felt the infection of him. He was grinning, and looked down at the carpet. Then suddenly he shook with mirth, and his face, like a woodcut of sunrise, broke into spreading beams.

"Dear, it's obvious to everyone that Zealy is jolly bad news," said Mother.

"You were just reading a different newspaper from everyone else," said Father, and again he laughed. "Oh dear, dear, I'm not laughing at you, Tommy, but you have to admit you walked into this one."

"Look, Zealy is a total crook, but he's also a total businessman. I have the paperwork upstairs. Unless I default on the payments, no one is going to come hammering on my door with baseball bats or shoot me in the street from a motorbike."

Strangely, my worldly but unworldly parents, for all their knowing talk about Zealy, were shocked by such language, and firmly resisted the idea that he was a crook.

"Zealy's a bit queer but he's not wicked. You mustn't put thoughts like that into our heads," said my mother.

"You're speaking like a criminal," said my father.

"Well, what on earth do you think Zealy is?" I said in frustration.

Peter sighed. "Oh, well, he's a bit sinister, he 'digs with the wrong foot,' as we used to say in the army, but he's certainly not a criminal. He wouldn't be in business if he was."

So my parents thought of Zealy as a kind of criminal while denying that he was one; and no doubt thought of me as one while reproving me for speaking like one. It made me laugh.

And then, as ever, after a few good weeks, work stopped going well. Suddenly I had nothing to say in my BAG, and every time I looked at the box of papers that constituted my Ph.D. I felt like being sick. All the bad behaviour began again. I lounged in bed until midday, stopped shaving, grew irritable and spiteful with my generous parents. Harboured by my parents' emotional stability, their resourcefulness and Christian optimism, I should have been able to relax into their sanity. Instead, I felt reproached, tormented, seduced, frustrated by the easiness with which they seemed to live. I kicked up a storm just to prove that the harbour was not safe. I'm sure I was not pleasant to have around in those months I spent with them. They stopped inviting parishioners to Sunday lunch. I longed to get to my bedroom so that I could get out my BAG and swallow a glass of whisky. Around the whisky I danced a set of routines. I would put, I told myself, one more entry in the BAG before I poured myself a little wave of amber. I lifted the bottle, felt its cold sliding weight, and suddenly a golden trench had filled the glass, sprouting sharp aromas. That, I thought, is just the amount of Scotch that *wanted* to be freed.

Unlike the childish glass of urine that my mother had never noticed all those years ago, she did find the bottle of whisky under my bed, at the end of February, and informed my father. Peter ambushed me in the car, on the way back from Durham one day. We seemed at first to be speaking normally. Peter was talking about the Thurlows, and how they had hoped that Max would go into academic work rather than journalism.

"Colin especially doesn't have any time for journalism. He dates the decline of the West from the year 1896." My father looked at me. "You don't know the significance of that date, do you?"

"Yes, Dad, I know all about it, thanks! Colin asked me exactly the same question last September when Jane and I went over to The Oratory. Since Colin doesn't take a newspaper and doesn't have a television, I don't know what right he has to comment on the news. He just fears the sting of something alien. It's like a . . . it's like a fish commenting on lemon."

"He says it's because news disturbs him too much. By the way, when did you last shave, old fellow?"

"How would he know? Have Max's parents actually ever seen a minute of TV?"

Father laughed. "Oh, Tommy, your memory's slipping. *The Forsyte Saga,* remember? How old were you then? Six or seven? The BBC did it, a huge series, it felt longer than the bally war but was getting awfully good reviews from all and sundry, and after the third or fourth episode Colin a bit shamefacedly hinted that his colleagues at the department were banging on about it, and could he and Belinda come and watch it with us? Mummy was terribly amused, if you recall, and imitated Colin's request—a cross between Oliver Twist and a student who wants an extension for his essay: 'Please, sir, can I have a little telly?'"

Father drove in the manner I had known all my life, with bursts of emotion, using the accelerator as a kind of church bell on which to register his irregular vitality. We were silent and awkward.

"It's been good for me to be with you and Mum," I said, half-meaning it.

"Has it?" said Father quickly. "Why do you say that?"

"Why would you doubt what I say?" I asked.

"Well, Tommy, because your mother found a near-empty bottle of Scotch in your bedroom two days ago, and I am old-fashioned enough to think that a man who snorts whisky on his own and in secret"—his voice had risen slightly—"is not at all happy."

We were now on the road to Sundershall. Father would not, could not, look at me, and used the road ahead as his excuse.

"If it's any consolation, it's not my parents who have driven me to drink."

"I don't find that as funny as you do."

"I'm stating a fact. In case you hadn't noticed, Jane and I seem to be in the process of separating. I suppose I have been drinking a certain amount since coming up here. But it's all perfectly controllable."

"That wasn't the sense your mother and I had at the Christmas party." Father became sad. "You were such a happy child."

"Was I?"

"Your mother and I thought so," he said, seemingly defensively.

"Oh, I'm not contesting you, I was interested, that's all."

"Yes, when you were a baby we called you Grinaldi, or sometimes the Duke of Grinaldi because you were always grinning." I raised my eyes from my lap and saw my father's hands on the steering wheel. Those hands had seemed large when I was a child.

"I'm not unhappy," I said slowly. "Obviously I'd like to get my Ph.D. finished."

Peter seemed very relieved by the turn of conversation. "Well, obviously," he said, with new vigour. "Once we get the Ph.D. out of the way, everything should resolve itself properly. How, ah . . . how . . . long do you still need, do you think?"

"Not long, Dad, not long now. It's very well advanced."

"Oh, I'm *so* pleased to hear that."

We were passing through Towmoor, the village before Sundershall. It was a dark, ugly place, as ugly as Sundershall was pretty. Mother used to joke that the two villages were like sisters, "but Towmoor is the one who never married."

Suddenly my father said with earnest passion, "So you give me your word of honour that you are not an alcoholic? I can honestly say this to your mother?"

"Of course not, Dad, don't be absurd."

We were silent again.

"But, Tommy, why would you *need* to drink?"

"I've told you, Jane and I have been fighting. Look, you and Mum wouldn't know anything about this kind of situation. To you, peering into our marriage is probably like opening someone else's electricity bill by mistake and thinking 'My god, that family uses a lot of electricity. I'm glad I don't have to write a cheque that large.' But we're the ones paying the bloody bill."

"You assume a great deal, Tom. I've been a parish priest for thirty years. One sees quite a lot of life, you know." His voice was stern again, and he was frowning in a way that reminded me of his angry face at my grandmother's funeral, as I lay on the grass of the cemetery and he strode towards me, black-cassocked, a column of night. Just the memory of that childhood moment made me shudder a little. Father's angry face, his striding legs, parting the black cloth. The driver in his grey cap, approaching from the other side. And Father's awful strange phrase: *Come back to the grave.*

"Since we rarely speak like this," he continued, "since we must be honest, I will tell you that your mother and I worry about your lack of spiritual resources. To me, a whisky bottle under a bed is . . . is a message in a bottle, really! And that message is telling me that you have no spiritual life."

"No spiritual life?"

"This is confusing, because Jane and I discussed you at Christmas, and she led me to believe that despite your doubts and scepticism, you were on a path towards God and towards Christ. She said she felt you were still 'seeking,' but at least seeking in the right direction."

I was astounded by Jane's untruth. So my wife, who had harassed me for years about *my* lying, had lied to my father about my atheism! For what? To tell him what he wanted to hear? To put his mind at rest? Or more likely as a way of attacking me, of putting me into difficulties. I suspected that Jane imagined that her lie would force me, at a moment such as this, to tell the truth to my father. For this very reason, so that she would not force me, so that *I would not be forced,* and because I had no inclination to argue with my father, I decided to go along with the lie.

It was a decision taken in less than a second; but once I had embarked on it, I had to see it to the very end, for that is the way with lies.

"Did you hear me talking to Tim Biffen?" I asked. "At the Christmas party?"

"I heard only Tim speaking. He seemed to be rather unsuccessfully getting you to agree that the cathedral was a mistake. I must say that it confirmed a few doubts I have about Tim."

Oh, these lies, these lies! I wasn't sure whether my father was now speaking the truth. He sounded a little cagey. But if he was telling the truth, I had entirely misinterpreted his collapsed sad face as he looked at me that evening. He had been sad for Tim Biffen, not sad for me.

"Well, Tim and I had been running through some of the old fundamentals, some of the obstacles to faith."

"The problem of evil, and so forth," said Father.

"Yes, evil, pain, suffering, the world that is so clearly not God's world."

"Well, my boy, I'm delighted that you might have found a way round these obstacles, if dear Jane is right. But you can know Christ all your life and still these obstacles don't disappear. There is no melting away, intellectually. The only hope is faith. Faith is the red flower."

"I like that," I said. "The red flower."

"I'm thinking of a little poem I used to know off by heart. 'My soul, there is a country, far beyond the stars.' Da da dee, I forget the next bit. Something about a winged sentry. It's all about heaven. 'If thou canst get but thither, there grows the flower of peace, the rose that cannot wither, thy fortress and thy ease.' Etcetera. I forget it. I think I'd like it read at my funeral."

We had arrived at the vicarage. In the dark, the house was represented by three yellow windows. On our right was the graveyard, where the permanently darkened residents would not notice the smaller imposition of night. Father stopped the car, but neither of us moved. He continued to look straight ahead at the windscreen, as if still driving.

"You know, not long before you were born, I had a crisis of faith. Curiously, it's why I became a priest. Or rather, I resolved the crisis by leaving the intellectualism of the university for the devotion of the priest's life. I didn't know the answers to any of my questions, and decided in the end that living a Christlike life was the only answer to them. It's why I am interested in Tim Biffen, because he so reminds me of myself when I was a young man. It's very very important not to be corrupted by theology."

"How were you being corrupted?" I asked, genuinely curious. Father had never told me about his intellectual formation. I imagined that he had always been the same kind of Christian, because he had been the same kind of Christian for the whole of my life.

"Theology was encouraging me to think of problems as intellectually soluble; and I saw that I needed instead to see life itself as a problem handed to me by God. I suppose you might say that I had a kind of vision, though Englishmen of my age are not allowed to admit such things. Sarah was pregnant with you—oh, about five months, six months. She was resting, and I went alone to the Christmas carol service at the cathedral. At the service I didn't feel like standing. I felt like sitting, even when everyone was standing and belting out those blasted carols. All I wanted to do was to sit and think. And the thing I was trying to resolve was not theological, really, but human. There I was, happily anticipating the birth of a child. Not God's child, Tommy, but mine!— you. Yet I was not sure that I had enough faith—faith in God, faith in the future—to be a father. I felt my faith in God flickering, with the danger of extinguishing itself altogether. I had been having doubts about just those questions which you mentioned just now—evil, justice, original sin, and so on. But how could there be such a thing as a world without God? I couldn't imagine it. So I tried to feel my way into a defence of God. The first answer I came up with was that if you take God away from the world, the world is no less horrid, no less painful or sinful or unsaved. It is simply painful and sinful *without God,* without the hope of salvation or succour. The second answer I came up with was that the creation of something out of nothing is an act of love. *Even* the creation of pain, the creation of evil. For this reason: we do not know why evil exists. We do not know the largest scheme of things, we cannot know God's plan. We know that evil is evil. But do we know that the *existence* of evil is evil? Do you see my point? In other words, do we know what evil exists *for*? We do not. And this is for the same reason that we do not know what the opposite of evil exists for. Why does goodness exist? Why happiness? Just as with evil, we don't have the faintest idea. But we do know that love cannot be a faculty that simply involves no pain at all. Love is not just kindness; love may also rebuke, command, punish. You don't know anything about this because we have never really had to punish you, you lucky thing! But you would know if you had a child, Tommy. And life is love. That we would rather be alive than dead, even if life is painful, is proof that there is more love in the world than pain."

I sat there in admiration of my father's mind, his absolute clarity. But I had to say something. I had to disagree.

"Is life love, or is it really power?" I asked. "And is God love, or is God merely power? Perhaps creation is just the tremendous exercise of power, the power to create. That's surely why Aristotle said that it would be very odd for citizens to love Zeus. Respect, fear, hate, perhaps, but not *love* him. Who loves power?"

"But, Tommy, Zeus is not our God. Power is not our God; love is our God. We have an intercessor whose name is Christ the Lord. And God so *loved*—loved—the world that He sent His only son to die on the Cross. Jesus suffered on the Cross, and suffers with us, and so God suffers with us every day, every minute. Our suffering is our love, our brotherhood."

"Do you remember," I said gently, because I was moved, "the old story Mum told about Terry's father and the doctor? He kept on going back to the doctor for a certain kind of pill. And then Mum went round once to his house and saw all these boxes of pills, unopened, and she asked him why he was hoarding drugs. And he said that the pills were not doing him any good at all so he had stopped using them. But he kept on going back to get more only because he 'felt sorry' for the doctor! He didn't want to hurt the doctor's feelings. Well, I think sometimes we make ourselves feel better if we also feel sorry for God a bit. You know, like the doctor, if God suffers as well as us, then perhaps things aren't as bad as they seem."

"Oh, Tom—is Jane right, *are* you seeking? For so many years your mother and I assumed you were indifferent, or bored, or just consumed by philosophy. You never mention Christian matters to us, you see, you have never really discussed them with us." He sounded reproachful.

"I was never indifferent, never bored! Look, I think Jane *is* right, I am seeking God," I said cautiously.

"Seeking God? Oh, that is wonderful to hear. It's far more important than your Ph.D., you know," said Father with a smile.

"Yes, Dad."

"Though your Ph.D. *is* quite important!"

And suddenly the moment had passed, our utterly unexpected, forever glorious intimacy and tenderness had arrived and moved away like a trade wind, stirring its little storm, and Father was returning to his buoyant, humorous, public self.

"We've steamed up the windows like a couple of desperate teenagers," he said.

And we went inside.

23

And so I sealed my father's lips with a final lie. The biggest lie. "Seeking God," eh? But it worked. Nothing further was said about the whisky bottle (my mother had removed it). Both parents seemed to abandon, or set aside, the habitual anxiety with which they had treated me for so many years. For I was on the path to Christ. I was a "seeker," and since I was a seeker the Ph.D. would suddenly be easy to complete. No mention was made of my rising late, or my afternoon trips to The Stag's Head. I was returned to innocence. As I walked into rooms, my parents' kindly, handsome faces opened themselves into smiles. Father told Mother, obviously, about my "new direction." By lying I discovered a great truth: I discovered what mattered most deeply to my parents, and what had worried them most deeply about me. It had nothing to do with the Ph.D.!

The next few days were spent in a characteristic Bunting limbo. Everything had changed, the house was full of the perfume of amnesty; yet it was understood by all that the subject could not be discussed again. It had had its moment, its accidental appointment, and was now returned to its place of reticence, a tiny English principality where no language existed. In some ways, this suited me; I wasn't keen to return to my lie; it was best left alone. But to be suddenly "innocent" and not to be able to speak of it, was painful, too. I longed to find again that charged solemnity with which Father had spoken to me in the car, a solemnity sweetened by his naiveté—I will never forget the way he quickly, earnestly said, "So you give me your word of honour that you are not an alcoholic?"

Instead, we all lived in what seemed to me a wordless time. Gestures spoke louder than words. From those days I remember my father coming to waken me one morning. He hadn't done this since I was a teenager. Alluding to his old story, he stood by the door and said, "Sorry, O'Brien." And I remember that one or other of my parents slipped a twenty-pound note into my pocket, while my jacket was hanging on the hook in the hall. I'm sure of it.

I was alone a great deal, as I had been in my childhood, and took notice again of the world around me while I was on my walks. Winter was ending. The silver ferns of morning frost on my bedroom window had become a gentler spring of dewdrops. Now that the ground was softer, Terry started serious work on my father's garden shed, and soon had the main structure up. (It was not for books but garden tools.) One day, Mr. Deddum's dog trusted the now tepid grass behind the pub enough to roll in it and juggle the air. The brass handle of the vicarage door lost its polish of cold. All around, the countryside was voyaging into its green abroad. On my walks I saw the sheep, now joined by collapsing lambs, on fields bordered and divided by loose, gap-crowded drystone walls, private versions of Hadrian's Wall, an hour to the north, built by the Roman emperor to keep out the Scots.

Speaking of Mr. Deddum, it was at this time that a curious incident occurred at The Stag's Head. I have known Mr. Deddum since I was a teenager, and have always liked him. Whenever I was up in Sundershall on previous visits I had looked in at the pub, and Mr. Deddum, in honour of the

rarity of these appearances, had always said the same thing as
I entered: "Eee, if I'd known *you* were coming, I'd've baked
a cake," in a slightly sarcastic way. Anyway, Mr. Deddum had
a young man, Simon, working for him; the boy could only
have been seventeen or eighteen. He seemed a little slow-
witted, with a permanently worried face like a gargoyle's
and a mouth which he never closed and through which he
breathed noisily. A clumsy, kind boy, who got to know
the brand of cigarettes and the whisky I liked, and gave
me a second shot of Scotch without charge on quite a few
occasions. On one of these afternoons, in March, as Simon
was handing me my drink, Mr. Deddum came out from
the back, said hello to me and watched Simon as he performed his duties. Then he said suddenly and rather sharply
to him, "Close your bloody mouth." As if he were Mr. Deddum's Labrador, Simon closed his mouth promptly, but
his face seemed to collapse as it contracted, and he blushed
savagely.

I felt sorry for him, felt ashamed, and was angry with
Mr. Deddum for making such a spectacle of the boy. I made
an anxious laugh or cough, and said, "Oh, he's doing all
right, you know." Mr. Deddum looked at me quite cheerfully and said: "What d'you know about it? There's nowt
wrong with your gob." I couldn't argue with this, and Mr.
Deddum, seeing me silent, continued: "I've already told
our Simon that if he wants to go to Newcastle and do this
line of work—ya kna, pub work—that open gob of his is going to be a winder for some hardcase to put his fist into, and
that's an end of it. It looks bloody stupid. Extra, don't think
I didn't see him giving you a pickle more of that Scotch
without charging you. The lad's on parole here, so don't
feel sorry for him."

Simon's humiliation affected me more than it deserved to. I found myself in a fury over Mr. Deddum's brisk cruelty, and I decided not to go again to The Stag's Head. The occurrence, which would seem trivial to most people, settled in me like a germ, and disrupted my sleep, and my now fitful work on the BAG.

24

THE REASON I eventually returned to London, in late
April, was that, despite my parents' warmth, I was getting
nothing done in Sundershall, and it seemed fairer to keep
my nothingness to myself than to inflict it on my parents.
Karl said that I could stay with him until Jane and I mended
things, and Max extended the same offer (of course I would
not have been able to stay with Max anyway, contaminated
as he was by Jane's information). So I went back to the city,
and my parents waved me off. We were at the Durham
bus station. The cathedral watched over us. My dainty parents stood very close to each other, like toy soldiers eagerly
arranged by a slapdash little boy. Father quipped, "Don't do
anything I would do," as he rather formally shook my hand.

I hardly noticed them, because I was in a "state" about
taking the bus, and yet was embarrassed to admit as much to
my parents. I very much dislike buses, but the train was
much more expensive, and I was saving the money Zealy had
loaned me. On long bus journeys I get afraid that the bus
driver will fall asleep at the wheel. I can't relax while this fear
grips me, and I feel compelled to try to keep the driver
awake. So on the trip to London I employed my usual tricks.
I sat right behind the driver. I could see his speedometer.
Then I spent the journey making various noises. I crushed
my newspaper, and noisily turned the large pages. (It was
Max's day to have his *Times* column, I noticed.) I coughed a
great deal, and shifted in my seat, and tapped the floor with

my feet. Above all, I kept my eye on the back of the driver's seat, and as soon as that head began to droop, I was ready to bring out my orchestra of effects.

Exhausted at Victoria Coach Station, I phoned Uncle Karl, and went to his house. Uncle Karl said he was not surprised that Jane and I were having problems. "You were looking too much at one another," he said, oddly. "I can always tell when relationships are on the rocks, it is all quite simple—they are always watching each other and saying 'Yes darling. No darling.' But look, this is just a cooling-off period. All will be well with the two of you. Anyway, you're welcome, Tommy. As long as you like. The last person to stay in your old bed at the top was a very early girlfriend of Lucian Freud's."

It was at Uncle Karl's, two and half weeks later, that Mother phoned to tell me the news. She was very calm. But I became hot and began to shake. The telephone receiver felt like a weapon which I wanted to bring down on my own head. Father had gone to the church, had not returned, and Mother had found him lying on the stone floor, face downwards. He had broken open the collar of his shirt. Dr. Braun said that he had had a heart attack. I could tell that my mother had already wandered into the bureaucratic wilderness of funeral arrangements and telephone calls and the undertaker's bills. By treading this arid ground she avoided drowning. It was no time for watery grief. But her voice was dull and weak. While she told me about the date for the funeral, Karl came up the stairs and stood inquiringly for a second. He smiled and so I smiled back and waved him on. He wrote a note and handed it to me: "Running out for the evening, back twelveish." The heavy front door was opened, a taxi could be heard drilling outside, and then there was silence. I told Mother that Karl was out for the evening, but that of course he and I would immediately drive overnight to Sundershall.

Karl came back at midnight, flushed and smelling of society. I told him the news, and felt oddly embarrassed as I did so, perhaps because I thought he would be full of sympathy for me. But his own grief was too strong for that. He crumpled, he bent over as if I had hit him, with the top of his head pushed towards me, almost in my nostrils, so that I could smell on him the royal aroma of good wine and cigar tobacco, which seemed to be souring as he shrank before me. "Oh, why did he do that, why that?" wailed poor Karl. I couldn't bear to see him so afflicted, I couldn't bear to see his rusty eyes full of tears, and so I wept with him, and rather than embrace we stood in his drawing room, holding hands like children.

Karl said he wasn't in a fit state to drive. I took the big Mercedes north, up the desolate A1, and he slept beside me. It was foggy; the strong headlights cut a world for us. We swiftly passed long articulated lorries, sighing and creaking their governed way north. They were covered with little lights like a starlet's mirror and as we passed them the car briefly glowed inside with rough glamour. Then suddenly they were gone, and we were silent again. Hatfield, Grantham, Doncaster. At York the dawn arrived very quickly, like something unimportant. At Durham, the cathedral seemed to be rising with the rest of the world, receiving light and attention as the morning grew. We were in Sundershall by breakfast.

It was painful to see my mother trying to assume a former politesse—grave smiles and "I'm sure you'd both like some breakfast." She seemed remote, like Karl, involved with her grief. She spoke to me immediately about the funeral, about the exact instructions he had left for hymns and prayers and music. I suddenly remembered that, in our conversation in the car, Father had spoken of a particular poem that he wanted read at his funeral.

"It was about a red flower, or about the flower of faith, or something like that. Does that mean anything to either of you?"

Mother looked at me as if I were lying. And also being a nuisance, an obstacle in the way of the proper rites.

"Mum, I'm not making this up! Dad mentioned this poem, and said he wanted it read at his funeral. I remember the phrase he used: 'faith is the red flower.' Then he recited the only bit he could remember—'If thou can get thither, there will be a flower of peace,' something like that. God, I've forgotten it . . . Oh yes! 'The rose that will not wither.' I remember that. Does that sound familiar? We must try to find this poem."

But Mother looked at me almost coldly, and said:

"He never mentioned that poem to me in more than forty years of marriage, and there's nothing about it in his instructions."

"But he said it to me, to me."

Karl pulled at my sleeve. "Come on, Tom, let's have breakfast, and then go to the funeral home." I took the hint, how could I not, and decided to drop the question of Peter's poem.

As we ate breakfast, Mother swept the kitchen floor around our table, something I had never seen her do. She seemed obsessed with getting us to go as soon as possible. "He's over there," she said several times. So we ate quickly and went to Pickering's Rest Home. Karl said I should go in first, and I walked into the room where the coffin lay on a trestle.

There he was. His nose looked prowlike, his brow forceful and almost glowing in the soft light. I realized how very
rarely I had seen him asleep; he was a spirit of wakefulness.
He was wearing a blue shirt I had never seen, and his tie was
not properly adjusted. But for the life of me I could not
possibly adjust it. I was terrified: he seemed so utterly alive.
Surely he was only dozing. I was afraid that at any moment
he would open his eyes and look at me and say "Tommy,
have you seen my cigarettes?" or "Everything all right?" or
"Sorry, O'Brien." My eyes went up and down the length of
him, searching for a sign. I was sure, for a horrid second,
that I saw his chest give a twitch.

Suddenly my eyes were drawn to his right hand, which
lay beside him, partly obscured by his body. I leant over the
coffin to get a better look. His hand was wrapped around a
small silver cross which I knew well. He had carried it everywhere with him, in his left trouser pocket. But there was
something else, the top of which could just be seen. It
looked like a piece of glossy paper. I willed myself to touch
the hand. I had to see what this paper was. Closing my eyes,
I felt the stiff hand. I could not move the fingers, and my
body was shivering with the vileness of the sensation. But I
tugged instead on the paper, and it gave way, and slipped out
of the dead fist. The paper was stiff too, as if it had also died.
Of course it was stiff: because it was a photograph. A photograph of my mother. Which she must have folded into his
hand, and which she must have thought obscured by the
closed fist. I looked at my father, and then at the photograph of my mother. And then I stuffed the photograph
back into the tight fist, pushing against both the unwilling
cold flesh of Father's hand and the hard silver cross, doubtless bruising and creasing the paper as I did so.

It was hard to think of Father's body simply stopped like a clock. Where had he gone? I firmly believe that "only burdock will grow upon my grave" and that the dead go nowhere at all; certainly not to hell; surely not to heaven. But the dead are fortunate; they have at least got beyond the ordinary celebrity of being alive. They are elsewhere, not here. Father believed that he would see his Maker in heaven, and his parents, and I suppose eventually his wife and his wayward son. But I won't be there, Dad, I won't be there, because I don't believe. I will be elsewhere, like you. And our elsewheres will be different in death, as they were in life.

One of the religious thinkers I had read instructed me that grief was not a properly religious emotion. All the world, except angels, must die, and to be distressed at the death of a person is merely to mourn the fact that your loved one was not born an angel. Certainly my father was no angel, but why should I not mourn him? I crossed the room to the dim corner where a table was set with many candles. I lit one and stood still for several minutes: I lit it for my father, for my mother, for my childhood, for my wife. The small flame flickered, retreated, and then remembered itself, filling out with light in a little golden rage.

The funeral was held two days later. Canon Palliser, who was taking the service, asked me to deliver a eulogy. My mother agreed with his idea, and I liked the notion very much. So on the eve of the funeral I stayed up, and spent all night madly writing: I had the idea of combining a farewell to Father with some of the material from my BAG, and was unsure if a proper fusion had been achieved. Deprived of sleep, oddly excited (I would share a little of my BAG with everyone for the first time), I kept on returning in my mind to the only other funeral I had attended, my grandmother's, when I had disgraced myself in the cemetery and Father made me stand next to him at the graveside.

Jane had arrived the night before from London, and together with Karl we accompanied Mother at ten o'clock in the morning from the vicarage to the church. I clutched eight pages of densely handwritten paper. Mother gave out a little cry as we entered, because the church was completely full—the "census-gathering" had come early this year. It seemed that the entire village was there. Paul Deddum had come; he stood behind the pew as if he were going to serve drinks. Shy, reclusive Sam Spedding—pale, bespectacled, and dressed in a green bomber jacket—was standing next to his mother, who had probably forced him to appear. Terry Upsher was there; he looked very sad. Miss Ogilvie, with the three canes, was also there, and Tim Biffen from Durham, and Mr. Norrington, who had pompously donned a black armband. He had the look of a sinister invalid. Susan Perez-Temple was standing next to a man I did not know. At the front were Colin and Belinda Thurlow, with Max. Colin had the calm, neutral stare of someone attending a second-rate lecture. Belinda, I noticed angrily, was disgracefully untidy; she seemed to be wearing her poorest gardening shoes. While on the subject of shoes, I should say I was wearing brand-new ones at father's funeral, as Socrates is at the beginning of the *Symposium*. They were a good Italian pair, bought in Knightsbridge with the last hundred pounds of my research grant, and saved for the right occasion—which had never come, since Jane and I had been going out less and less in the months before our separation in December.

Mother, Jane, Karl, and I took our seats. The coffin lay in the middle of the nave, at the front. Canon Palliser began:

"We are here to say goodbye to Peter, Peter who illuminated all our lives, who tended to his flock like no other priest I have ever known, and who was loved in return, not only in this village, or this county, but wherever he went. Everyone who met Peter loved him. I know that there are many friends and family here today, and that each of us was touched in some way by Peter's faith, hope, and charity." Palliser spoke of Peter's "gift of simplicity," and the "quiet certainty" of his faith, and I found myself resisting his pieties. Was Father's faith so simple? I remembered the jokey notice stuck to his Bible: "This is an advance copy sent in lieu of a proof." It surely hadn't been just a joke, but some hint of anxiety, of complication, of philosophical sophistication. Yet at the Christmas gathering Tim Biffen had said that Peter was not "wily," that he would certainly say, like Job, "I know that my Redeemer liveth." I was thinking these thoughts when Jane nudged me with her elbow. It was my turn to walk up the small church's nave and deliver the eulogy.

I was a little shaky on my legs as I walked towards the pulpit; clearly the ghost of my old adolescent self-consciousness— that horrid era of being "born again"—was teasing me. I could feel a hundred faces appraising my back. Then I climbed the five steps, and turned, and saw Jane beautifully looking at me, and poor Mother with her eyes closed, and Max rubbing his glasses, and Colin Thurlow superciliously waiting, as if for a student's *viva voce*.

I had decided to begin, as my teacher Mr. Duffy would have advised, "with a bang"—in this case, a joke:

"I feel, standing here, a little like a man I once read about in the newspaper who won a competition: he was given one minute to remove as much money as he could from a bank vault, money which he would be allowed to keep. Instead, the excitement caused him to hyperventilate, and he

collapsed." There was a rustling amongst the congregation—
the sound of laughter anxiously displaced onto movement.

"Like that man, I don't know if this is a moment of victory or defeat. I mean—for both my father, and for me.
When I was a boy, I often dreamed of walking up into this
pulpit and delivering a fiery sermon—the kind of sermon,
thankfully, my father never gave—and here I am, standing in
the pulpit of his very church, delivering, in effect, a sermon, and my father is not here to witness it. Like the man
who won that competition, I have simultaneously lost the
competition, too. I have the money, as it were, but I don't
get to keep it, and so it is worthless, ashes in my mouth.

"A great idol of mine, the free-spirited and freethink-
ing Heinrich Heine, wrote that Martin Luther forgot that
Christianity demands impossible things from those who
follow it. But Catholicism *did* understand this, said Heine,
and had worked out a comfortable contract between spirit
and matter, between spiritualism and sensualism. In that
sense, and that sense only, Father was a Catholic. No one in
this parish ever felt that he was being judged by Peter
Bunting. He used to joke about the Ten Commandments
that it was not very impressive simply to observe the ten
commonest elements of human nature and put 'not' in
front of them. Can't you hear him say that?"

There were some awkward laughs—I heard Max's slow
chuckle—and I felt, now, that I "had" my audience. At UCL
I was never important enough to give a lecture, but had always
imagined doing so in the big lecture room there. But here
everyone was four feet below me, sitting like willing babies.
Colin, Belinda, and Max Thurlow were staring up at me.
The prospect of all those babyish tilted faces went to my head.

"Nevertheless, he and I did not agree about everything.

Fundamentally, we were opposed. I am a very theological philosopher—as some of you may know!—and he was a somewhat philosophical theologian, and yet the width of our overlap was small. Yes, I must be honest here: it was small and grey. Did we ever talk about our differences? Only once, about two months ago, and it was frankly too little, too late. My father was an optimist, as many of you gratefully recall, but I am not an optimist. Schopenhauer said, towards the end of his life, that a philosophy where you do not hear between the pages the tears, the wailing and gnashing of teeth and the fearful tumult of general mutual murder, is no philosophy. I agree with that statement. My father by contrast believed in the calming grace of God, as well he should. I apologize, by the way, for all these necessary allusions, something that I have inherited from Peter Bunting, of course. We both of us at various times resembled the fabled scribe, Denys the Alexandrian, mentioned in various ancient texts, who is said to have received orders from heaven to read all the books in the world. Obviously, I am still following those orders, even though I don't believe in heaven; my father, some of you may choose to believe, is now catching up by reading all those books *in* heaven."

But now there was complete silence in the church. I looked around, for ballast. But Max would not let me catch his eye, and Jane was fiddling in her handbag, and both Belinda and Colin were looking down at the floor. Tim Biffen was overcome by a convenient coughing fit. I sensed that my audience had turned against me, that I had alienated them. Why? I was being frank, for sure, but wasn't that a virtue? It seemed essential, at that moment, to speak the truth, to tell my father certain things I had not been able to say to him. Holding my sheets of paper with a sweating grip, I continued:

"Anyway, I have spent the last year writing something which I have provisionally entitled 'The Book Against God.' A big project. In recent months, up here alone and without a wife, I have had a lot more time than usual! Too much time. One of the arguments I make in my Book Against God is that life is essentially what I call a bowl of tears. In some people the bowl overflows; in others, it seems hardly full at all. Yet all suffer. Now, my father did suffer, I think, even though he used to joke that he was absurdly happy, that unlike most men he was seeking for the key to *un*happiness. It may surprise you, but my father was no angel, that's for sure—"

But I stopped because Jane had left her pew and was walking towards the pulpit. Her tightly persuaded ponytail swayed ominously. At the same moment, Canon Palliser left his seat and moved towards me. He and Jane converged at the foot of the pulpit steps. It was Granny's funeral all over again! Jane beckoned to me, and I descended reluctantly.

"Tommy, darling, you're overwrought," she whispered. "You can't go on with this. Please make it stop."

Canon Palliser added more pacifically that there were several parishioners who wanted to say a word, and that time should be given to them, as well as to me. Perhaps I could finish my remarks at the graveside, or in the vicarage at lunch?

I was dumbstruck. I thought my eulogy had been going well; it balanced respect for my father with respect for the truth. I glanced from Jane and Canon Palliser to the congregation. Some were now whispering. Max had his head in his hands. My mother's eyes found mine, and she gently summoned me with her little finger to return to the pew. She looked very sad, and I knew I had to obey her. But I was furious with Jane for initiating this humiliating course of events. Turning to the congregation, I said: "I think I am being told by various . . . organizers here that I have gone on too long—that's what years of academic seminars will do to you! Please forgive me. All of you know how much my father meant to me." And I returned, boiling with rage, to my pew. My mother took my hand and held it throughout the rest of the service, and I was grateful to her. It felt oddly familiar; the touch of her hand reminded me of something I could not quite recall.

Once the service was over, I learned, outside, that Jane's version of the events inside had taken hold. I was apparently "overwrought"—Jane's word was repeated by Mother—and this explained my rambling, unfinished speech. Everyone assumed that I had been forced to make the speech. Susan Perez-Temple approached, and quietly said:

"We all understand why you couldn't go on there in the church. Personally, I disapprove of this modern tradition of children giving so-called 'eulogies' for their parents. It asks far too much of them at a very vulnerable moment. But don't get me started. You should be allowed the privacy of your grief."

I was most struck by Terry's sadness. For once, his high voice was quiet, almost averagely pitched. He, too, felt sorry for me.

"It's not proper that you had to make that speech. You cannat control yourself when yor da's just gone. Remember me at my da's own service?"

"Thanks, Terry. But, you know, I wanted to make that speech. No one forced me."

"Aye, but it's not right that you had to make it, still."

I didn't argue with him, but again thanked him. Terry lingered.

"Mary and I wanted him to marry us, now we have to get someone else." Then he added, mysteriously: "I'm ganna push on with that shed, anyways."

I was still angry with Jane for marching up to the pulpit in her most imperious manner. I was determined to reproach her, but first we had to bury my father. We stood in the northwest corner of the churchyard, where three closely planted cherry trees form a mesh and shade the grass. It was a clear, sunny day, the best kind of May weather. The trees were at the end of their brief bloom, but still full enough to frisk the sunlight before its entrance, which dappled us. The coffin was lowered, and as it hit the ground I thought of how many hundreds of unredeemed corpses lay around us. Terrible to contemplate: hundreds of dead souls, all or most of them believing in the prospect of heaven, and none of them getting any nearer to heaven, as far as I could see, than this piece of dead ground. Canon Palliser began to speak. Suddenly a mild wind blew, and hundreds of little white cherry blossoms, wingless white cloths, fell. They were missionaries sent to convert the ground to white. My mind wandered as the words sounded: "I know that my Redeemer liveth, and that He shall stand at the latter day upon the earth. And though after my skin worms destroy this body, yet in my flesh shall I see God: Whom I shall see for myself, and mine eyes shall behold, and not another . . . We brought nothing into this world, and it is certain we can carry nothing out. The Lord gave, and the Lord hath taken away; blessed be the name of the Lord . . . O death, where is thy sting? O grave, where is thy victory? . . ."

The coffin was docked, the earth was shovelled in. This would not be a bad place for Buntings to rot. Peter had a favourite Sundershall anecdote about this graveyard. In the middle of the nineteenth century a Sundershall farmer, Enoch Stott, was courting a local girl. But he was shy and had not yet put the question to her. So he took her for a walk in the churchyard, and said to her, "My folks lie here, Mary; would you like to lie there with them someday?" She took the hint and married him, said Peter. And indeed, the Stotts had a cluster of graves at the back, behind the church. I smiled through my angry tears as I remembered Father's pleasure at this story.

I cornered Jane at the funeral lunch. She looked at me defiantly with enormous dark eyes.

"What were you playing at?"

"What were *you* playing at? What was that speech?" she asked.

"I'm . . . I'm furious," I said impotently.

"There's no monopoly on anger, you know. Why can't we be furious with you?"

"Who is 'we'?"

"Well, Max said to me just now, 'Did Tom come to praise or to bury his father?' So I'm not the only one to think that speech a total disgrace."

"Well, well, Max agrees with you, how very nice. You and Max. That explains why he's been avoiding me since the end of the service."

"Max agrees with me, and I'm sure your poor mother does, too."

"Actually, she has been very sweet to me, unlike you," I said.

"Don't be such a baby." Guests were glancing around at the frozen intensity of our postures and our fierce whispering.

"Come here," said Jane. We walked out of the dining room. "Come upstairs."

We entered the double bedroom we had shared at Christmas. "No, not this one," insisted Jane, and so we went to my childhood room.

"Tommy, I stopped you speaking because you were embarrassing yourself. You were ranting. And *then,* when you mentioned our marriage, and got onto how Peter was no angel—"

"That was the beginning of a reference to a lovely sentence by a seventeenth-century theologian, but you stopped me before I could finish it! It's all about how we shouldn't mourn people, because their death proves only that they are not angels. The point is that none of us is an angel."

"I don't care if it was a reference to Gandhi, Einstein, and Mother Teresa rolled into one. It sounded as if you were picking a fight with the coffin. People were laughing."

"I wanted them to laugh," I protested.

"Laughing *at* you. Did you want that? Well, I don't."

"Janey, maybe you'll find this odd, but I spoke those words because I wanted to be truthful. Don't you understand that everything else in my life is a lie? The Book Against God isn't a lie. I wanted to tell the truth to my father about my lack of faith. I was speaking to him, not to anyone else."

"But, Tommy darling"—she was softening—"you, of all people, believe that your father is dead and gone. *He* couldn't hear you, and *we* could. And your speech was awful, awful. You mentioned *our marriage.* You lie at the wrong times, and then you tell the truth at the wrong times, and it's all such a terrible mess."

I sat down on the bed and looked at Jane.

"Do you love me?"

"I love you very much."

"What do I have to do to make you want to live with me again?" I asked.

Jane sighed; her thin chest rose and fell.

"I can't live with a liar."

"Of course not."

"I can't live with a liar, and you are a liar. Admit that."

"I am a liar."

"Furthermore, you would have to be honest with me about Christmas, about that disgusting incident. And you would have to be honest with me about children. Do you want them?"

"Well, I can tell you—"

Jane stopped me.

"I don't want to hear it now, and now is not the place. I don't want suspiciously easy fluency. Now everything has changed. Now you have to *think* a bit before you spout words. Yes, I want you to think, and then prove to me over the next few months that you can be honest with me, honest about absolutely everything, from the highest matter to the lowest. Above all about children. I'm not interested in philosophical truth—all that Schopenhauer mush you were quoting in the church. I want daily, practical, ordinary, living truth."

"And over these next few months, however long this process takes, will I live with you or not?" I asked.

There was a long silence.

"I don't think that would be a good idea, do you?" said Jane, gently.

"So when do I get the chance to be honest with you if I don't live with you?"

"We'll meet regularly, we'll have lunch and dinner, we'll go to concerts, we'll do most things except actually live together. Think of it as several months of probation."

"Does this probation start right now?" I asked, inwardly joyful that Jane might be giving me a second chance.

"Yes, right now. Admit to me that the speech was monstrous."

"The speech was monstrous." I was lighthearted.

"Don't just parrot me," said Jane, smiling. "Be *actively* honest. I don't want to just pull truths out of you like someone forcing open a handbag and rummaging around for a penny."

"Okay, here is something," I said.

"Yes? Oh dear."

"When I heard from my mother that Dad had died—remember, I was at Uncle Karl's—I immediately had the shameful thought that now you might take pity on me and let me come back. I can honestly say that you were the first thought I had on hearing of Dad's death."

Jane looked away, and bit her lip.

"Oh Tommy."

She stood, and I eagerly stood with her. We embraced. She was gentle, and held me gently—starved of her, I couldn't help letting my hands move down her thin back. But she pulled off.

"Let's go downstairs, shall we?" she said.

Thanks to Jane's offer, I was ecstatically happy throughout the rest of the funeral lunch.

It was quiet once everyone had gone. I was desperate to leave and to begin the new era of marital "probation" in London, assuming I could find somewhere to live. Mother and I said little to each other, though we had one sharp exchange about the BAG, in which she confessed her dismay that I had not been working on the Ph.D., and urged me to finish the thesis "to honour Daddy's memory." In Peter's presence, she and I had been his suitors, always petitioning for his vital, difficult attention. Without him, we were both husbandless. And both kingless, too—each room of the large house seemed to be dominated by an empty throne. Terry continued to work on my father's shed; now I understood what he had meant at the funeral. "I don't have the heart to tell him to pull it down," said Mother. "Let him keep his tools in it." When he was not working on it, Terry would sit in the shed, hunched on a little wooden stool he had brought with him.

My mother abandoned the kingless palace; she spent as much time as possible visiting villagers to thank them for flowers and food, or planting and weeding in the awakened garden. I often watched her from the sitting room window. She and Terry spoke quite a lot. He seemed to need to keep her informed about each tiny development of the shed. One afternoon, while she was in the garden, I went into my father's study. It was frozen in squalor; not a thing had been touched. But already, without its daily renewal, the air was losing its scent of tobacco. I sat at the desk, fingered some books. Then more systematically I went through the drawers, and found an intriguing little notebook, half-full with jottings. One of the pages read as follows:

Polanie—the Poles; literally, "people of the plains"
shul—proper Yiddish word for synagogue (lit. "school" in Old German)
"bone-orchard" Terry Upsher's phrase for graveyard
Ranke: "I am an historian before I am a Christian."
Ranke on Michelet: "he wrote in a style in which the truth could not be told."

St. Bede's dying prayer to God: "O leave us not as orphans!"

Aristotle: Why is it that he who confers benefits loves more than he who receives them?

Celia Johnson = Mrs. Peter Fleming = Ian Fleming/James Bond (Mr. Norrington)

Sums are not set as a test on Erasmus.

I read this page again and again. The last entry was nonsensical to me, but the others, types of which appeared on every page, clearly formed a particular kind of commonplace book. There was a whole section marked "Karl," with entries such as this:

"The Slovakian officials offered their Jews to us like someone throwing away sour beer" (Eichmann)

Inventor of the word anti-Semitism: Wilhelm Marr

Inventor of the word genocide: Raphael Lemkin

So this was a book of promptings, in which Peter stored away little pieces of found knowledge, where he prepared privately for his public successes. For a moment or two, I thought: the cheat! Look how he cribbed! But I reflected that surely I had always known him to be a performer, even if the mechanics of the performance had been invisible to me.

On my last morning at home, as I was making for the bathroom, I heard my mother behind the door. The water was running, and it was only because I was so close to the door that I heard, amidst the other water, the sound of crying. When I was little I used to hear her doing her "reciting" in the bathroom. Those freezing, wintry mornings, years

ago, when I used to take a few extra minutes in bed while
Mother was in the bathroom . . . Father, seemingly irre-
pressible, rose first, and was always up and about by the time
I began to stir in my sheets; I never saw him unclothed, as if
he were a commanding officer who could not be seen out of
uniform by the rank and file. Once he or Mother had
woken me—she ghostly in her long white nightgown, with
fretted panels in it that looked acoustical in function, as if
designed to let the body speak—I turned over for a few more
minutes, in the delicious knowledge that she would now oc-
cupy the bathroom. In winter months, I eventually stretched
out a hand, parting the air for my clothes. Then I pulled
them in, like an animal feathering its nest, and dressed under the blankets in the trapped warmth. So by the time I
even approached the bathroom door I was fully dressed—
perhaps that is where I developed my disdain for bathing?
But it was a good thing I was dressed, because often Mother
was still in the bathroom. I could hear her talking to herself.
For seven years she taught religious knowledge at a junior
school in Durham, and at weekends or in the evenings she
sometimes gave speeches to town or village societies, or
opened garden fetes and speech days, and for all these different forms of presentation her method of preparation was
the same: she learned things by heart, reading out aloud a
textbook or the speech she had written, in a low gentle voice
as she sat in the bath or at her dressing table, calmly, as if
speaking to a loyal pet: "Leaving Corinth, Paul continued
on his travels to Ephesus and Antioch, where he addressed
the congregations there, which were large in number." But
now she was crying, not reciting.

25

IMMEDIATELY AFTER THE FUNERAL I found this place on the Finchley Road. It's cheap, but Philip Zealy's firm has been admirably businesslike and professional in its pursuit of my monthly payments, and it is all I can afford. UCL do not want me back, so I have been living off my weekly dole cheque. I had to get some work. For the month of June I was employed by the local council. One of my tasks was to lock the park gates at the foot of Primrose Hill "at dusk." Roger paid me to stuff envelopes for his early music choir. Then I got a job as an underground porter-packer for Harrods, during the July sales, in busy catacombs underneath the Brompton Road. The sooty tunnels lead from the shop under the street to an enormous loading area, where green, liveried vans are parked under old-fashioned wooden signs, on which are written different destinations: Kensington, Hammersmith, Chiswick, Hampstead. The work was tedious and subterranean, and there was a peculiar torment in being so close to so many luxurious unaffordable items. The manager of my section liked me and asked me to stay on after the sales. But I had had enough of working underground as a kind of miner for Mayfair sheiks, and told him that I had to take some time off because my father had just died. He didn't seem to believe me.

It is late October now, five months since the funeral, and Max and I are still wary with one another. Of course, his extraordinary recent behaviour at Roger's music evening did not help. Last week he told me that he is getting married to Fiona Raymond, which will surely take everyone by surprise; perhaps marriage will make him sweeter. He has not asked me to be his best man; I am waiting, without much optimism.

And so life continues, and my rhythms are not so different from those I had as a student, or those I had when I was married to Jane. I wake, I lie on my bed (and try not to think of Jane or my father), and then I rise in my little bedsit and brew my coffee (and try not to think of Jane or my father). Recently, I have had great difficulty getting up. Now that summer is properly over, it is getting cold in this room. When I do rise, I put on the paisley dressing gown, have a cigarette. I look at my books, I write this Book, and sometimes continue with the Ph.D. The familiar optimism, the familiar fatigue. On really bad days, if I have the cash, I have lunch at the Olympus, because Theo's gloominess cheers me. He never has any good words to say about the country he has lived in for seventeen years. Today, his peculiar turn of speech reminded me horridly of last Christmas and all my troubles. Theo looked phlegmatically through the Olympus's smeared window at the street and said, "I think England is one big sperm bank, that's what we are."

God Almighty first planted a garden: and now England is in a mess.

Last night, Jane invited me to supper at her flat—our old flat. This was very exciting; our last, awful meeting, three weeks ago, was at Roger's, when we argued so. None of our meetings since the funeral has taken place in her flat. So I was as excited as I had been before Roger's music night, and I made sure that I bathed thoroughly and used the sunscreen. This might be it, I thought, this might be the moment of truth.

At the flat, I kept looking for signals. She cooked, we ate, felt warm and tender, and then Jane put on a record.

"This is Richter. A live performance of Beethoven 109. This is the slow bit, a beautiful theme, with variations."

I listened, heard first the noise of steady background hiss, and then, cleanly abolishing it in a way that made me think of opening my eyes for the first time on a brilliant morning, the piano's chords sounded. It was a beautiful tune, oh yes, simple and hymnlike, broken into sets of two repetitions. There was something about that first chord which made everything following it less exciting. That first chord was pristine, and pushed its successors out into an ordinary exile. Nostalgic for that first annunciation, I asked if she could stop the record, and start again. She did. Again, the first chord broke through the background noise and announced itself. This time I listened properly to what followed. The melody was, above all, very stable, neither joyful nor melancholy; instead, it seemed to be the essence of knowledge itself, the gold of truth, constant behind our stormy extremes as the sun is behind clouds. Yet there was another sound, not musical. Something like a man sniffing. It was the pianist breathing!—heavy, almost impatient, as if he were wrestling with the music to secure its great medial serenity. The pianist was breathing quite hard through his nose as he wrestled with this sweet sound. It was the sound of hard work, but it was also the sound of existence itself—a man's ordinary breath, the give and take of the organism, our colourless wind of survival, the zephyr of it all.

The evidence of human effort, of pain, was intensely moving, and I hung my head as I listened. How strange, this combination of Richter's strong, masculine, working butcher-breath, just audible to the microphone, and the delicate impalpable music.

"Thomas, my darling, you have tears in your eyes?"

"It's the pianist breathing," I said simply. "That's what you wanted me to hear."

"What are you talking about?"

"I can hear Richter breathing, the struggle of it . . ." I wanted to be as truthful as possible with Jane.

"I didn't hear that," said Jane. Sadly, she looked at me, and said: "All I wanted you to hear was the simplicity of the tune. It's so soothing. Does it mean anything? I played that piece at the concert."

"Which concert?"

"The one at which you first met me."

"Well, put it on again, and this time I promise not to hear Richter breathing." So we sat together, as the music repeated. But the moment was lost, somehow, and once I had finished my drink, Jane shook her ponytail with a familiar, irritable flick, and I knew that I was being dismissed.

This morning, thinking over the events of last night, I sat in my room and once again heard in my head the sound of the pianist struggling, the zephyr of it all. I thought about Max, and something he had said to me at Roger's, when we argued, which at the time I had interpreted as merely hostile. "If the Book Against God is your own little secret, your own private crime, then think of your dad's death as the removal of the last witness, the one who could have seriously testified against you." But what if I still needed the witness? And I recalled Father's funeral, and the mild wind that blew as the coffin was docked, a wind as invisible as the future, and my mother holding my hand. And suddenly I

realized why the experience of having my hand held by my
mother seemed familiar. Because I think perhaps that my
father held my hand all the time that I stood next to him at
Granny's funeral. Is that right? Could that be? Why, then,
did I only remember Father being cross with me and striding towards me in his black cassock? But the more I think
about it, the more I convince myself that Father took me
back to the graveside and held my hand at Granny's funeral.
I am sure he held my hand. All my adult years I only held his
hand to shake it, to say hello or goodbye. I would like to put
my hand out now, and touch his.

Oh, Father, there were days so exciting when I was a little boy that each morning was a delicious surprise, a joy
adults can only mimic when they are fortunate enough to
make a long journey by night and rise in an undiscovered
place in the morning and see it in the first light. When anyone asks me, I say that my childhood was happy, and for once,
for once, I am not lying. Wasn't it an orchard, my childhood? But why, then, the worm? Why the worm? Tell me.